THE
HIDDEN
TEMPLE

K. N. TIMOFEEV

For my stalwart writing companions. Thanks for keeping my feet warm. And sorry for all the times I kicked you in the face.

ACKNOWLEDGMENTS

It's a funny thing when you have to split up a story. Technically, this was supposed to be the 2nd half of The Serpent's Coils, but as I reached the part where Mirra was forced to make a choice, I felt as if that was a better stopping point for that story than the climax of this part of the story. It was a touch choice, but I can definitely say that I made the right choice. Either way, we've made it to the end! Of this bit, not the total story.

This story has definitely been one of love and iron grit. Between Covid 19 and the resulting decline of my mental health, I had to completely change the timeline for this story. But I made it, no small in part to Dmitry, who is always there to cheer me on or beat me over the head for being too hard on myself.

I also need to take a moment to pause and give a hearty shout out to Christina for bulldozing back into my life like my personal motivational speaker. You changed the game girlie! Believe me when I say that where I'm at now is because of you and I hope that one day I can be there for you the way you've been there for me.

Shout out to the amazing authors in the indie writing community across all platforms. You guys are my favorite people and I love being apart of such a welcoming and helpful community.

And as always, before I leave you to continue on with Mirra and the others, thank you my lovely readers. I love each and everyone of you. My greatest wish for you is that you find a place for yourself in the world of A Tale of Blades and Darkness. And try to forgive me for the emotions I'm about to put you through.

Exit stage left with a cape flip and cackling like an evil queen.

CHAPTER ONE

THE WORLD WAS MADE OF NOTHING BUT LIARS AND daggers hidden in the dark. Sometimes, if the gods were merciful, you were able to see the traitors before they struck. But it was more likely that you would find yourself bleeding out on a cold hard ground with a dagger in your gullet, staring up at someone you thought was a friend. Gaitlan wished he'd been so lucky. Instead, he had survived by running away like a coward.

Everything Gaitlan once held dear was gone. All that remained was an empty shell of a body functioning purely on instinct and a gaping void where his heart used to be. The only reason he had that much was all thanks to the woman riding ahead.

He glowered at the woman, swaying slightly in her saddle. She lashed his legs to the saddle, poured water down his throat, along with some bitter herbs. She cursed his name while urging him onward. He wished she would let him die. He hated her.

"We're nearly there," Mirra shouted over her shoulder.

She ground her teeth, questioning her sanity, peering over her shoulder, staring at Gaitlan's blank face. She hated him. If he couldn't get his head out of his ass, then so be it. She never cared for him—the spoiled, selfish prick. It might be easier to dump him in the nearest village and disappear, but then, an image of Braelyn's bruised but hopeful face danced across her mind. She couldn't turn away now; not yet. If she could get the prince into a position where he could fight for himself, her debt to the princess would be repaid.

She looked over her shoulder at prince Gaitlan again. His head rolled listlessly on his shoulders, his eyes vacant and empty. Now and again, flashes of pure hatred or anguish would ripple across his face, but they never lasted for more than a moment.

Braelyn left her brother and the kingdom's fate in Mirra's hands like the heroes of old. But she wasn't a hero, no matter what her recent actions might say. Her skill set was more suited for thievery, spying, and assassinations. And Gaitlan ...Gaitlan wouldn't be helping anyone anytime soon.

Her horse stumbled over a rock in the road, forcing her to grab the saddle horn to keep from falling off. She cursed, righting herself, rubbing her burning eyes. Dawn wasn't too far off. She hoped to reach the village by then, but it didn't look like that would happen. Scanning the surrounding woods, Mirra spied a small trail leading into its depths. She dismounted, palming one of her daggers, and crept toward the opening.

Lingering nighttime shadows clung to existence beneath the canopy of the trees. In the pale light, Mirra followed the trail further into the woods and listened. Birds had started to stir in their nests, filling the air with their melodies. Other smaller daytime creatures rustled in the underbrush. All signs that the way was safe, but Mirra knew that dangers lurked in all sorts of places.

She closed her eyes and reached into the place where her magic dwelled. Exhaustion stole the strength from her body and mind, leaving her magic to feel like water slipping through her fingers. She gritted her teeth and dug in deeper. Sweat broke out across her forehead as she clawed a large enough thread to serve as her eyes. She flung it out into the woods before it could fade away like smoke on the wind.

Energy rolled through her consciousness. Mirra felt the dwindling energies of the nocturnal creatures and the rising energies of diurnal creatures but nothing else.

Pulling her consciousness back within her skin, Mirra faltered, grabbing onto a young tree for support. Black dots swam across her vision. She clung to the tree, gasping for air until she was no longer in danger of fainting.

Gaitlan remained atop his horse, staring blankly into the distance when she stumbled out.

"We're stopping for some rest. Can you manage it?"

Gaitlan didn't respond, though he did turn to look at her. She took his silence as a yes, loosening the knots that kept him in place. For half a heartbeat, she thought that she was going to have to drag him off his horse and carry him into the woods, but the prince swung his leg over the horse's head, sliding out of the saddle. He took the reins of his horse, waiting for Mirra to lead the way.

Gaitlan's silence bothered her, but the ache in her bones and the way the road swayed beneath her feet demanded her immediate attention.

Once nestled in the safety of the trees, Mirra picked up the faint sound of running water. The trail seemed to be going in the same direction, so she followed it. After a short walk, the path opened up to a small clearing just large enough for them and their horses. Next to the small patch of grass was a small stream running bright and clear. Mirra eyed the stream and sighed in disappointment. She had hoped to perhaps fish for their meal.

She dropped her pack and set about tending to the horses. Gaitlan had already unsaddled his horse, setting it free to graze. The tired beast shuffled straight to the water for a well-deserved drink. Mirra's horse joined it a few moments later.

Gaitlan stood in the center of the clearing. Mirra dug around in the pack to retrieve the herbs that helped his body clear away most of the narcotics Lord Julian had given him. Gaitlan saw the herbs and scowled.

"No more." His voice was hoarse from screaming, dust, or grief—most likely all three.

"As long as you act like you're drugged, I'm gonna keep shoving these down your throat," Mirra growled.

"Fuck you."

Mirra clenched her fist. The air around her became aromatic from the herbs. "Fuck me? Without me, princeling, you'd be on your way to the executioner's block for the murder of your parents, leaving the throne wide open for Lord Julian."

A bit of his old self sparked in Gaitlan's eyes at the mention of Lord Julian's name. "Don't mention that traitorous bastard's name."

Mirra sneered. "We had to leave your sister in the hands

of Lord Julian. Lord Julian is probably sitting in your father's seat. Lord Julian is probably sleeping in your parents' bed."

"Stop," Gaitlan growled.

Mirra squared her shoulders, lifting her chin. "Lord Julian. Lord Julian. Lord Julian."

Gaitlan crossed the distance between them in three strides, stretching to his full height to loom over Mirra.

Mirra didn't back down. She tilted her head back to meet him in the eye while her other hand drifted to the knife at her side.

"Don't. Say. His. Name," Gaitlan growled.

"Lord fucking Julian," Mirra said, baring her teeth in a feral grin.

Gaitlan lashed out, but Mirra was ready. Sidestepping, she brought her knee into Gaitlan's unprotected sternum, knocking the wind out of him. He fell to the ground, gasping for air.

Mirra stood her ground, her whole body quivering. As much as she wanted to, she couldn't beat him into a bloody pulp. He was angry and had every right to be, but where he placed his anger ... Mirra refused to be an easy target.

Gaitlan scrambled to his feet, going after Mirra again. She dodged his attacks with ease, her hand still resting on the hilt of her dagger.

"Stop dancing around and fight me, you conniving bitch! Stop toying with me. Finish what your master started."

Mirra weaved under his guard, taking the prince down with a well-placed leg sweep. However, Gaitlan managed to snag her upper arm, dragging her down with him. Mirra shifted to maintain her advantage, landing on Gaitlan's chest, knocking the air from his lungs.

Mirra's blade kissed his throat before he had the opportunity to regain his breath or organize his thoughts.

Mirra used every ounce of her remaining strength to keep him down. She brought her face to his so close that their noses nearly touched. She saw the hurricane of emotions raging just behind his eyes. He saw a cold fury that chilled him to the bone.

"He's not my master, not anymore. My task that day was to kill your sister, not you. Julian wanted your entire family gone."

Gaitlan moved to throw her off, but she pressed her blade harder against his throat, drawing a tiny droplet of blood.

"I didn't. I went against a man that I am terrified of in ways you can't even imagine. All for her. She's ten times the noble you are, and frankly, she should get the crown."

Mirra sat up, resheathing her dagger. "I am on her side, and she sacrificed herself so that you could escape. So you could escape." She stood, glaring down at the prince. "What are you going to do with the freedom her life gave you?"

She extended her hand toward Gaitlan. He looked from the hand back to Mirra before taking it. After helping him to his feet, she shoved the crushed medicinal herbs at him. "Take these, then gather some wood. I'll set up camp."

Gaitlan took the herbs, shoving them into his mouth, and grimaced against the taste and grit. He chased the herbs with a healthy swig of water from his waterskin. The water helped the thready mash of plant matter down his throat but also intensified its sharp flavor. Making faces and smacking his tongue to erase the lingering taste, he gathered fallen limbs from the forest floor.

Mirra eyed the prince sharply before turning to assess their paltry supplies. She grabbed the small rucksack, emptying its contents onto the ground. In addition to the bedroll and thin cloaks given to them at the tavern, they had enough dried foods to last them a day, maybe two if they didn't mind going hungry for a while. They also had a single flint and wet stone and a pitifully small bag of coins. It wasn't enough for a single person, let alone two. Mirra took out a small strip of dried meat, throwing it into her mouth whole. It was as tough as leather and just as tasteless. She splashed her face with water from the stream a couple of times before cupping her hands for a drink; then she hobbled the horses.

Gaitlan returned, dropping the wood near the center of the clearing. "Do we have flint?"

"There's no need for a fire," Mirra said after swallowing.

Gaitlan's face went dangerously still. "Then why did I have to gather wood?"

"It gave you something to do, didn't it? And while I doubt anyone is looking for us yet, I'd rather not risk it any more than we have to."

"How do we keep warm?"

Mirra shrugged, unfurling her bedroll.

Ire flashed in Gaitlan's eyes once he realized Mirra had sent him on a useless errand. He opened his mouth to argue, but a wave of exhaustion crashed over him. Grudgingly, he snatched one of the bedrolls and curled up on the softest piece of ground the farthest away from Mirra.

Mirra watched him, wondering how far she should push him to keep his darkness from swallowing him whole. Too much effort, she thought, grabbing the other bedroll, curling up in the center of the clearing, her hand lightly wrapped around her dagger's hilt.

So far, the city watch has found no sign of the prince or your niece, my lord."

Lord Julian shuffled the reports without reading them, knowing they all said the same thing. "I'm not surprised. If the prince had half a brain, he would have left the city before the watch sealed the gates."

The other nobles seated around the long table shifted uncomfortably in their seats. "And your niece," one lord ventured.

Lord Julian twisted his face into the perfect example of pained disappointment. "My niece was never the same after her husband's death. I had hoped that the princess would help her return to her former self, but it is clear that the wrong royal has influenced her. I don't know why she went with him; perhaps she was coerced, but I cannot ignore her hand in the untimely death of the king and queen."

The tension around the table was palatable. The death of a monarch was never easy. But to lose both in such a bloody way at the hands of the heir was something the lords could not have fathomed, even on their darkest of days.

"Shouldn't the princess be present?" asked a young lord, breaking the silence.

The lord was young, inexperienced in the position he

recently gained, thanks to the coup. Lord Julian didn't know the young lord's name at the moment, but if the young lord continued to press his luck, Lord Julian would ensure that no one would ever learn it.

"Princess Braelyn has confined herself to her chambers, mourning for her parents and her brother. She has asked that I lead in her stead until she is ready to assume her role as leader of our nation." The young lord frowned, pressing further. "A number of the court have recently lost people as well, and yet here we are. She is our princess and the last remaining member of the royal family. I may not have had the pleasure of meeting her in person, but her reputation is well known, even in the holdings along the mountains. She has always prided herself on the care she gave to her people. I find it suspect that she'd suddenly find it too much to bear locking herself away from the people she, up until now, always fought for."

Eat this proud little lord urged the dark part of Lord Julian's soul. Suck the marrow from his bones; then raise his lands to the dirt, salting the fields, and burn everyone—down to the last living thing. He took a deep breath, subduing the violent presence beneath his iron will.

"I understand your frustration, lord ..."

"Tolin Hastings. My lands are to the south of the Border Mountains."

"Ah yes, as I said, young Lord Tolin, I understand your frustration, but the princess, while having a stout heart, has never had to face the hardships she does now. It has shaken her to her core. And we all know that women do not have the same stalwart resolution as men."

Around the table, the older lords chuckled and nodded

in agreement. The newly minted lords, including Lord Tolin, kept their own counsel.

There's one that will cause us trouble.

"My lords, thank you for your time. I know that we all have much to attend to. We will convene again in a fortnight. I trust that gives you ample time to ease your people's fears and get your affairs in order? Until we meet again."

The council of lords stood, murmuring their farewells and affirmations. Julian watched Lord Tolin turn and storm out of the council room without speaking to anyone. He would deal with the lordling soon, but he had more pressing issues to handle at the moment.

All around him, people wore either black clothing or black bands around their arms. The general mood in the castle was somber, with many of the servants bearing red-rimmed eyes. A slight satisfied smirk tugged at the corners of his mouth, but he would never let it show. It wouldn't help him keep his position if the people thought The King's Viper took joy from the death of his masters.

The two guards outside the massive gilded doors snapped into attention as Julian approached, opening the doors with a bow. Julian smiled as he strode through the doors. The royal wing. Admittance to this part of the castle had been strict before the massacre. Now no one came or went without Julian's express permission.

A lone guard stood outside a simple white door. Julian opened the door, walking into the main chamber of Princess Braelyn's room. The princess wore a simple black mourning dress and veil for her hair. Her face was free of all cosmetics, making her face look wain and pale. Grief lingered around her eyes, but the sight of Lord Julian standing before her brought out a bit of fire.

"Just because you've stolen the throne doesn't mean you can walk into my room announced."

Julian chuckled. "Yes, it does, princess. But that's not why I'm here." Julian sat down in a wingback chair, stretching his long legs out in front, one ankle crossed over the other.

Princess Braelyn carefully shifted in her chair, one of her hands slowly sliding to reach into the folds of her dress. Julian knew that she kept a sharpened letter opener within her grasp. He nearly laughed at the absurdity, but her spirit was admirable. Much like another young woman he knew.

"Then, why are you here?"

"Your absence has been noticed amongst the nobles."

Braelyn scoffed. "I wonder why."

Julian scowled at the princess. "Don't be pert. Your continued existence in this world depends on my good graces."

"And your grip on the throne comes from mine." Braelyn leaned forward, placing her hands in her lap. The perfect picture of a demure woman, except for the wicked gleam in her eyes.

"The people are only tolerating your presence. They know who has the right to the throne. I may only be seventeen, my lord, but I am the crown princess. And since you've smeared my brother's name, the rule of the kingdom falls to me."

"You're still a child in the eyes of the law."

Braelyn leaned back, her face hardening into the mask of the queen she would one day become. "Only for another year. The weak-willed nobles will follow you until then. They know the law as well as we do. All the power you gained at the expense of my parents' lives, you'll lose. One way or another, I swear on their graves, you will lose everything."

The darks of Lord Julian's eyes spread to encompass the entirety of his eyes. The shadows lengthened and darkened, reaching out for her. Braelyn gasped, reaching for her sharpened letter opener once more. Julian stood, stretching his hand between them. Black ichor pooled in his palm, coiling around his fingers before dropping to the floor with a heavy wet sound.

To her credit, Braelyn kept her composure, with only her wide eyes giving away her true feelings.

"A lot can happen in a year," Julian said before turning to leave, the coiling darkness disappearing into smoke just as he crossed the threshold.

Spirited women are only good for breaking, and soon before, she makes good on her promise.

Brimming with barely checked aggression, Lord Julian made his way through the castle to the former king's chambers. The servants that carefully packed the king's and queen's personal effects jumped as he barged in but kept their eyes to their tasks. The King's Viper was a mysterious and dangerous man. Though they may not have ever met him, they were well aware of the tools at his disposal that assisted his climb to his seat at court. To catch his eye was to risk vanishing into thin air, never to be seen or heard from again.

"I'm going to the study," Julian growled. "No disturbances."

A massive mahogany desk took up most of the space, along with several straight-backed chairs. Only a single wall hadn't been claimed by ebony bookcases, brimming with books that most likely hadn't been opened in decades. A great hearth took up most of the remaining wall. Its mantle was covered with bits of shells, heavily creased finger paintings, and other remnants of the family that no longer existed.

Julian picked up a miniature, rough-hewn carving, turning it this way and that with mild interest as he tried to determine what animal it was supposed to be. With a disgusted snort, he chucked the carving amongst the kindling before scowling up at the painting that hung overhead.

"A colossal waste of space for such an insignificant man."

Stepping into the cold fireplace, he placed his hand along the back of the hearth. For several minutes, he ran his hands over the back of the hearth, heedless of the soot coating his hands. He only worried about finding a particular image carved into one of the stones. It was difficult work because the centuries of fires had smoothed many of the stones. At last, his fingers traced over a seven-pointed star, and with a toothy grin, he pressed the stone. Behind the fireplace, ancient mechanisms came to life, rolling and grinding against centuries of dust and cobwebs.

The back of the fireplace swung inward, revealing a gaping maw of darkness. Julian walked through it with no hesitation, the wall slamming down afterward, encasing him in total darkness. Julian didn't mind the dark. It was his home, his bones, his lifeblood.

The air was stale and dusty inside the passageway. The thick layer of dust muffled Julian's footsteps on the stone. The narrow corridor led to a long, winding staircase. Up and up, he climbed until he reached a small landing at the very top. Once, there had been a door, but it had turned to dust and crumbled long ago. Julian stepped into the small room, his grin stretching wider.

Darkness blacker than the shadows of the room pooled around his hands. Julian pointed into the void, firing an arrow of night. Crimson light blossomed from a glass orb suspended from the ceiling by a rope, emitting light onto a room that hadn't been used in an age.

In the age when Mystics roamed the lands, one or two served as mages for the crown. They built secret rooms throughout the castle to wield their gifts in secret and safety from those who mistrusted their talents and race. Over the centuries since The Purge, many of the places have either been destroyed or forgotten. As far as Julian knew, this was the only room still standing in the palace. He'd stumbled across an old schematic during his youth.

The years had wreaked havoc on the once sacred space. Most of the shelves were dry-rotted and broken, and the work table was beyond salvaging as well. None of that mattered, not to Julian. He only needed the residual magic that still clung to the stones, all thanks to the runes carved over every inch of the room.

Closing his eyes, Julian connected to the lingering magic. It slammed into him with the force of a cannonball, drawing black blood from his nose. The ancient magic surged against him in waves, seeking to either dominate or eradicate. Gritting his teeth, he attempted to force it to his will.

The magic recoiled against Julian's command. His nails dug into his palms, spilling more black blood from his skin. Seconds stretched out into eternity until a lifetime later, the ancient power bowed its head, fully submitting to his will.

Julian shoved up the sleeve on his left arm, drawing a dagger from his belt. He slashed his forearm, spilling more black blood on the stones by his feet, where it stayed frozen in place by the power humming in the air.

The wound on his arm closed in an instant, not even leaving a scar. Julian took a deep breath to calm the pounding that blossomed at the base of his skull. He held both his hands over the pool, eyes going black, chanting in a voice that carried the cries of hundreds of lost souls. He started chanting a guttural language in a voice that wasn't entirely his own. The pool rippled as if a stone had been dropped into its inky depths, eventually separating into six equal pools of night.

"Go forth and find the crown prince and the woman traveling with him. Kill him and any witnesses; capture her and bring her to me alive. I have plans for young Mirra."

The inky pools moved, stretching into the shape of serpents speeding down the stairs and out the castle gates without a soul noticing.

The inky serpents slithered through the Noble and Divine districts in search of hosts that were best suited for their task. A small band of mercenaries sat outside a tavern in the Merchant District, roaring drunk. Pockets loaded with coin, they had every intention to drink, feast, and whore until their bodies gave out, or the coin, whichever one came first.

"Here's to another successful job, boys," said the leader, the largest of the band, his voice slurring. His men hoisted their tankards into the air, shouting. "Enjoy these next few days 'cause I got another job already lined up."

A cheer went up again. More jobs meant more coin, and more coin meant more fun for them to enjoy.

The young serving girl tried to gather the empty tankards without drawing attention to herself. But as soon as she reached out to take the first tankard, the leader's hand wrapped around her too-thin wrist, pulling her into his lap. She bit back her squeal as she pressed her hands against his broad chest. It was hard as stone beneath her too-thin fingers. His thick arms, corded with the most muscle she'd ever seen on a human, encircled her waist, effectively trapping her within his grasp.

"Sir, please," she said, her voice already shaking. "There are Painted Women inside for use."

The men around the table laughed coldly at her feeble attempts to free herself from their leader's grip.

"But none as sweet as you," the leader said, burying his face into the crook of her neck.

The serving girl pushed away, looking for the man the owner hired for moments precisely like this.

The six creatures huddled together in the lea of a building, the one place where the lantern's light didn't reach, excitement sending ripples of pleasure down their long bodies. Finally, a promising group of meat sacks. They slithered forward, ignoring the stinging light from the city lanterns and shop windows. The light would lose its power over them once they settled inside.

It was first come, first serve as the creatures raced toward the mercenaries that continued to laugh at the prey they had caught. The men's ill intent scented the air, driving the creatures into a frenzy. The creature that reached the band first headed straight for the leader, slithering up an opening in his pant leg. The burly man was too far gone into his drink to even notice. The creature then flattened itself, pushing itself into the pores in the skin, mingling with the man's blood, spreading its essence to every portion of the mercenary's being.

Roaring in pain, the leader of the mercenaries flung the

serving girl from him, leaping to his feet, his hands slapping all over his body. His men surged to their feet, hands going for their weapons, eyes scanning the streets and rooftops for any signs of the assailant.

Another among the group began screaming, his dirty nails raking down his face.

Four more men fell victim, adding their screams of pain, destroying the calm of the night. People in the street scurried away, locking themselves behind shop doors or carriages. The serving girl crawled away, scuttling on her hands and knees to the entrance of the inn, leaping to her feet, only to throw herself inside, bolting the door behind her.

The remaining mercenaries encircled their screaming comrades, calling out to them in vain.

The six screaming mercenaries stopped screaming as one, their silence falling as sharply as the blades strapped to their sides. They stood completely still. The others were unsure if they even breathed.

"Sir," one of the mercenaries ventured, reaching out.

His screams filled the air as he pulled back the bleeding stump where his hand used to be, the burly leader's blade dripping red. The five others turned as one and joined their leader as they slashed down the men they'd fought and drank besides for years. A few of the mercenaries managed to escape, leaving everything they owned behind.

The remaining mercenaries fell to the ground in a bloody heap; the six possessed mercenaries stilled again.

A pair of city guards cautiously approached, their hands wrapped around the hilt of their swords. "What's going on here?"

The mercenaries remained silent.

"I asked you a question."

The guard grabbed the mercenary leader but was stopped short by a dagger thrust into his stomach.

The other guard shouted in alarm, reaching for his whistle to call for backup. His lips wrapped around the silver whistle and blew. Blood poured out the open end of the whistle. The guard fell to his knees, blood pouring down the front of his uniform, the whistle clattering to the street before rolling into the gutter.

The creatures in their new bodies looked toward the city gate, the expression on their faces blank, and their eyes as black as the deepest pits of hell.

CHAPTER TWO

GAITLAN WOKE FIRST, JOINTS STIFF AND NEARLY FROZEN despite the bedroll. He glowered at Mirra sleeping peacefully, curled up like a cat in a patch of sunlight. The gentle light of dawn filtered between the leaves of the trees, giving her porcelain skin a warmer hue and bringing out the variations of color in her dark hair.

Beautiful.

Gaitlan shook the treacherous thought from his mind, easing to his feet, rubbing the warmth back into his fingers. Stiff-legged, he shuffled over to the pile of wood he collected the day before. Shifting through the boughs, he gathered a fistful of twigs, arranging them into a small pyramid. But his frozen fingers were stiff and clumsy, knocking over the pyramid down several times before his temper got the better than him. Cursing, he snatched the bundle of twigs and threw them across the clearing.

"Feeling better?"

Gaitlan spun. Mirra stood, rolling up her bedding with an amused smirk on her mouth. Scowling, he turned back to the cold, empty fireplace.

Mirra's smile took on an edge. She stretched her arms over her head, arching her back, the movement drawing Gaitlan's attention. Her movements were as graceful as a dancer as she leaned and stretched. His eyes lingered on the curve of her chest, beneath her shirt, and the lines of her waist and hips.

"Time to go, princeling," she said, dusting off her clothes.

"Where?"

Power rolled behind her unnatural ice blue eyes. Gaitlan fought the urge to shift into a fighting stance. The power disappeared as quickly as it appeared, forcing a fresh wave of suspicion about his savior.

"The road. We have quite a bit of distance to go yet before we reach the village."

"Village?"

Mirra rolled her eyes. "Yes, princeling, a village. You know, the place where most of your people live? They tend to be small, mostly farming communities."

Heat pooled at the nape of his neck. "I know what a village is," he snapped. "What I meant was, why are we going to a village? Shouldn't we head to the nearest estate? Gather allies and take back the city?"

"What allies? I know you were lost in your own little world for a few days, but even you should have noticed that nobles fought on both sides. Do you know who you can trust? Who will turn us over to Lord Julian?"

Gaitlan's strength crumbled to dust, nearly sending him to his knees.

Mirra scrunched her face, internally groaning. "I'm trying to help. For your sister."

Gaitlan said nothing, choosing instead to ready his horse. Thoughts and emotions swirled around his mind like dead leaves ripped from the limb during an autumn wind. He struggled to keep a grasp of any single idea or feeling before it was torn away to be replaced by another. Begrudgingly, he knew that Mirra was right. He didn't know who he could trust anymore.

Gaitlan eyed Mirra over the back of his horse. He may not remember much from the days leading up to his parents' death, but he did remember the look on that bastard's face when he saw what side Mirra had chosen to stand on. She'd betrayed The King's Viper, the most dangerous man in the kingdom, and if she could betray him, she could betray anyone. There was no reason for her to help him. He could offer her no gold, no title or land. She didn't even like him. Was this all a play by that traitor to force those who would remain loyal to his family out into the open?

Flashes of blood spreading across a black and white floor and shadows taking form played across his mind's eye. The smell of smoke and burning flesh singed the delicate skin inside his nose. The ground beneath his feet rolled and pivoted, sending his thudding into his horse.

"You ready, princeling?"

"Stop calling me that," Gaitlan growled.

Mirra laughed as she led her horse back onto the road.

Gaitlan watched her through narrowed eyes. How far was he willing to trust this woman?

BRAELYN TRIED TO IGNORE THE WHISPERING THAT

trailed after her, no matter where she went. Keeping her eyes trained ahead, she was the perfect picture of calm, when in all actuality, she wanted to scream and lash out against the oppressive air closing in around her.

To make matters all the more disheartening, the public readily accepted the lies Lord Julian spread about her brother. How could they so easily believe the worse of her brother? A man they'd known for years and, until now, were going to accept as their new king.

But to show these questions, to even ask them aloud, would only bring more suffering to herself and her people. They didn't want to delve into the truth of it all. They only wanted a simple answer that would allow them to go back to their lives.

"The men may sit on the throne and wield swords, but it's the women that keep a kingdom together by knowing when to speak and when to remain silent and watch."

Her mother's words have echoed many times through her head over the past few days. She would have to maintain her composure as the crown princess, becoming the stone to which they clung to, until she found a way to set everything right again. If that was even possible now.

"Princess, it is good to see you."

A deep crease formed between her brows at the arrival of a young nobleman. He appeared close to her brother's age. His mourning attire was more straightforward than most other nobles, preferring clean cuts with no adornment. His eyes were kind as they stared down at her from his open face tanned from years spent outdoors. A faint scent of spruce clung to him mingled with a sharpness she couldn't quite place. He bowed deeply to her, light from the windows catching the streaks of auburn in his hair.

She took his offered hand, noting the large calluses on his palm and fingertips as he brought her hand to his lips.

"Lord Tolin at your service. Perhaps you might like to take a walk in the gardens. I find that the presence of growing things helps to ease the heart, if only for a moment."

Braelyn hesitated, chewing the inside of her cheek before cautiously accepting his arm, letting him lead her away. The silence grew heavy between them. She let it grow, partially enjoying the young lord's unease.

"My father lost his life during the incursion. From what I heard, he died trying to get to the king and queen before they were slain."

"By my brother's hand."

From the corner of her eye, she saw Lord Tolin clench his jaw.

"There's still a great deal of uncertainty about that night. I'm certain that the truth will be revealed one way or another."

"Truth?" Braelyn laughed bitterly. "What is truth but the victor's voice. It means nothing and changes as frequently as the winds blowing across the Lorcean plains."

Lord Tolin stopped, placing his other hand over Braelyn's arm. "Only if good people do nothing. We must always strive to discover the truth in ourselves and others. Don't let the injustices of the world harden your heart, your grace. We need it."

Braelyn looked at the young lord in earnest. She nearly dismissed his words as nothing more than an empty comfort until she met his eyes. He did not believe Lord Julian's lies, or at least wasn't ready to accept them in full.

Braelyn willed her face into a bland smile, her court smile, a mask to hide her thoughts. They continued their walk toward the gardens in silence. All the while, she chewed the inside of her cheek until she tasted blood. Lord Tolin warned her not to harden her heart, but she'd recently learned that a bit of hardening was essential for survival. She would never trust so easily again. She'd put her trust in Lord Julian until he showed his true intentions. She'd even trusted Mirra until the moment she appeared in her chambers, backed by two beasts of men ready to take her life.

Mirra.

The woman Lord Julian placed to watch her until he was ready to strike her family down. The woman who had taken her for pastries talked to her like she was her own person. Someone who wasn't swayed by her connection to the crown, who went against her master, revealing her biggest secret to save Braelyn and her brother.

Gods, magic.

Mirra and Lord Julian both had magic, dark magic. Magic was supposed to have with the Mystics.

Braelyn massaged one side with her free hand. It was all too much.

"Are you all right, princess?"

"I'm not completely sure," Braelyn replied without thinking. "So much has changed. I'm struggling to make sense of it all."

Lord Tolin placed his hand on top of hers once more. She turned and was met with a kind smile. "That's what I'm here for if you'll let me."

Braelyn lost herself in the depths of Lord Tolin's eyes and found herself wondering what Mirra would do in her position.

THE VILLAGERS OF CROGLEN DIDN'T BOTHER TO LOOK UP when Mirra and Gaitlan rode into town. This close to the capital, and on the main road that crossed Undros, they received dozens if not hundreds of travelers at any given time. A perfect place to resupply and come up with a plan. Probably why it was a stopping point on The Shadow Road, the covert series of pathways generated to help royals escape the kingdom in times of need.

The structure of the village was similar to the village she lived in with Brian and Ylanna. The local temple sat near the middle of the square; a large, wooden platform constructed in front; a place for religious plays, justice, and other important events. Several shops made up the rest of the square. She spied a tanner, blacksmith, butchers, clothier, cobbler, and a postmaster's station. She spurred her tired mount toward the postmaster. She wouldn't get much out of the horse for much longer if she kept pushing it the way she was. If she traveled alone, she would have ridden the horse into the ground, abandoning it to disappear on foot in some wooded area.

Her eyes narrowed at the sound of Gaitlan's mount approaching hers. Swinging her leg over the horse's head, she dismounted, stopping short as she read the closed sign on the door. Mirra groaned, digging the heel of her palms into her eyes.

"Expecting a letter?"

"No."

The prince sidled up next to her horse. "Then why stop?"

Mirra ground her teeth, swinging back into the saddle, pulling on the reins with more force than necessary. "No reason."

The prince paused, then followed her to the Iron Cross Inn.

The inn was a decent size. Its sign swinging in the breeze appeared freshly painted, and the windows were free of dirt and grime. From the modest attached stable, a young lad came running eagerly to take their horses.

"Room for the night or a hot meal?"

Mirra reached into her pocket, drawing a silver coin, flipping it at the boy. "Both and a hot bath if it's not too much trouble."

The boy caught the silver coin, tucking it away before bowing deeply. "I canna' speak for the bath, lady, but the meal and room are easy enough. Speak with my master, and he'll set ya up."

Mirra shouldered her bag and made her way toward the door that the boy had pointed to. Though the prince followed quietly after her, she felt the force of his questions rising to the surface. She prayed he'd hold his tongue until they were in their room rather than airing them in the open, risking exposure.

The owner of the inn was a plump man with ruddy cheeks. He beamed when he saw Mirra and the prince walk through the door, hustling to greet them.

"Greetings, travelers! What can I do for you today? Our food and beds cannot be beaten by any other inn from Eastport to Verance."

"A room for the night, with meals and baths."

The innkeeper's smile lost a bit of its luster as he rubbed his stubbly chin. "The food and room can be managed easily enough, but the baths ... that's a bit trickier and costly."

Mirra and Gaitlan answered at the same time.

"Don't worry about it."

"Just hot water, then."

The innkeeper stared at the two, attempting to puzzle out their dynamic and whose order to follow. Mirra spoke again before the prince could spend the coin they didn't have.

"We haven't been traveling for long; hot water is fine."

The innkeeper nodded, his smile turning his cheeks into apples. He pointed them toward the bar, where he drew a thick book from under the counter. "Name?"

"Shaw," Mirra said quickly. "Abby and Gregory Shaw."

The innkeeper scratched the names into the ledger. "Let's see a single room, two meals, and a stable fee."

Mirra tapped her foot, eager for the room key. The longer they remained in the common room, the more time someone had to recognize the prince. After what felt like an eternity, the innkeeper spouted out the fee for their stay. It was a tad high, but Mirra didn't want to waste more time haggling the owner down. She handed over the coin, barely refraining herself from snatching the key from the innkeeper's hand.

Their room was decently sized, with a large bed taking up most of the space, a medium-sized chest for storage, and a small bedside table. Mirra dropped her bag on the floor before falling back onto the bed, the scent of musty straw wafting around her.

"Are we supposed to share the bed?"

Mirra lifted her head to glare at the prince.

At least Gaitlan had closed the door before speaking; though she wished he kept his comments to himself. All she wanted was a few hours of uninterrupted sleep in a halfway decent bed before hitting the road again ... to where ... she hadn't gotten that far yet.

"If it bothers you, then you can have the floor."

A petty jab, she knew it, but the prince's flushed space and sputtering speech gave her the tiniest sense of satisfaction.

Her ability to tolerate Gaitlan's presence had become nearly nonexistent since he regained his consciousness. The stress of the past weeks had finally begun to wear on her. And their current situation did nothing to quell the ire steadily growing inside her every time the prince spoke.

Mirra closed her eyes and took a deep breath, releasing her anger on the exhale. It wasn't the prince's fault. He couldn't have stopped Lord Julian any more than she could.

"We'll be sleeping in shifts. So, no, we won't be sharing this bed."

"Shifts?"

Mirra pinched the bridge of her nose and flashed the prince an incredulous look.

"Right, we're on the run. Sorry." Gaitlan walked further toward the middle of the room. When he reached the bed, he stood awkwardly, tugging at the hem of his tunic, running a hand through his tousled hair.

A knock at the door spared Mirra from having to interact with the prince some more.

Gaitlan reached for his dagger. Mirra stilled him with a

light touch of her hand. He stiffened, staring after her when she answered the door.

"Warm water and soap."

"Thank you," Mirra said to the maid, stepping aside to let her in.

The maid briefly made eye contact with Gaitlan, swiftly nodding in his direction. She placed a picture of steaming water on the bedside table along with a chunk of plain soap. "The washbin's outside the door. Leave it all there; someone will come by and get it later."

Mirra thanked the maid again, handing over a copper coin. The maid smiled brighter, curtsying before closing the door behind her.

"Just how are we supposed to bathe with this?"

"Face, neck, hands."

Gaitlan's face contorted into disgust.

"Before we go any further, I need to make some things crystal clear. One, I don't give an unwashed horse's ass about your royal status; not that it matters much anymore. Two, you're going to have to deal with certain 'discomforts' for the unforeseen future. And three ..."

"What's number three?" Gaitlan growled.

"You have to trust me."

"Trust you? You worked for the bastard that killed my parents! I can never trust you, no matter what my sister thinks."

"I wasn't given a choice!" Mirra spat back. Hopefully, the noise from below would drown out their words.

"You didn't have a choice," Gaitlan scoffed. "That's what

they all say." He strode toward Mirra, his long legs allowing him to cross the room in a couple of strides.

Mirra stood her ground, widening her stance as her hands curled into white-knuckled fists.

"What did he have on you? Drugs? A favor? Or did you serve him for the money?"

A red haze fizzled at the corners of Mirra's vision. "My god's damned life! That's what he 'had on me.' What would you do if you were facing the death penalty at twelve for a crime that you were forced to commit!"

Shock replaced anger on Gaitlan's face. Mirra spun on her heel and stormed out of the room before she could see the pity that undoubtedly took over. She didn't need his pity. She didn't even need him.

She walked right through the common room, heedless of the noise and glances her way. Winter's chill still lingered, turning her breath into little clouds in front of her face. All around her, windows glowed with lights from candles and crackling hearths. Seeing them from outside made the bite of the cold all the more potent. Mirra wrapped her arms around her and let her feet take her wherever they willed.

Croglen wasn't that large, and before too long, she found herself standing in front of the inn again. Laughter and life poured out from the windows on the main floor, while the upper floors remained dark, save for one window—the room where she left the prince.

He doesn't need me. He's a prince. He can find his own way, and if not, he didn't deserve the crown, anyway. I could leave him here and disappear. Maybe I could go north to Lorcea or Nealet, find work on a ship. See the world before Lord Julian finds me.

Mirra shuddered. She didn't want to know what fresh rounds of torture he'd put her through now that he knew she had magic and lied to him about it. She'd gotten the prince this far. She could leave a note explaining how to find stops along Shadow Road. That should silence the nagging voice in her head calling her a coward. The prince didn't trust her; he made that abundantly clear. She didn't want to spend the rest of her days locked into a battle of wills with some stuffed-up man-child.

Mirra turned to fade away into the night when a melody coiled out from the inn, encircling her. It filled her, chasing away all her fears and thoughts until nothing remained but the song. A song without words, yet, somehow, she knew it as surely as she knew her name. She turned and entered the inn, swaying slightly to the rhythm of the melody. It carried her upstairs, where the prince had fallen asleep waiting for her. On the chest sat her meal, still warm. She sat and ate, only realizing after finishing her meal that she never saw a single person playing the flute in the room below.

CHAPTER THREE

THE MORNING LIGHT HADN'T BREACHED THE TOPS OF THE trees, and yet, the villagers were already up and going. And so was Mirra after sneaking out of the room she and Gaitlan shared. The job she needed to complete would undoubtedly go smoother without the prince's questioning or disapproval.

A bell hanging over the door frame jingled merrily as she walked through. A clerk looked up from a small mountain of letters with a bright smile, if not a little bit sleepy.

"Greetings on this fine morning. How may I help you today?"

"I'm here to pick up a package."

The clerk paused, checking a large, leather-bound ledger. "I haven't received any parcels for some time now. Are you sure it was sent here?"

Mirra stepped closer, bracing on the counter, staring coldly into the clerk's eyes. "I am sure. There wouldn't be a name on the package; just a drawing."

The clerk's cheerful expression; a deep furrow appearing between his brows. "Of what?"

"This." Mirra pulled back her sleeve, exposing Lord Julian's brand, the mark of servitude to the King's Viper.

All color drained out of the clerk's face. He stepped back, casting his eyes to the floor. "Forgive me. I was mistaken."

Mirra withdrew her wrist and took a step backward, tilting her chin. "My package, if you please."

The clerk murmured something that Mirra took as a yes before disappearing through a door.

As soon as the clerk vanished, Mirra relaxed her stance, looking over her shoulder to check for approaching customers. Her hands traveled from her waist to her belt, to the hilt of her daggers. The itch to be on the road grew to the point of pain. She needed to put as much distance between herself and Lord Julian as possible. In all honesty, she should have left the night before, but … Her mind was blank. Why hadn't she abandoned Gaitlan? The last thing she remembered from the night before was … She couldn't remember that either.

The clerk arrived, stopping her downward spiral of panic.

"Sorry for the wait. It took me a moment to find it. We've had this in storage for as long as I can remember." The clerk hefted a long wooden box onto the counter with a grunt.

Mirra took the box and hoisted it onto her shoulder. It was heavier than she'd expected, but hopefully, it would carry them further than to the next village. She chucked a couple of coins on the counter before walking out of the post office, the bell jingling as she went.

As soon as Mirra rounded the corner, a shudder ran

down the clerk's spine. He'd wished the postmaster had been on duty instead of sleeping off his hangover. He really didn't want his name to be attached in a way to the message that had to be sent, but the protocol was protocol. Messenger birds greeted the clerk with a chorus of noise, expecting their breakfast. Some of the birds' wings were painted, indicating where they'd been trained to fly to. Red wings meant they flew to Lorcea. Green, Nealet. Purple for the capital, and white for the Holy Isle. The clerk chose a white bird with black-tipped wings, the only one with such coloring.

The clerk scratched a scripted note onto a slip of paper, binding it to the bird's leg with a black thread. After giving the bird a bit of breakfast, the clerk gently tossed the bird into the air, watching it soar over the treetops. The clerk's mind briefly went back to the young woman who claimed the box. She was the most beautiful woman he'd ever seen, even with the unnatural shade of her eyes. Too bad she was one of his people. That world was not for the likes of him. The clerk dusted his hands off the matter, returning to his simple but safe life.

WHERE THE HEL HAVE YOU BEEN?" GAITLAN SNAPPED the moment Mirra entered the room. "And what in the hel is that?"

She threw the box onto the bed with a grunt. "Presents courtesy of Lord Julian."

Gaitlan eyed the box with suspicion.

"Relax, princeling, it's part of the Shadow Road."

Gaitlan's eyes widened with recognition. The light lasted

but a breath before narrowing with suspicion. "And you still trust the validity of that path?"

Mirra shrugged. "It was made to get royals out of the city and to allies quickly. It changes with each spymaster, but even still, it's practically impossible for him to find us right away."

The prince peered at the box. "That may be. Where does this box send us?"

"Let's open and see."

She reached out to undo the latches. Gaitlan wrapped his hand around her wrist. She cut her eyes to him, with a sharp retort already forming on her tongue. But the sight of Gaitlan's colorless, sweat-soaked face and wide eyes killed them like a spark caught in a strong wind.

"What if it's a trap? What if he already knows? How can we be sure that man won't find out where we are?"

Mirra scrunched her lips, mulling over Gaitlan's concerns.

"What choice do we really have?" she asked. "The only thing that I know for sure is that we need to get as far away from Lord Julian and the capital as possible if you're going to have a chance. This is the only way."

Gaitlan closed his eyes and swallowed. Mirra watched the bob of his Adam's apple with a twinge of sympathy. She closed her eyes and released a heavy breath, already regretting the words clawing at her mouth.

"If you feel that strongly, then we can figure out something else."

Gaitlan stared up at her in surprise, taken back by the sudden show of empathy from her. His face was a wild mix of a hundred different emotions, thoughts, and fears. Each one skipped across his face too fast for Mirra to read.

Gaitlan closed his eyes and made peace with his ultimate decision. He released the clasps on the box, flinging the lid open. Reaching in, he pulled out a long wrapped bundle. He uncoiled the wrapping, revealing a medium-length sword. It was wider than the blades wielded by knights and nobles, with a slight curve at the point. Intricately interwoven artwork had been etched along the edge.

The design stirred something within Mirra's mind. She reached out, running her finger along the pattern. "A horse lord blade?"

She turned her attention to the fabric that the sword had been wrapped in. "Nealitian fabric."

She dug around in the box, ignoring the dried food stores and other helpful items until she discovered two sizable bags of coins. She opened one, emptying its contents into her hands. Coins from all over the continent filled her palm.

At the bottom of the box sat a small envelope bearing a black seal. Mirra set the coins aside to pick up the envelope, breaking the seal.

"What does it say?"

"Eastport and Rythos."

Mirra pulled the end of her braid over her shoulder. "There may be a ship for us to board at Eastport, but Rythos; I've never heard of it."

"It's a trading village near the northern road that passes through Mystic Wood and the Border Mountains."

"Impressive," Mirra said with a smirk.

Gaitlan made a face. "Joys of being a prince; hours and hours of my life dedicated to the scholarly arts, including learning the basic geography of my future kingdom."

"At least you had an education," Mirra muttered.

Gaitlan took the note from her hand, turning it this way and that, looking for any signs of a hidden message.

"Rythos is closer, only a three- or four-day journey on horseback. Eastport would take us a week if we pushed the horses."

Mirra rubbed her chin. "Eastport's too risky. The way there is too well-traveled; too many eyes to avoid. It puts us at a greater risk of someone recognizing you."

Gaitlan reflected on Mirra's words. "Rythos it is, then."

Mirra poured the coins in her hand back into the bag, synching it tightly to her belt with a few extra knots to deter pickpockets.

"Take that," she said, jerking her head at the bag in the prince's hands, "and get yourself some more gear; a waterproof cloak, flint, and whatnot. Whatever you'll need on the road, within reason. See if you can purchase a few bags of feed for the horses while you're at it."

Gaitlan looked down at the small bag of coins, a slight frown on his face. "What are you going to do?"

Mirra yawned and stretched, her back popping in several places. "I'm going to take a nap. We leave just before sundown."

"Is it safe to ride at night?"

"Safer than waiting for guards or whoever Julian sends after us to catch up."

Gaitlan watched Mirra take off her boots before curling

up in the middle of the bed, appearing to fall asleep instantly. Her face softened as her breathing slowed and deepened. He didn't believe it for a second. Still, recognizing a dismissal when he saw it, Gaitlan left, closing the door softly behind him.

Gaitlan stood out front of the inn, at a loss of what to do. He never had to manage his funds before now. How did one go about the acquisition of items without completely depleting their funds? He didn't even know what else he might require on the road. Every aspect of his life tended to by a small army of attendants; his every want and need taken care of, sometimes before he even knew of them. His hand slid to the paltry amount of coins at his side, the nature of his inadequacies becoming woefully apparent.

Perhaps my father was right, after all?

Reality crashed into Gaitlan, stealing the strength from his limbs, causing him to stumble into the pillar of an open-air workshop.

"Ya all right there, lad?"

Gaitlan lifted his head. A husky man with the largest arms he'd ever seen stood just to the left of a massive anvil, various hammers strapped at his waist. Heat and the acrid scent of scorched metals curled around him, reminding Gaitlan of the god Haptos, the armorer of The Dark Court.

"I have to be."

The blacksmith cocked his head, unsure of what to make of Gaitlan's response.

The blacksmith turned to his work, pulling a glowing red rod from the fire. The sound of his hammer striking the anvil chased away the crippling thoughts running through Gaitlan's mind. Sparks flew from the rod like tiny embers, some catching stray strands of straw alight before puttering out into ash. After beating the rod a few more times, the blacksmith returned it to the fire, his apprentice using great billows to stoke the fires to sweltering heights.

Splashing himself with a ladle of clean water, the blacksmith turned to Gaitlan. "Ya want some advice?" He carried on without waiting for Gaitlan's response. "Life is pain. That point is fair easy for most of us to ken. But even still, it can throw us sideways. It the gods way of teachin a lesson. All ya gotta do is ask yaself two questions. Tell em, Nate."

"Are ya gonna stay down, or are ya gonna get up swinging?" Nate, the apprentice, bellowed from his position.

The blacksmith nodded proudly, crossing his massive arms across his broad chest. "Well, son, which are ya gonna choose?"

A shy smile tugged at Gaitlan's mouth as his spine straightened. "I guess I come up swinging," he said.

The blacksmith's smile made his face less like an impassive god and more like a stern but caring father.

Gaitlan reached into the bag at his side, flicking a silver coin at the blacksmith. "For the advice," he said before striding down the way with a little bit of his old swagger.

Some time later, Gaitlan returned to the inn, a rucksack slung over his shoulder. Inside sat his newly acquired traveling supplies. He purchased a weatherproof cloak as Mirra had suggested. He also purchased flint, fishing hooks and a bit of line, and another set of clothes. The feed he was sent to buy already sat in the stables, ready to go. Though he was satisfied overall, the cost of everything still gnawed at him. He wasn't entirely sure he hadn't been taken advantage of.

"Took you long enough," Mirra commented when he opened the door.

Gaitlan caught sight of her long black hair cascading down her bare back like a river under a moonless sky. All the air was sucked out of the room. Time stopped. Even his heart froze at the sight before him.

She turned to look at him over her shoulder with eyes the color of a glacier's heart that bored right into the very center of his being, completely exposing every fault, every deficiency.

Mirra arched a brow, wholly nonplussed by her partial nakedness.

"I had things to buy." His face twisted the words that flew out of his mouth.

Mirra pulled on her shirt, gathering her hair into three locks, weaving them around each other with deft fingers. "That, you did." She turned around and quickly braided her hair. "My turn. See you in a bit."

She walked out of the room without another word, leaving Gaitlan behind, crippled by a fresh wave of confusion. Only when her footsteps retreated down the stairs was he able to move.

What the hel was that?

The bell chimed the hour, and Mirra had yet to return. Granted, he had been gone much longer when it had been his turn, but Gaitlan's trust in her was still unsteady. His mind rotated between thoughts of her deserting him to his enemies and unwrapping her braid, savoring the way the dark locks rippled down her porcelain skin.

He collapsed onto the bed, throwing an arm over his eyes. Perhaps a few moments of sleep would relinquish Mirra's hold on his thoughts.

The straw from the bed poked through in some places, yet he still found it comfortable. His limbs grew heavy, and his breathing slowed. It only took a matter of minutes for sleep to claim him, sending him to a place where dreams come to life or nightmares.

Smoke filled his senses along with the coppery tang of blood. He stepped forward and lost his footing, falling hard on the floor. His hand came away red, and he looked up in horror at the sight of his parents bleeding out, his mother's hand reaching out for him. His bowels turned to water as he scuttled away from his parents.

Lord Julian emerged from the recesses of the room, larger than life, laughing at Gaitlan's feeble attempts to escape. Braelyn came into view, clasped tightly in Julian's black hand, tears streaming down her soot-streaked face.

"Brother, why did you abandon me?"

"I didn't," he cried.

Julian's cruel laughter crescendoed, drawing out all other sounds. He lifted Braelyn to his face. His mouth opened wider than humanly possible to swallow his sister whole.

Gaitlan shot up, drenched in sweat, the echoes of his nightmare still clinging to him. "A dream. It was just a dream. She's not dead."

He turned to the window to gauge the time, the sky a gentle orange. It would be time to leave soon. He would need his wits about him on the road, especially once night fell. Gaitlan pulled on his boots, hoping that a brief walk about the village square would clear his head.

A pair of riders thundered past the inn, leaving a cloud of dust in their wake. Gaitlan starred after them, dread coiling in his stomach. Their clothing and the crest sewn on the backs of their capes marked them as royal messengers. His feet moved of their own volition, following after the messengers.

A small crowd already gathered at the local temple, worried whispers rising and falling like winter wheat. One messenger dismounted, conversing quickly with the high priest, who paled and took a step back. His weathered hands were clasped tightly in front of him. The other messenger scowled as he scanned the crowd. Gaitlan held his breath when his eyes met the messenger's, but the messenger's eyes slid over Gaitlan without any signs of recognition.

The first messenger stood in front of the temple and removed his helmet. He looked out at the gathering crowd with a solemn expression before retrieving a scroll from his bag—a scroll bound by a black ribbon. Muffled cries of alarm rolled through the people. Their fear and confusion carrying them forward.

The messenger held up his hand, signaling for calm and silence.

"Woe to the kingdom of Undros. Woe to its people. Our beloved king and queen were betrayed and slaughtered by their own son, Prince Gaitlan. He brought foreign forces into the castle to subdue loyal and honorable agents of the crown."

The remnants of his nightmare roared to the surface, digging its claws into him, drawing up details from his darkest day.

Horror and disbelief painted every face gathered, the villagers crying out for it all to be a lie, a fallacy.

The messenger continued, raising his voice to finish reading the proclamation. This was his last stop of the day, and all he wanted was a mug of cold ale and a clean bed. In the morning, he'd ride out, reading the same message over and over until he reached the eastern shore.

"Yet, even with purchased steel and assassins, those loyal to the crown defeated the prince's forces, reclaiming the palace for the crown."

Gaitlan's ears were deaf to the ruckus around him. Numb to the growing violence around him, the way the crowd had started to sway and roll.

"Like a coward, Prince Gaitlan fled the capital like the coward he is, disappearing with what remains of his forces. With the full support of the Council of Lords, Princess Braelyn has declared the prince a traitor. With the matter of Mirra Ó Broin, Lord Julian's niece, while the full extent of her participation is unclear, she is as guilty as the prince. Warrants of arrest have been issued for both. Approach with caution."

A man jostled Gaitlan, sending him to the ground. There he remained, unseen by the mob. A foot crushed his hand, while an elbow sent stars dancing across his vision.

Someone pulled Gaitlan up, freeing him from his waking nightmare. His mouth was full of the bitter tastes of smoke and sorrow. Still half caught in memory, Mirra dragged him away from the crowd toward their horses, already packed and saddled.

Numbly, he climbed into the saddle and followed Mirra out of Croglen. Behind him, no one took notice of their departure. The mood of the once peaceful village had turned into a horde hungry for the traitor prince's blood and any who dared to align themselves with him.

CHAPTER FOUR

SMOKE FROM THE NEARBY INCENSE BURNER CURLED upward IN the dim light. Braelyn watched its journey to join the massive cloud of perfumed smoke roll and billow amongst the eves of the temple with burning eyes. If anyone asked why, she'd blame it on the smoke.

Yulla, Dark Mother, I beg you to reach out your hand and guide my parents to their place by your side. Forgive the mistakes they made, for we are mortal and stumble from time to time. Please keep my brother and Mirra shielded from those who would harm them. Please guide them to safety.

Braelyn didn't bother with prayers for herself.

A priestess glided past, her semi-sheer black robe whispering across the dark gray stones. In other shadowed alcoves, whimpers and soft cries mingled with low hymns for the dead and lost. A single tear trailed down Braelyn's face. She let it fall, knowing that the black lace mourning veil obscured her face. She would only allow herself to shed that single tear. She had no way of knowing who watched her from the shadows.

To prove her point, heavy footsteps approached from behind. Braelyn made the motion for the end of a prayer to wipe away the tear without drawing attention. With a heavy heart, she stood, slowly turning to face the person who disturbed her rare moment of peace.

"Forgive me, your grace," Lord Tolin said, bowing deeply.

"Lord Tolin."

He swayed side to side. He clasped his hands in front, then he crossed arms but quickly uncrossed, finally settling with them behind him.

"Do you need something, Lord Tolin?"

Lord Tolin shifted under Braelyn's gaze, unease pouring out of every fiber of his being.

"I want to express my condolences again for your loss."

Braelyn bit back a frustrated sigh. "Yes, my lord, you've expressed it repeatedly." She stepped around Lord Tolin, her veil fluttering behind her like the wings of a raven.

Behind her, she heard Lord Tolin sputter nonsense before turning to follow after her. She rolled her eyes.

"I know, and I do apologize for the awkwardness, but it's the only thing I can think to say. For days, I've tried to talk with you. To ask you … well … you are a fine woman with a sharp mind and …"

Braelyn's tightly reined emotions finally snapped. Spinning around, she came face to face with Lord Tolin. He stopped short, taken aback. She threw her face veil over her head, letting him see the full extent of the fiery storm raging inside.

He took a step back. Braelyn pressed forward to the point where their bodies were flushed against each other. He looked down at the tiny storm of a woman scowling at him. A shiver ran down his spine, setting into the lower portions of his body.

Through clenched teeth, she hissed, "You think now is the proper time to come forward as a suitor? My parents are gone, not even cold in their tombs. My brother is accused of their murder with only an assassin for an ally."

Lord Tolin's brow furrowed. "What assassin?"

The fire in Braelyn's blood fizzled under a crashing wave of ice. Gods above, what have I done! Quickly, she schooled her face into an emotionless mask. "While I appreciate your condolences and continued support, I must ask that you respect my wishes and allow me the time and space to grieve and pray."

Braelyn walked as fast as she could without running out of the temple and into the waiting carriage. She was blind to the looks and whispers of the common folk. Her stomach soured, rolling like a ship at sea. She'd let her emotions get the better of her. What if Lord Tolin took what she let slip to Lord Julian? What would he do? Braelyn worried her thumb the entire ride back to the castle. She could only come to one conclusion—she had to get out of the city; the sooner, the better.

THE SETTING SUN FORCED MIRRA AND GAITLAN TO FIND A place to make camp after only a couple of hours on the road, more for their horse's sake than their own. The prince's silence was equal parts of a curse and a blessing. She knew what it was like to have the rug ripped out from under you, but that didn't mean she knew what to say to make him feel better or if that was even possible. Bao or Em would know what to say to ease some of the prince's pain; they were the gentle ones. Mirra clenched the reins, leather crackling in her grip. She'd expected Lord

Julian to twist the truth for his benefit. Still, Mirra hadn't expected him to turn the entire kingdom against them. If she didn't get the prince somewhere safe soon, there wouldn't be any allies left.

Mirra spied a small trail leading off into the woods just as the sun disappeared behind the treetops. She dismounted and walked a few steps under the canopy, stretching her ears and her senses for any signs of danger.

"Let's stop here for the night."

Gaitlan dismounted and followed after her without a word. The prickliness of worry fluttered about in her chest. He was slipping away, going deeper into the darkness.

"It's going to be chilly tonight, but I don't think we should light a fire. Our bedrolls and cloaks should keep us warm enough." Mirra chewed her lip, then added, "What do you think?"

Gaitlan shrugged his eyes like twin voids. Silently, he unsaddled his horse, seeing to its needs before unrolling his bedroll. He crawled inside, pulling the coverings over his head.

Mirra starred at Gaitlan's prone form for several long minutes until growing shadows forced her to tend to her own needs.

Crickets came to life, filling the night with their melodies. The soft sounds of sobbing soon joined them. Mirra turned to take care of her own horse, pretending to not hear the prince's sobs. Everyone needed space to process the shattering of their world. She would speak to him in the morning.

Mirra bundled up her cloak, stuffing it under her head like a pillow. She spared the prince one final pity-filled glance before falling asleep.

MIRRA STOOD IN THE MIDDLE OF A BATTLEGROUND. ALL around her, people screamed, holding their arms over their heads in a pitiful attempt to protect themselves from falling debris. After a moment of panic, she recognized some of the horrified faces around her. She'd seen them before in a dream.

She slowly spun, taking in as much as she could. She didn't recognize any of the buildings. The people running around her could be from Undros or even from the Stone Clans of Lorcea. But there was something about them that was familiar. It gnawed at her consciousness like a sore tooth.

Mirra walked through the chaos, heading toward the temple. Perhaps, there, she would find some answers. The longer she walked, the quieter the streets grew until she was alone, surrounded by the city's funeral pyre. On and on, she walked, but she couldn't seem to find any street that would take her to the temple. She could make out its domed roof looming over the tops of the others, but no matter how far she walked, she never got any closer. Mirra groaned, throwing her hands up in frustration. She turned to try another street but stopped short, her heart rising to her throat.

At the other end of the street stood a tall, dark, imposing figure. Mirra squinted against rolling clouds of smoke and ash. The hairs on the back of her neck stood on end. There was something different about this being than the others.

"Hello," Mirra tentatively called out.

The being flew toward Mirra, death white claws reaching

out as it released a blood-curdling screech.

Mirra turned heel and ran as fast as she could down a joining street. Vaulting over burning debris, she scanned for any place to hide, only looking behind her when she could muster the smallest fragment of bravery.

The demon was nothing more than billowing black robes with startling white hands and face. Though Mirra never focused long enough to register anything more than the gaping maw that continued to scream.

An errant basket proved to be Mirra's downfall. It split, tangling around her feet, sending her crashing to the ground.

The demon hovered over Mirra for a heartbeat before diving down; its claws aimed for her heart.

Mirra summoned a shadowy whip, flinging it at the demon in a last-ditch effort to save her life.

The demon broke off its attack, veering off as smoothly as a hawk.

"Rise," commanded a voice echoed with masculine and feminine tones. It carried the lightness of a child and the weight of one heavily burdened by the ages.

Mirra rolled over, calling on her shadows. The demon's form shifted, dropping its monstrous form a young woman not much older than Mirra herself. The woman stood as a silent pillar of darkness against the glow of the fires.

Mirra slowly rose to her feet, taking time to study the woman more closely. Midnight black hair floated around an impossibly pale face marred by dark marks. Mirra took a small step forward.

The woman remained still, ancient power fluttering her

hair into the air. Mirra crossed the distance between them, stopping an arm's length away.

The markings turned out to be intricate tattoos nearly covering every inch of the woman's face. They were beautiful in a savage way, swirling around the woman's face, accenting her features, including eyes the same shade as Mirra's.

As Mirra studied the woman's face, cold dread pooled in the pit of her stomach. The woman's face transformed, turning into her own before shifting again to her original form.

"Who are you?" Mirra asked, her voice barely above a whisper.

The woman's expression turned sad. "You cannot escape your destiny."

"What destiny?"

Tears poured down the woman's face as she drew a dagger from thin air. The blade was nothing like Mirra had ever seen; it radiated pain, hunger, and regret. Its black blade swallowed up the light around the woman, leaving her shrouded in darkness.

The woman raised the dagger high in the air before plunging it into her heart. She gasped, her blue eyes turning black, before crumbling to the ground in a pile of ash.

MIRRA FOUGHT WITH HER SLEEPING ROLL. SHE LURCHED to her feet, hunting daggers in each hand. Her breath was ragged, and a cold sweat turned icy in the evening air.

"Nightmare?"

Mirra turned toward the prince. He sat on the ground

across from her, a short sword across his lap. He gave off the impression that he'd been waiting a while for Mirra to wake up.

She sheathed her daggers and straightened her clothes. "Not really."

Gaitlan made a noise in the back of his throat like he didn't believe her, watching intently while she put her bedroll back together.

"Do you want something?" Mirra asked through a stiff jaw.

"You heard those lies that bastard said about me. About you."

"What of it?" she said with as much calm as she could muster.

Gaitlan surged to his feet; the knuckles on the hand that held his sword were nearly as white as the young woman's face from her dream.

Who was that woman? What did she mean by 'her destiny'? Was she going to die if she kept going on her current path? Or did it mean something else altogether?

"What of it? That's not what happened! That bastard is the one who plotted against the crown, not me! And I left ... we left Brae there with him." Emotion choked Gaitlan's words, his sword clattering to the ground. He followed shortly afterward, burying his head in his hands.

Mirra pressed her lips together. "Your sister is stronger than you realize. She's been handling people for years while you were off, gallivanting around with your friends. Don't underestimate her."

Mirra turned and saddled her horse, giving the beast a

friendly pat. "Now, pull yourself together, princeling, and let's go."

"To what end?"

Mirra's horse tucked its head over her shoulder. She stroked its nose absentmindedly. "I was hoping that you'd be able to fill in that part once you pulled your head out of your ass." Gaitlan shot her an incredulous look. "Do you have friends outside of Undros that might be willing to help?"

Gaitlan's gaze turned distance as if he could see the other kingdoms. "Yestin of Eddany. He's the youngest son of Morí Dwelyn. I spent a season with them when his sister was anointed as the heir."

Mirra continued to stroke her horse's nose. "Sounds good to me," she said after some consideration. Fragments of the dream still clung to her. She couldn't shake the feeling of dread.

Wordlessly, she walked back to the road, mounted, and continued north. It was still early, yet the road was already starting to fill with merchants and other travelers. Nearly everyone wore a black armband.

Mirra was painfully aware of how exposed they were on the open road. She pulled the hood of her cloak over her head. A quick glance behind her revealed that Gaitlan had followed suit.

Mirra opened up her senses, stretching her awareness to the masses surrounding them. The moment someone started to recognize the prince, they would be off. However, it appeared that the common folk was more interested in gossiping about the king and queen's demise than looking for the supposed guilty party.

"The prince slaughtered his parents with his own hand

because they denied him the crown on his birthday. Their concerns well-founded, it seems."

"The Viper's niece practiced black arts learned from her time as a war chief's whore after he slaughtered her husband's family."

"The only reason why the princess is still alive, I hear, is because The Viper himself saved her. He may be a spy, but at least he's true."

Mirra grimaced. She couldn't care less about what people thought about her, but the prince ... She risked a glance over her shoulder to see how he was handling the conversations around them.

He stared at the pommel of his saddle, hands clenching the reins tightly. His face was like a storm cloud, threatening to release at any given moment.

Another feel ran like an undercurrent in the crowd. Bands of roving men armed with hunting knives, pitchforks, and shovels stop random people, questioning and emptying wagons. Mirra spurred her horse faster, eager to put some distance between them and the mob.

By some miracle, they made it to an inn without any incidents. Mirra chalked their luck up to the fact that they had started to look like a pair of brigands, especially when they kept their hoods up. Gaitlan objected to the warmth but relented when she pointed out the other people with their hoods up too.

"Any'ing else for ya?"

Mirra growled out a no, flinging a few coppers onto the table. The serving woman eyed Mirra before snatching the coins off the table, muttering a soft "bastard" under her breath.

Gaitlan stared at her like she had grown a second head. "What?"

"How did you do that? You sounded like a man."

Mirra smirked. "Assassin, school."

"Yeah, right." Gaitlan chuckled lightly until he realized she'd meant it. "Is there really an assassin school?"

Mirra shrugged. "I don't think there's anything official like, but Lord Julian did arrange for me to learn a fair number of things before bringing me to the palace."

Gaitlan stared at her in disbelief, his mouth slack-jawed. He quickly closed it and lowered his gaze. He pushed the tasteless boiled potatoes around on his plate.

"What did you learn?"

"All sorts of useful things—how to mingle in any class, poisons, hand-to-hand combat. The stealth and stealing, I learned early on as a kid."

Gaitlan pushed his food around on his plate. "What about magic?"

The noise of the room evaporated, leaving her in a vacuum of silence. She set her fork down with care and precision, her face blank.

"There's no such thing as magic. Not anymore."

Gaitlan narrowed his eyes. "I remember that night."

Mirra scoffed, waving her hand. "You were out of your mind from whatever Lord Julian gave you that you could have probably seen the gods."

Gaitlan scowled at her. "I know that I saw, drugs or no drugs. There's the matter of when you saved me when I was attacked by those nobles."

Mirra laughed. "Again, you were drunk off your ass."

Gaitlan wasn't deterred. "I know you heard what those people on the road were saying. I have ears too. I heard what they were saying about you."

"Peasants will believe whatever they want. Of course, they're going to whisper about dark forces because, otherwise, no one will want to listen to them. It's all just rumors to bring life into their little lives. Listen to it if you want to, princeling. I, on the other hand, have far more pressing things to worry about here in the real world."

Gaitlan's scowl deepened, and he turned his attention back to his food, stabbing his potatoes violently with his fork. Mirra kept her face neutral for the remainder of the meal.

She should have worried less about the prince finding out her secret and worried more about the dangers surrounding them.

Across the room, tucked around a small table near the stairs that led to the rooms for rent, a trio of grizzled men sat half into their pints. Bloodshot and greedy eyes had marked Mirra and Gaitlan the moment they walked through the door. At first, they had pegged them as a potential mark, each man silently claiming a sword, blade, cloak, and even Mirra for themselves. Then they caught a glimpse of Gaitlan's face and matching cruel grins spread across the table. They recognized him as the crown prince from the wanted posters now in circulation. If they managed to capture him, they would be set up for months.

When Gaitlan and Mirra headed for the door, the men stood, tossing a few coppers on the table before exiting out a smaller, less used door that led straight into the stables. They knew the roads around the inn and the surrounding roads like the back of their hands.

In the common room, Mirra had felt a prickling at the back of her neck. It persisted on the road, even though Gaitlan was the only other person she saw. She wasn't sure if it was because of how close the prince had come to exposing her secret, or if it was something else altogether. It bore her down until she felt the weight of everything in her bones. Just further proof that she was not meant for the life of a hero. People like her were meant to live their lives in the shadows, surviving off their wits, disappearing, and reappearing at will.

Stop! Stop! Stop!

She halted her horse, scanning the road with her senses, physical and magical.

Gaitlan pulled up next to her, lowering his hood. "What is it?"

"I'm not sure, but I think ..."

A bloodthirsty roar killed the remainder of her thought. A single rider came barreling around the bend with a short sword already aloft. Before Mirra or Gaitlan had a chance to go for their own blades, two more men erupted from the underbrush on both sides of the road, reaching for Gaitlan and Mirra.

Mirra was pulled from her saddle before she could reach for her daggers. But Gaitlan managed to kick his assailant in the face, sending him careening back into the underbrush. His expression was torn as he looked from Mirra to the mounted third attacker.

Mirra struck her attacker in his solar plexus with her fist, knocking the air from his lungs. His breath smelled of rotting teeth, causing her to gag. Rolling, she tossed him off, drawing her blades in a fluid motion.

"Go, I got this!"

Gaitlan turned, drew his blade, and charged, letting out a roar of his own. In it, he poured all of his hatred, guilt, and despair. He felt it tear at his throat, tasting blood. At the same time, the edges of his vision disappeared into a red haze until all that existed was his opponent rushing to bee his blade. The two met with a clash of swords, striking hard and fast before disengaging to attack again.

Mirra and her opponent circled each other with wary eyes. He kept a hand over the place where she struck, still struggling to regain his breath. He eyed her suspiciously.

She wouldn't let him get the upper hand again. Twirling her long daggers so that the blades were against her arm, she surged forward, spinning under his guard to slash at his exposed side.

He roared in pain, swinging his arm blindly, but Mirra already had moved, delivering two swift slashes. She heard the clashing of swords behind her. She trusted Gaitlan to hold his own until she took down the man in front of her. The other assailant still hadn't reemerged from the brush.

Her opponent ran at her, rage fueling his strength. Mirra brought her daggers up in a cross pattern, catching the downward swing of his sword. A brutal smile broke out across his pockmarked face as he bore down, using his height and weight to his advantage.

Mirra gritted her teeth, struggling to keep the tip of his blade from inching closer to her face. Pain blossomed at the back of her neck as she felt a force pulling her back to the ground. The other bandit had finally recovered, her long braid wrapped around his filthy fingers.

Mirra took an awkward fighting stance. I can't use magic, not after telling the prince he was wrong. I just need to hold out long enough for the prince to finish the other guy. I can do this.

A sharp cry drew her attention. A flush of red blossomed along Gaitlan's shoulder. He dropped his sword, pressing his hand to the wound. The mounted bandit howled in victory, making a broad swipe meant to remove the prince's head. Gaitlan threw himself from the saddle, landing in a painful heap on the dusty road.

Mirra's distraction cost her. One of her opponents pressed on her. She moved but not fast enough, the tip of the blade slicing across her thigh, marring the delicate skin beneath.

Sensing a change in the fight, the bandit holding her braid pulled harder, forcing her chin toward the sky, exposing her pale neck fully to his partner's blade.

Mirra strained against the downward pull of her braid, feeling strands of hair ripping away from her scalp. Sunlight caught the edge of her assailant's blade as he raised it into the air for the final blow.

No, she screamed in her mind, I will not go out like this. I won't die at the hands of these backwater thugs.

Gritting her teeth, Mirra twisted one of her daggers around, bringing upward. Warmblood splattered across her forehead, followed by a cry of pain and the sweet release of tension on her scalp. Mirra rolled away from the would-be-killing blow, brushing the hair out of her face. In freeing herself, she'd cut more than a couple of filthy fingers.

Gaitlan's grunts let her know he hadn't crossed into the Dark Mother's Realm yet.

He managed to get to his feet, diving for his fallen sword, drawing a fresh wave of blood from his wound. His face already lost most of its pallor, though his eyes lost none of their intensity. He wasn't going to last much longer. He knew it, and so did the bandit, who smiled, exposing his rotten teeth.

Mirra drew a small dagger hidden in her belt and threw it at the bandit. But a fresh attack from the remaining bandit forced her to dodge, throwing off his aim. She neither had time to see the look of mockery on the bandit's face nor the sad acceptance that took over Gaitlan. Her opponent had come at her again in earnest. It took everything she had to deflect the dual attacks.

Seeing no other option, Mirra tried to calm her mind enough so that she could draw up her magic from the place where it dwelled.

The fletching of an arrow blossomed in the center of her attacker's forehead. She blinked at it numbly.

"Mirra, get down," shouted a familiar voice.

Mirra dropped to the ground as another volley of arrows flew over her head. She heard three impacts, followed by a grunt and the thud of a heavy body falling. A pair of sturdy but weathered leather shoes came into Mirra's line of sight.

Mirra lifted her head to see her savior with trepidation.

Beaming down at her was a face that was still as familiar to her as her own.

"Em."

CHAPTER FIVE

MIRRA COULD BARELY FOCUS ON KEEPING HER SEAT IN the saddle. Next to her, Em, a person she never thought to see again, rode in the wagon beside her. Bits of loose hay flitted in the breeze, lazily trailing after the wagon. A large lump of hay shifted, revealing Gaitlan's incensed face.

"Do I really have to stay here?"

Em chuckled, not bothering to look back. "Your face is plastered all over the kingdom, princeling. If you want to get caught, then, by all means, get out. We'll even give you your horse back, but Mirra stays with me."

Em's voice took on a sharp edge, stirring memories from another lifetime. A small smile splayed across Mirra's face, grateful her friend's new life hadn't dulled her edge.

Gaitlan swore softly, disappearing beneath the hay.

Em flashed Mirra a crooked grin that stabbed her in the gut. Mirra was torn between joy at seeing her friend again and guilt over how they had parted ways. Never in a thousand years would Mirra ever regret giving her life for Em or any of her friends. But she'd be a fool not to think that the woman riding calmly in the wagon hadn't ripped herself apart with guilt.

Mirra groaned, tilting her head toward the sky. She heard Em chuckle.

"Wanna talk about it?"

"I don't even know where to start." Mirra tucked a loose strand of hair behind her ear. "I guess I should start with I'm sorry."

Em pulled her gaze away from the road, fixing it on Mirra.

Mirra struggled against the urge to shrink under the weight of her friend's stare. Em's face appeared calm, but Mirra knew just how strong emotions could run underneath a pretty surface.

Em turned back to the road. "Bao sent me a letter a while back, telling me everything. I'm still pissed about it. I thought that I got you killed, my sister."

The tightness in Mirra's throat kept her from offering words of comfort. The Shadow Guild had been her family, even when she had been too stubborn to admit it to herself.

"But if Bao can forgive you, then I guess I can too."

"I don't think he has fully."

Em made a reserved sound. "If I had been in your place, I probably would have done the same thing. Though I lack your 'natural gifts,' so I doubt I'd gotten the same offer."

Mirra stared at the pommel of her saddle, silently cursing Bao for spilling her secrets. Yet equally grateful she wouldn't need to figure out how to broach the subject.

The rest of the journey went by in total silence. Mirra's unease faded to the background of her mind as she tried to imagine the new life her friend had carved out for herself.

Em veered off the main road just as the sun neared its zenith onto a path with deep ruts made from wagon wheels. Tall trees ran along the sides of the path, their branches curving overhead, shielding them from the sun. They traveled for a few more miles before coming to a piece of cleared-out land.

As soon as her home came into view, Em's shoulders relaxed. A small pack of mutts came barreling from their hiding places, yipping, barking, and howling in joy over the sight of their master. Laughing, she dismounted, kneeling to return the affection, disappearing beneath the shaggy bodies.

Mirra smiled, bracing her forearm on the pommel of her saddle. A small smile broke out across her face, a moment of true peace in a never-ending storm.

Unable to withstand hiding beneath the hay a moment longer, Gaitlan emerged, cursing and swatting away the loose strands as well as he could with one arm.

The dogs' attitude changed instantly, putting themselves between Em and the trespassers.

Gaitlan drew his sword to only drop it, grunting in pain. The dogs bared their teeth, a low rumbling in their chest.

Mirra sighed, sliding from the saddle. "Easy, boys. We're all friends here. Isn't that right, Em?"

Em tapped her mouth before stepping forward. "I don't know. I see two dangerous criminals standing on my land. Your capture would set us up for years."

Gaitlan swiveled toward Mirra, his mouth open wide.

The corner of Mirra's mouth tugged upward. She licked her lips to hide her smile.

Em sighed dramatically before snapping her fingers. The

dogs halted, sitting calm and quiet. Their tails thumped in the dirt, awaiting further commands. "You might as well come in," Em said with a careless wave of her hand.

Gaitlan recovered his sword, shooting a worried glance at Mirra. She shrugged his concern off, following after her friend.

Em's home was small, a bit rough around the edges, but overall, a welcoming home. Em kicked off her boots and slipped on a pair of simple leather slippers. "Boots off. I cleaned the floors this morning."

Mirra tugged her boots off, placing them by the door. She unbuckled her short sword and daggers next, hanging them on the pegs that ran along the wall.

"Are you mad?" Gaitlan whispered through clenched teeth.

"Em and I go way back. We may not have seen each other since we were twelve, but I trust her more than I trust you."

"Well, I don't trust either of you."

Running the tip of her tongue over her lips, Mirra inched closer to Gaitlan. Bracing her hands on her hips, she stared up at him with a wicked gleam in her eye.

Her teasing remark was halted by Em's return. "You know it's not nice to play with your food, Mirra. Whatever did that man teach you?" Em set a wooden box onto the table, jars and bottles clinking inside. Em opened the lid of the box and pulled out a wad of linen strips. "One word, and I'll use a hot poker to cauterize the wound instead of nice smelling ointments and stitches. Now, sit."

Mirra pressed her lips together to keep herself from laughing as Gaitlan sat down on a stool, eying her friend warily.

Gods, she'd missed Em.

SINCE WORD OF THE KING'S DEATH, EVERY CITIZEN OF
Croglen was on edge. Uncertainty about the future stirred up
feelings of discontent and anxiety. Violence simmered just
beneath the surface, threatening to boil over at the slightest
provocation amongst the typically calm patrons of the Iron Cross
Inn.

"I'm tellin' ya," Hawn bellowed, swinging his hands
wide, heedless of the ale he splattered. His words were slurred
and filled with venom, "dem pampered, trussed-up bastards take
der golden carriages an' ride through da low streets o'the capital,
offering coin to poor mums for a night with dem babes."

"Ah, sit down, you drunkard," shouted the barkeep over
the roar of the room. "If ya can't keep it down, you can take it
outside."

Hawn grumbled, tumbling back into his chair, tipping
his cup back to only find it completely empty. He snagged a
haggard-looking barmaid, shoving a copper coin into her hand.
"Give us another, love."

"I dunno, Hawn," she said, pocketing the coin. "You've
had a fair amount already. You remember last time, don't cha?"

Hawn's face hardened as he squeezed her wrist harder,
drawing a wince.

"Get me a drink, woman, before I knock yer teeth in."
He shoved her roughly, sending her stumbling into another table
occupied by several men playing a game of cards.

The men cheered as the barmaid ended up half sprawled

across their table. The closest man pulled the barmaid into his lap. She struggled to keep his hands from going down the front of her dress, which drew a wider, predatory grin from the man. He pinned her arms behind her with one hand while the other loosened the ties that kept the front of her dress closed.

"Jarl! Help!"

The barkeep swore, grabbing a club with metal studs from underneath the bar. "Hands off the girl, lads."

The men at the table eyed Jarl and his club, weighing the risk. In the end, they decided one skinny barmaid with no tits wasn't worth getting their skulls cracked. They let her go, turning back to their drinks and game.

Jarl gave the men a curt nod before turning and pointing his club at Hawn. "You've had enough, Hawn. Get out."

Hawn's eyes blazed with drunken rage as he slowly rose from his table.

Jarl stood his ground, bracing his feet, with his studded club hanging loosely by his side.

In height, strength, and mass, the men were equally matched. Hawn had crippled a man once in his youth. Jarl used to work security for the trade caravans that traveled through the Border Mountains. As the two men continued to size the other up, bets were whispered sharply, and coins passed to impartial hands.

Jarl's grip on his club tightened at the same time that Hawn seemed to swell in size. The barmaids hunkered down behind the bar, regretting their choice to not marry a farmer and settle down. Just when the room felt as if it would burst like an overripe fruit, the door to the inn banged open. Everyone turned to see who had the misfortune to disrupt the violent spell that still lingered in the air.

Six men, clothed in worn leather and road dust, strode through the door, heedless of the tension around them. They scanned the room with dark, disinterested eyes before heading toward the stairs that led to the rooms.

"Now, hold on one minute, friends," Jarl said as he put himself directly into the men's path. "You gotta pay for a room, and we don't have any free, sorry."

One of the men looked down his nose at Jarl, his upper lip pulling back into a silent snarl. The man went to move toward the stairs again, but Jarl stopped him—this time, placing his club in the middle of the big man's chest.

"I said we don't have any rooms. Now you need to leave, or I'll make you."

The man looked down at the well-used club—with its tarnished and dented studs still stained with the blood of those who failed to heed Jarl's warnings in the past—with disinterest before ripping it from Jarl's hands. He flung it behind him, sending patrons scampering for safety. The club crashed through a window, annihilating the last ounces of civility that held the patrons in place.

The room erupted into chaos. Bowls, plates, tankards, and wooden eating utensils flew through the air, crashing into the writhing masses. The sounds of fighting reverberated up to the rafters, adding to the overall sense of chaos.

Three men surged at the mercenaries, their faces flushed with blood lust. They raised their makeshift weapons high in the air, shouting obscenities. Three mercenaries stepped forward, their faces void of any emotion. Moving as one, they unsheathed their weapons, cutting down the men like winter wheat.

Jarl stared at the chaos around him in disbelief. Never in his twenty-odd years of running the bar had a brawl ever broken out like this. Shock gave way to indignation as he clenched his jaw. This was his home, and he'd be damned if he let it burn to the ground without a fight.

The barmaids cowered behind the bar, covering their heads. The most senior maid crawled on her hands and knees toward the kitchen, hoping that the cook hadn't already barred the door. If she and the others could get to the kitchen, they could make a break for the marshal's office and hopefully bring back some lawmen to calm everyone down.

Her hand slipped, her face landing hard onto the wooden floor. She cursed and sat up, licking her lips, tasting blood. She raised her hand to brush along her mouth but stopped short, her face going pale.

"Olina?" The barmaid who had been assaulted earlier crawled up to see what caused her friend to pause and let out a scream.

Jarl's severed head stared back at them from a pool of coagulated blood.

A thick pair of legs came around the bar, followed by a bloody sword. The women behind the bar cowered together in one final attempt to save themselves, gazing up into the blackest pair of eyes they'd ever seen.

Oh, it was wonderful to have a physical body once more. Swinging his broadsword, the creature hacked the women cowering behind the bar into bits before gazing out at the beautiful chaos around him. It didn't take much to send the meat sacks into a frenzy. Their true nature was one of destruction, much like his kind. The only difference was that his kind didn't try to convince themselves they were anything else than what they were. Only humans pretended to be something else, something kinder, wiser, foolish.

The creature spat, eyeing the closed door. He wanted to kick it down and continue bathing in the blood of the useless, but he had a task to complete for his master.

Leaving his comrades below, the creature stomped up the stairs, his nostrils flaring as he scented his prey. The trail was faint, a day or two old.

He kicked down the door with the greatest concentration of the scent behind it, carelessly walking over the broken door.

The room was vacant, with a sharp tang of vinegar and lemon over everything, muddling the lingering scents of his target. The only place where the smell remained was the musty straw mattress.

He buried his face into it, inhaling deeply. Thousands of scents and messages filled his nasal passages. The creature carefully sorted through each one until he found the two he had been tasked to find.

Pain and anguish tempered the prince's scent into fine wine. The creature breathed it in deeply, savoring the flavors dancing in his mouth. The woman's scent was different. Its flavoring was bitter on his tongue, yet there was something faintly familiar about it.

"We're finished downstairs."

The creature turned, facing his offal-coated comrade. "Let us be on our way, then. We're closing in."

The feral grin on his face was matched by five waiting beings below.

MIRRA WAS IMPRESSED. GAITLAN MANAGED TO REMAIN silent the entire time Em tended to his wound. Perhaps she should threaten him with bodily harm in the future. His silence continued as Em had tied the last knot of his bandage and put away her supplies. Nevertheless, as soon as Em retreated out of sight, Gaitlan turned to Mirra.

"Are all your friends psychotic and antagonistic?"

Mirra gave him an impish smirk. "Pretty much."

"I have some old clothes you can change into. You both smell like horse shit."

Gaitlan's face crimsoned. "We bathed in Croglen."

Em puffed. "Splashing some hot water over yourself doesn't count as bathing. The wash room's out back. There should still be some hot water in the scald. If not, then I hope you don't mind cold baths." Em left the clothes as well as some wash things on the table.

"Where are you going?" Gaitlan rose to his feet, hissing when he tried to move his injured shoulder.

Em cocked an eyebrow at him. "Tending to my farm. What else would I be doing? I'm sure you noticed all that hay in my wagon? Someone's gotta put it in the barn."

Mirra slid off the corner of the table, walking over to Em.

"Let me give you a hand. That way, his highness can have a bit of privacy while he baths his royal bits."

Em's eyes fell to the front of Gaitlan's pants and made an unimpressed expression. Gaitlan flushed blood-red, snatching the clothes off the table before barging out of the room, muttering under his breath.

Mirra and Em waited until they heard the door to the washroom slam before falling into a fit of cackles.

"Oh my gods! Is his ego really that fragile?"

"Pretty much; even more so before his parents ..."

The mirth in the room faded away, leaving a bitter taste in Mirra's mouth. Even Em looked unsettled. The two women entered the yard and set about their task, working silently until the last of the hay was secured in the loft of the barn.

Mirra leaned on her pitchfork, watching the stray bits of straw that floated in the air. Her arms were sore, and a pool of sweat had formed in the small of her back. Yet, there was a strange sense of peace in her heart. How many years had it been since she'd done an honest day's work?

"So, what's your plan?" Em's question washed away Mirra's sense of peace.

"Get him north as fast as I can. We're using The Shadow Road."

Em cocked her head.

"It's a network of routes plotted out but unknowable."

"How?"

"There are two or three routes a person can choose. So, unless you tell someone what path you've chosen, there's no way they can find you. At least for some time."

"Is that smart? Didn't The Viper make it?"

Mirra sighed, hanging her pitchfork on the wall. "Yes, but even he can't track every possible route. There's not much else I can do right now."

"Get off the trail."

"Like it's that easy," Mirra scoffed. "The prince has a friend in Lorcea. I gotta get him there before Lord Julian's story can reach him."

Em hung her pitchfork next to Mirra's and placed a hand on her friend's shoulder.

"You know that will never happen. All that Julian has to do, if he hasn't already, is send messenger birds. No matter how fast your horse may be, nothing is faster than a bird on the wind."

Em completely eviscerated the last sliver of hope Mirra had desperately clung to with a few short words.

Mirra put her face in her hands, sliding down the rough wall of the barn. She was doomed.

It was only a matter of time before Julian's forces caught up with them. They would kill the prince. However, she had kept secrets from her master, thwarted his plans, and stole his prize. Her fate would most likely have her begging for death long before it arrived.

She heard a shift on the floor and felt the warmth from Em's body and the reassuring weight of her arm fall around her shoulders. In the quiet privacy of the barn, with no one to witness her weakness but Em, Mirra allowed herself to cry.

She was going to be locked away; this time, for good. Julian delighted in her suffering when she belonged to him. There was no telling what he would do to her now that she had defied and betrayed him. All she ever wanted was freedom. The freedom to live her life the way she wanted. Perhaps look more into her 'gifts.' None of that mattered now; nothing mattered now.

A FARMER GROANED, GRITTING HIS TEETH AS HE PUSHED up the edge of his wagon. His son scrambled to stack crates, rocks, and whatever else he could get his hands on to keep the wagon tilted before his father's strength gave out.

"All good, da."

"Aye," the farmer called, gently lowering the wagon down. His shoulder screamed in agony. The farmer rubbed it, wishing his wife was there to tend to it with her physics and gentle touch.

"It looks easy enough," the son said, peering underneath the wagon. "Maybe an hour's work."

The farmer huffed. "Nothin' ever as simple as it looks."

The son kept his face turned away from his father so that he wouldn't see the way his eyes rolled. His father constantly spouted nonsense like that. All that needed to be done was brace the joint where the axel met with the wagon's bottom. He could do a rudimentary job on the road, enough to get them to the inn just a little way up the road. Once there, he would spend most of the night replacing the weakened braces so they could be on their way in the morning, finishing the last of their deliveries.

The thundering of hooves drew the son from beneath the wagon. A group of six riders down on them, kicking up a flurry of dust behind them. The riders slowed as they neared the farmer and his son, both of whom grabbed a potential weapon as nonchalantly as possible. One never knew what the road would bring.

The men were clearly mercenaries. Their clothing was dark, rough, heavily patched, and stained with something the farmer and his son pointedly pretended they couldn't see.

The largest of these men stopped his horse right in front of the broken wagon. He was close enough for the son to see the sweat stains across the horse's flank.

"Can I help ya, sirs," the farmer asked, putting himself in between the mounted mercenary and his son.

The man looked down at the farmer with a face void of any human emotion. "Have you seen a young woman with black hair and unnaturally blue eyes? She may have been in the company of a young man, bright hair and green eyes."

The farmer shook his head. "Haven't seen anyone since leaving for the market this morning. But there's an inn a few hours up the road. Perhaps they stopped there for a meal or a bed."

The man looked toward the direction the farmer indicated. The son watched over his shoulder. As the mounted mercenary stared off into the distance, the son could have sworn that the blacks of his eyes grew until the man's eyes were completely black. The son must have made a noise because his father and the man looked at him. But the mercenary's eyes appeared as normal as any human's.

"Thank you," the mercenary said, spurring his exhausted horse onward. The rest followed after, kicking up dust and small stones in their wake.

The farmer turned to his son, bothered by the paled expression on his face. "Nothin' can't be fixed by a few hard hours of labor."

This time, his son didn't roll his eyes. He gladly devoted every bit of his waking mind to solving the wonderfully mundane task of fixing the wagon. With any hope, he'd forget the mercenary's eyes or the way death clung to them like a delicate perfume.

GAITLAN WATCHED MIRRA INTENTLY. SOMETHING HAD changed in her. He couldn't quite put his finger on it, but she seemed ... smaller. Whatever happened while he bathed had stripped away her ever-present armor, making her look younger in his eyes, surprising him.

Though he knew that Mirra was only a few years younger than him, perhaps the same age as his sister, the way she carried herself and her aura always made her appear older. A strong urge to protect surged through his being. He shook his head, scattering the odd emotion to the dark recesses of his consciousness.

"You'll meet my husband tomorrow," Em said, breaking the silence. "He's on the road, making deliveries with his son."

Mirra turned sharply. "His son?"

Em nodded, a slight smirk on her face. "Micha had a wife before me. She died during childbirth. His son is almost the same age as I am. Made for a bit of a rocky start, but once he saw that I truly loved his father, we came to a truce, of sorts."

"How'd you meet him?"

"I swindled him naturally."

Em and Mirra broke into a fit of laughter, garnering a frown from Gaitlan.

"Don't get your moral sensibilities all twisted, princeling; he got me back. I still don't know how Micha found me. But when he did, he said that the only thing a beautiful woman should steal is hearts, not goods or gold."

"So what?" Gaitlan asked.

"We made a bargain. Since I couldn't return what I'd stolen, already spent, I would pay him back with my time. Micha paid for a nice meal, and we spent the rest of the evening talking. We shared our stories, the good times, and the heartaches until the sun came up. At the end of it all, he kissed my hand, wishing me good fortune in the future."

A dreamy look fell over Em's face. "I dreamt about him every night after that. I was a mess. I made careless mistakes, got into more fights than ever before. In the end, Bao pulled me aside, demanding to know what had changed. I told him about Micha."

Gaitlan leaned forward. "Was he angry with you?"

Em shook her head. "That bastard laughed at me; laughed. He tossed me a bag of money and told me to go find Micha. He said that I would never have peace or balance in my life until I faced him and spoke the truth in my heart."

Mirra made a face. "What kind of Zallino bullshit answer is that?"

Em waved her hand. "You know how he can get."

"Who's Bao?"

"Our friend and the leader of our old gang," Em

answered before continuing with her story.

"It took me two weeks to find Micha again. He was just as surprised as I was. I stayed with him for five days, helping him in the markets. He didn't ask about my sudden reappearance. He just accepted the help I offered with the same kindness he showed me on our first meeting. But then, one day, it finally dawned on me. In him, I saw a life that I never thought possible. With Micha, I could be a person who lived, not only survived."

"Isn't that the same thing?" Mirra asked.

"Not always," Em said. "Sometimes, the person who survives is a completely different person from one who lives. People will do whatever it takes to survive. We lie, cheat, steal, even kill. I think that you know just how strong the drive to survive can be."

Mirra frowned, looking down at her hands clasped on the table.

"I returned to Verance one more time. I walked right up to Bao and said I wanted out. I was prepared to pay any price to get a chance at the life I saw with Micha. But Bao; he let me go with his blessing, wishing me a good life. The only thing he asked was that I stayed in touch."

"Was it worth it? Do you have a good life?"

A warm glow of happiness shone through Em's being as she smiled. "Yes."

Gaitlan spent the rest of the day resting while Em tended to the needs of the farm. Mirra filled the time walking around the house, running her hands over the items that made up Em's new life. Every room carried warmth, comfort, and peace. A small smile formed on her face as she reminisced about her experience on a farm not too different from this one. Em deserved it after everything she'd gone through as a child, and perhaps, so did she.

"So, is everyone you know a criminal?"

Mirra screamed internally. Just whenever she'd thought she was starting to get along with the prince, he'd open his mouth, revealing the depth of his ineptitude.

"Everyone is a criminal in one fashion or another, princeling. Might I remind you that right now, you're a villain charged with parricide?"

The thread of Gaitlan's control finally snapped. Mirra raised her arm to prevent Gaitlan's hand from crushing her throat, but only just. His eyes stared at her without seeing her, completely taken over by his anger. Fear coated her tongue. This was a side of Gaitlan she'd never seen before. She doubted he even knew this side of himself.

"What the hel," Mirra snarled, attempting to throw him off.

His lips pulled back into a silent snarl as he used the differences between their height and weight to his advantage. Gaitlan wrapped his hand around her braid and pulled.

Mirra brought up her knee at the same time Gaitlan pressed his advantage, striking him firmly in the privates.

"Gods in hel," Gaitlan bellowed, releasing his hold on Mirra, his hands going to cup the delicate parts hanging between his legs. "What the hel is wrong with you, woman!"

"Wrong with me? What the hel is wrong with you! You attacked me."

Gaitlan blinked at her as he replayed the last few

moments over in his mind. "I don't remember that. I only remember you saying I was the one who killed my parents."

Lingering fear made her tongue sharp. "You might as well have, walking around like the world owed you everything, then throwing a fit when it didn't. Julian may have been the one who orchestrated it all, but you still played your part beautifully."

Gaitlan moved against Mirra again. This time, she was ready, stepping back and raising her fists. "Go ahead, your highness; show me how wrong I am. Show me you aren't what everyone thinks you are—a spineless coward who tears down anyone who dares say anything against you."

Gaitlan muttered a curse before flinging the door open and stomping down the wooded path.

Mirra watched his retreating back, a hand going up to massage her scalp. It might be better if I cut my hair. Less chance for someone to grab it.

"I see you're still a bit of a bitch." Em placed a woven bowl full of eggs on the table. She twisted, placing her hands on her hips, her eyes full of reproach.

"Excuse me?"

"You heard me right," Em said, her voice chipped. "Whenever one of us got too close to your wall, you'd snap at us, causing a fight until that closeness was gone."

Mirra made a face. "This wasn't like that."

Em arched a brow. "Then how is it?"

Mirra sputtered, struggling to find the right words to convey why she'd pushed the prince to his breaking point. Eventually, she gave up, hanging her head in shame.

"I'm not made for this," Mirra said to her feet. "I'm not a

planner like Bao, kind like Sorro, or able to change the way you and Tul have."

"You're not us," Em said. "But we never expected you to be. You have always been simply Mirra to us. The person whose instincts were rarely wrong; the one who could move undetected like a ghost; and the one we knew was softer than the persona she put up to protect herself."

Em closed the distance between them, gently lifting Mirra's face. "Your entire life, you've had to be someone else, anyone else to survive. That sucks. But unlike the rest of us, you're refusing to move forward."

Mirra swatted Em's hand away. "How am I supposed to move forward while I have that millstone of a person around my neck and knowing what that man is capable of?"

Em shook her head, a silent laugh on her lips. "Stopping that bastard from getting his way is moving forward. For the prince," she shrugged, "try to be patient. This is probably the hardest time of his life, while it's a normal day for us."

Mirra remained silent, a stubborn scowl on her face.

"Think about what I said. Really think about it."

Em disappeared to the back of the house, leaving Mirra alone with her thoughts. Realizing her friend was correct but not fully committed to accepting it, Mirra dug through the pantry, searching for wine, ale, or anything that could dull her mind for a time.

GAITLAN STUMBLED ONTO THE MAIN ROAD BEFORE HE realized it. Blinking against the brightness on the open road, he walked out the center of the road, spinning slowly.

"There's no way that woman isn't working for that traitor. Clearly, she's trying to drive me mad, to break my soul."

Oh, asked a harsh voice from a dark corner of his mind. Then why did she risk her own life to face him? He seemed pretty surprised to see your sister alive, and Mirra standing against him.

Gaitlan covered his ears, hoping to drown out the bitter truth.

"It's all a ploy, an act," he whispered. "She's a manipulating bitch, just like Julian, just like ..."

Your friends? Your friends that were so willing to spill your blood when you denied them their fun? She saved you that time too. She might be the only person who actually cares for you—after your sister, of course. Yes, she's rough around the edges, but she's a survivor. Could you have survived half of what she's been through, still going through?

Hot, bitter tears streamed from his eyes while shame spread through his chest. Dropping to his knees, Gaitlan screamed at the sky, at the gods themselves.

"Hey now, son," said a gentle voice, bringing Gaitlan back to his senses.

Gaitlan turned, heedless of the tears running down his cheek, spying a middle-aged man staring down at him from the bench of an empty wagon. The man's son peered over his father's shoulder, worry etched across every pore of his body. Gaitlan took one deep breath, drawing in the peace and serenity that seemed to roll off the man.

"Are ya lost, lad? Not much out here but a few farms and

an inn about a half a day's ride that way." He gestured over his shoulder with his thumb. When Gaitlan remained silent, the farmer pressed on.

"I'm Micha, and this here's me boy, Tom. Our place isn't too much further. If ya want, you can rest with us for the night. I'm sure my wife won't mind overmuch."

"Micha," Gaitlan breathed. "You're Em's husband."

Micha's easy-going demeanor changed at the sound of his wife's name. "And how do you know my wife?"

"Not like that," Gaitlan coughed, spreading his hands wide. "My ..." he stumbled briefly over what to call Mirra, "companion and I ran into a bit of trouble on the road. Your wife was kind enough to offer us aid and shelter."

Micha relaxed, a broad smile breaking out across his face as he gazed in the direction of his home. "What a big heart my lass has." His smile retreated as he looked back down at Gaitlan but lingered in the corners of his mouth like a coil ready to spring free. "I take it, then; you're responsible for that mess up the road?"

"Not intentionally, sir. We were simply riding along when attacked. I don't even know why. It's not like we have anything worth stealing."

"You're alive. That means that you have something, even if it's just the clothes on your back or the horse under you. And speaking of horses; is this yours?"

Mirra's horse peered around the wagon. Its ears perked up when it saw Gaitlan, recognizing him.

"It's my companion's; thank you." Gaitlan walked around to untie the horse. He was just about to mount it when

Micha's son cried out in pain, a black arrow jutting from his shoulder.

"Get down!" Gaitlan shouted, taking shelter after sending Mirra's horse into the underbrush with a firm slap.

Micha tumbled backward, reaching for his son. "Don't worry, Tom. It will be all right." A comforting lie from a father to a wounded son. Micha knew it, and so did Gaitlan. All his weapons were back at the cottage, and they were too far away to shout for help. Just another hopeless situation. Gaitlan shook his head. That wasn't entirely true. Yes, they were weaponless but not defenseless. An arrow struck the bench where Micha had sat with a thud. They had some semblance of protection as long as the horse strapped to the wagon wasn't spooked.

With the utmost care, Gaitlan crept alongside the wagon until he reached the hitch. He peered out from around the corner, nearly catching an arrow in the eye. Six mercenaries emerged from the shadows. Gaitlan swallowed. Each man was massive, with thick cords of muscles running the length of their bodies. But it was their eyes that turned his bowels to water. There was something about their eyes that brought up the scent of smoke, blood, and the sharp taste of fear on his tongue.

Another arrow flew, striking Micha in the chest. He let out a gurgled yell that was sharply repeated by his son. Gaitlan shook his head and moved forward. It took him several tries, but eventually, he could disconnect the horses from the wagon. Sensing their freedom, the horses bucked and ran down the path toward their home. With any luck, Mirra and Em would see and come running. All he had to do was keep everyone alive until then.

Tom sobbed inside the wagon, urging his father to stay

with them, his hand pressed to his bleeding shoulder. "Do you have any weapons?" Gaitlan shouted.

"Just my hammers," the boy replied.

"Toss them to me."

A heavy bag flew over the edge of the wagon, nearly hitting Gaitlan in the head. He bit back a curse, knowing that the near-miss wasn't intentional. His heart fell when he opened the bag and saw that all the sizable hammers were wooden and not the steel that he'd hoped for. He grabbed the two largest, giving them a few swirls, testing their weight and balance; not ideal but better than nothing. He edged forward, peeking out from behind the wagon.

The mercenaries discarded their bows, stalking toward the wagon with bright, hard steel glinting in their hands.

"Whatever you do," Gaitlan said softly to Tom, "stay down, and don't draw any attention to yourself."

Gaitlan adjusted his grip on Tom's hammers, taking several deep breaths before launching himself at the mercenaries with a roar.

He aimed for hands, wrists, elbows, and knees. He knew that the hammers would be no good against battle-hardened steel and did his best to avoid them. He spun and dodged, weaving through the mercenaries, all the while keeping an eye out for aid. It seemed Tom took his advice to heart, meaning the boy might survive in the end. His father, not so much. Gaitlan got a glimpse of where the arrow struck, and very few men ever survived such a blow.

Hurry up, Mirra. I need you.

MIRRA KNEW SOMETHING WAS WRONG THE MOMENT SHE SAW THE horses. She leapt to the side to avoid being trampled to death. She cast a worried glance down the road before turning to run back to Em's house. If there was trouble, she was going to need her weapons.

Em and Mirra collided in the doorway. Mirra quickly strapped her weapons on her before tucking Gaitlan's under her arms.

Em mounted one of the horses, wrapping the long reins around her hand. She extended her hand to Mirra, swinging her up on the horse behind her. Em spurred the horse into action before Mirra had a chance to fully seat herself.

Mirra wished she had her bow, but her knives would have to do, and she still had the poison darts that had been meant to take Braelyn's life. It would have to be enough. When their horse burst onto the road, Em and Mirra slid off its back, diving headfirst into the fray.

Em went straight for her husband and stepson, vaulting over the side of the wagon, sliding to a stop on her knees.

"He won't wake up," Tom wailed, tears spilling down his face.

"Micha!" Em didn't like how pale his skin had gone or the way that his head rolled on his shoulders as she shook him. "We need to get him home."

Em peered over the edge of the wagon; two mercenaries fell, the fletching of Mirra's poisonous darts in their necks. Mirra locked blades with a mercenary twice her size. Em's body seized, torn between a lifetime of friendship and a new love. The tension in Em's shoulders eased a fraction when Mirra sent her opponent to the ground with a leg swipe. Mirra knew how to take care of herself. Em needed to take care of her family.

Mirra was in trouble. It took everything in her to keep the mercenary at bay. He was a lot stronger than he had any right to be. Every blow he landed reverberated down to her bones. In between strikes, she glanced over to Gaitlan, her stomach souring.

He was doing well, fending multiple attacks, armed with only wooden mallets, but for how much longer? One well-placed strike would be all it took to eviscerate his only means of defense.

As if her thoughts came to life, the largest of the mercenaries maneuvered out of Gaitlan's guard, bringing down his sword with a mighty blow, shattering the mallet.

Time slowed as Gaitlan was kicked to the ground. His head bounced against the road. The two mercenaries circled the fallen prince, their black eyes glinting with predatory glee.

Ice pooled in the pit of her stomach. She parried her assailant's attack, taking a few precious seconds to study his face. He, too, had black eyes, and the truth settled like a stone. These men were agents of Lord Julian, magically enhanced to trace her and the prince down. Movement at the corner of her eye made her decision for her. Drawing upon the wellspring where her magic dwelled, Mirra cast a smokey wave of darkness in every direction.

The mercenaries went flying through the air, landing with heavy thuds a few feet from where they'd stood only a moment before. Gaitlan rolled over, eyes glazed, and mouth wide with surprise.

Mirra stalked forward, her magic rippling around her.

With a dagger in each hand, she put herself in between the mercenaries and the prince. "Tell your master, if he wants us, he'd better come himself."

The mercenaries said nothing. They regrouped and rearmed, standing silently as if waiting for something or someone else.

"Mirra!"

Mirra risked glancing over her shoulder to look at Em. Her heart sank as the two mercenaries she took down with the darts awkwardly got back to their feet. They'd been encircled. Those darts should have killed them.

"When you see an opening, run for it," Mirra said, adjusting her grip on her weapons.

"But how?"

"For once in your life, Gaitlan, do what you're told."

Mirra closed her eyes and dove deeper into her magic. The air around her grew darker, spinning like the wind funnels that tore through the Nealitian plains. Dust and small stones were picked and joined the swirling vortex around her.

The mercenaries slowly rose from the ground, their lips pulled back into a snarl. They spat at Mirra before raising their weapons high to deal a killing blow to the still prone Gaitlan.

Gaitlan could only watch, throwing an arm over his head in some final attempt to protect himself.

Mirra opened her eyes, flashing an icy blue light edged with black before settling down to a constant shimmer of white. She flew; her body became translucent, leaving trails of shadows in her wake.

The mercenaries released an unearthly screech, turning

their black gaze on Mirra.

It wasn't his near-death experience or the way his palms were stained red from their screech that kept Gaitlan frozen on the ground. It was the young woman disappearing and reappearing from smoke like a specter from a nightmare.

"Magic," he breathed. "She has magic."

Mirra slashed and stabbed, moving through shadows and propelled by her desire to keep everyone safe. Each breath was a stab to her lungs, her limbs growing heavy. She wouldn't last much longer. Even more alarming, the mercenaries refused to stay down.

Stripes of crimson stained the road, their clothing in tatters, and still, they fought on. They swung their weapons wildly, leaving themselves exposed to Mirra's blades.

If ordinary weapons were useless, then she'd make a magical one.

Mirra ducked under the swing of a battle-ax, the force of the swing kissed the top of her head, ruffling her hair. She let her momentum carry her to the ground, rolling away from the mercenaries.

She came up, gasping and cursing. Gaitlan still lingered on the road, gaping at her like a fish. She wanted to shout at him to move his ass, yet didn't want to draw attention to him. She only hoped that the death glare she gave him would be enough to get him moving.

The mercenaries surged forward again, forcing Mirra into action. She was slower than before, her body more solid with fewer shadowy trails. It was harder for her to focus. Pain flared from the successful strikes they managed to land, but she couldn't dwell on them for too long. While she fought on pure muscle memory from years of training, her conscious mind was strained to its breaking point as she funneled as much of her magic as she dared into one of her daggers.

An unseen kick sent her tumbling to the ground.

Now or never. Mirra flipped to her feet, stabbing the nearest mercenary in the side.

Unlike before, the blow had its intended effect. Black, putrid blood erupted from the wound, spurting with each heartbeat. Mirra retched her dagger free, sending him to his knees, slashing his throat as he fell. The mercenary let out a garbled roar, reaching for his throat. Mirra let go and scrambled away, already forcing more of her magic into her other dagger. She stopped when the others bellowed in pain, their hands going to either their sides or throat.

"What one feels, so do the others."

The mercenary she struck convulsed on the ground until black ichor oozed from his neck and fell still, the others following shortly afterward.

Mirra's strength gave out at last, her legs crumpling underneath. As her vision clouded, she heard a gut-wrenching cry that could only mean the death of one's heart.

CHAPTER SIX

I AM GREATLY DISTURBED BY THESE REPORTS."

The speaker was an elderly lord whose hands shook slightly from their folded position on the table. His voice was soft, quivering with age, yet it had enough strength to travel down the length of the table to Julian's ear.

He bit back a sneer. "As I am, Lord Hamal. Such violent acts are unforgivable."

"Then perhaps we should remove the bounty on Prince Gaitlan's and your niece's heads?" Lord Tolin met Julian's eyes in a silent display of dominance.

Julian checked his rage by biting the inside of his cheek. The coppery tang of blood filled his mouth, quieting the savage side of his consciousness that was always close to the surface these days. A vein throbbed at his temple, a sure sign that a migraine was not too far behind. The council of lords had been making more and more demands as the days went on, sniffing around the rotting carcass of the former king's power. He'd have to deal with them. Eventually, a certain lord would suffer first.

Julian plastered a vacant smile on his face before answering. "Don't you think the people will find it odd? It might make it look like we no longer care about catching the regents' killers."

"That may be, but removing the bounty, at least publicly, will weed out most of the unsavory characters. Effectively sparing more innocent lives."

The following words out of Julian's mouth flickered with an invisible fire. "Valid point as always, Lord Tolin. I will bring your concerns to the princess and return with her decision by our next meeting."

Lord Tolin didn't lower his eyes. "Shouldn't she tell us with her own voice? She is the last member of the royal family. She should be here with us."

A low murmur went out across the other nobles. Several nobles, both newly appointed and long-standing, nodded their heads.

A muscle feathered in Julian's jaw. He envisioned his hands wrapping around Lord Tolin's neck, squeezing the light from his eyes.

"Princess Braelyn is in mourning and has given me the authority to act in her stead. She knows little of what it means to manage a kingdom and wishes to leave her family's kingdom in the hands of those more capable than hers. After all, she's only a young girl, not even eighteen yet, who'd spent her entire life surrounded by peace and prosperity."

And just like that, Julian gained control over the room. The tufted-up old men smiled at each other, diminishing the princess in their minds to nothing more than a simpering young woman who knew nothing beyond how to make things pretty. A pretty face, empty-headed girl child, not a tigress tirelessly pacing in her cage with eyes that burned with indignation. Julian's smile was edged with malice as he bid the other lords farewell. He marked the faces that carried lingering doubts or thinly veiled hostility. He would seek them out later.

After the last of the lords had gone, Julian gathered the various reports into a single pile. Assault cases rose steadily across the kingdom as people turned on one another for the mere prospect of gold.

In Croglen, an entire tavern had been slaughtered. Shortly before the discovery of the massacre, the provost's reports noted that a small band of mercenaries had been seen fleeing town.

Julian smiled. His creatures had picked up the trail; they would not stop until they had their quarry. The prince had served his usefulness. Julian had no more need of him, but Mirra; she was completely different.

The little thief had kept her magic hidden from him. He suspected her since the day he paid that blowhard Bossman Jax to remove that troublesome high priest, but the smoke in the room raised enough doubt. But now, he knew. An oily smile spread across his face. A power like hers hadn't been seen in over an age. A priceless tool he needed to bring back into his possession, lest it be used against him.

Julian scoffed, removing a sealed envelope from his inside pocket. Two points along the Shadow Road had been used; one, a simple tavern near the easter gate of the city, and the other, in Croglen. Based on that, Mirra could be heading north to Nealet or Lorcea or east to Zallino. He'd need another report before he could be entirely sure.

He tossed the reports into the fire and spent some time watching the flames consume the pages. When the reports were nothing more than ash in the hearth, he turned to formulate the following stages of his plans.

A sharp pain shot through his neck, drawing a hiss from between his teeth. He clasped a hand to his neck and wiped, expecting to see blood, but it came away clean. The pain rolled through him again, stealing his breath and the strength from his limbs. Only a quick thrust of his hand kept him from falling entirely to the floor. His jaw locked, keeping back the screams building in his mouth. His vision came and went with flashes of a tree-lined road stained by blood.

The pain vanished as quickly as it had appeared, leaving him gasping and sweating on the ice-cold floor. "What the hel was that?"

In all his years of existence, Julian had never experienced such pain. It was as if a portion of himself had been burned out of him. He rose shakily to his feet and pressed a hand to his face. Images played through his mind too fast for him to clearly make out.

A field.

The laughter of two boys.

A young woman standing in the middle of dark swirling clouds.

The cry of a woman.

The sound of breaking glass.

Blackness took over both his eyes as a feral growl escaped from between his clenched teeth. "So be it," he growled. "Let the games begin."

MIRRA WOULD HAVE RIPPED HER OWN HEART OUT IF IT meant that Micha could come back. She'd travel through the Dark Mother's realm to retrieve his soul to completely erase the image of her friend clutching a cooling body while screaming to the sky. She'd done this. She'd brought on this suffering.

Tom clutched his father's other hand. His face was tear-streaked, and his eyes vacant. The shock of losing his father had proved too much for him.

Gaitlan stood off to the side, his whole demeanor torn between wanting to offer comfort and fleeing from the raw display of emotion in front of him.

Someone needed to move, needed to break the spell of grief and take the next measures.

Mirra forced herself to take a single step forward. She took another, and then another, until she stood in front of the hearth. She poured water into a kettle, throwing a handful of fragrant herbs in before setting it to boil over the fire.

One task done; onto the next.

She dug out a clean sheet from the linen chest, stopping to grab a clean set of clothes. She laid the items at the top of the table. Em didn't acknowledge Mirra or anything she did.

"Em."

Em lifted her head. Her eyes were red and swollen and so full of hurt that Mirra had to swallow back her own tears.

"Let's get him clean."

Em blinked, confused. She turned her head slowly, spying the sheet and clean clothes placed by her husband's head. She turned again, finally registering the utterly lost look on Toms's face. Life slowly returned to her eyes as she took a large swallow, pushing down her anguish to be the rock her stepson needed her to be.

"Tom, go with Gaitlan and see to the animals. Your father wouldn't want us to forget. Make sure the coop is locked 'cause we haven't caught that fox yet. Give the horses a good brushing and extra feed. Don't forget to milk the goats."

Tom let go of his father's hand and numbly shuffled out the door. Gaitlan shot Mirra a quick glance before following after the youth.

Together, Mirra and Em stripped Micha of his dirty, blood-caked clothing until he was as naked as the day he came into the world. With the water from the kettle, they washed away the filth. Em cut the arrow shaft, leaving the head behind. There was no need to remove it now.

Once his skin gleamed in the firelight, they dressed him in his best clothes, the very ones he wore when he and Em pledged to spend their life together, their hands bound by white silk.

Hot, bitter tears streamed down Em's face throughout the entire process, yet she uttered not a single sound. Once dressed, they carefully wrapped Micha in the sheets. Em and Mirra stood side by side when they had completed their task, clutching the other's hand for dear life.

Onto the next task.

No one had much appetite. However, they all accepted the warm bowl of stew Em made from whatever she had left in the larder. They held it in their hands as if the heat would chase away the chill of death that clung to every pour, every fiber.

"We will send for a priest in the morning," Em said.

Mirra gripped her bowl tighter over the hollowness of her friend's voice. "You should be gone before he arrives."

"I want to stay. I don't want to leave you."

Em looked up, her eyes clearer than they had been for hours. "You have to finish your job. If you're discovered before you get the prince to safety, exposing Lord Julian for the snake that he is, then Micha, my husband, will have died for nothing." She shouted the last bit, pointing a finger at the white wrapped body on the table.

"Avenge him. Avenge them all."

Mirra hung her head. "I will, I promise."

The sky was dark. Not a single star could be seen. Silence pressed around Mirra as she saddled her horse. She looked over the back of her mount at the dark, gaping windows of Em's house.

"Will they be all right?"

"I don't know," she said, cinching the last strap. "Em has a good head on her shoulder, so, maybe."

Gaitlan shifted on his feet and fiddled with the pommel of his sword. "Can we trust her to keep our secret?"

Mirra spun and pressed a dagger against the prince's neck. His eyes went wide, and he took his hand off the pommel of his sword.

"Her husband lays dead because of us, and you dare to worry about her keeping out secrets?"

Gaitlan swallowed. Mirra's blade moved along with his Adam's apple.

Mirra pressed her dagger harder in a silent warning before returning it to its sheath. "She'll keep our secret, princeling. Have no fear of that."

Mirra stopped down the road, pulling her horse behind her.

Gaitlan followed after her. He glared at her back, saying in his mind what he was too afraid to say aloud.

We took the only thing in this world she actually cared about. I've seen people betray others for less.

Any sign of their battle the day before had been wholly wiped away. Even the bloodstains. Mirra and Gaitlan shared one worried glance before mounting their horses, heading north. They rode in silence for most of the morning, constantly scanning their surroundings. They wouldn't be retaken by surprise. They couldn't afford to.

A sharp pain coursed through Gaitlan's shoulder with every loping step of his horse. Mirra's entire body was sore from her battle yesterday, and though she didn't want to admit it, her magic was acting up. It flared up like the embers from an abandoned fire. A time or two, it slithered out of her like a snake, running for the woods. On top of all that, her skull felt three sizes too small and pounded like a drum. The light from the sun was a thousand times brighter, stinging her eyes, burning her skin that was already raw from the fabric of her clothing.

"Perhaps we should take a break?"

Mirra rubbed her eyes until dots swam across her vision. "No, we need to get further along before we abandon the horses."

Gaitlan pulled his horse to a halt. "What?"

"Em was right. We can't keep going like we have been. It will be only a matter of time before he spreads his lies across the land, leaving us to only find closed doors in our faces and swords at our backs."

"By my friend ..."

"We can't count on him or anyone else. The only people we can trust are each other and your sister. And none of us are in any position to do anything but lay low and keep living."

Gaitlan's face blanched. "That's a coward's plan."

"No, that's a survivor's plan."

"Well, who says that you're the one in charge? I'm the prince. I'm the one who has been trained since birth to plan, strategize, and lead. If we stop now, we'll never regain traction. We must keep moving forward and as quickly as possible."

The pounding in Mirra's head increased, increasing in force and frequency; all the while, she felt a growing pressure beneath her skin. Gaitlan continued to speak, but the drumming in her blood drowned him out. She wouldn't have been surprised if she exploded like an overripe plum.

"Fine," Mirra snapped, sliding off her horse. "Go rescue your damn self, then." She unfastened her pack and threw it over her shoulder. She gave her faithful mount a quick brush along her nose before sending her onward with a slap to the rear. She didn't watch as her horse trotted down the road at a leisurely pace. Someone would find the horse sooner or later and take care of her, grateful for the gift.

Mirra stomped past Gaitlan, barreling into the underbrush. She heard him call after her, but she kept pushing forward, letting her rage carry her. She walked for several miles, stopping only when she came up to a fast-moving river. She stopped at the bank, studying the water.

Rough and choppy, filled with debris and froth, the spray

that hit her face was as cold as ice. The river was undoubtedly filled with spring melt from the mountains. To cross at this point would be foolish and most likely result in her death.

"Bloody hel, woman!" Gaitlan shouted. "What devil possessed you?"

Mirra scowled at him over her shoulder. "Why are you here? I thought you didn't need me, being the highly educated prince you are."

Gaitlan made a face and loosened a strained breath. He rolled his head and shoulders. "I didn't mean it like that, and you know it."

Mirra closed her eyes, rubbing her temples with her fingers. "I know. I know. I don't know what's the matter with me."

Gaitlan rubbed the stubble growing in his face with his free hand, looking off to the side. "Maybe...it has something to do with the magic you released yesterday."

The dam burst.

Power danced along Mirra's bones, drawing a cry from her lips. She fell to her knees, a wave of shimmering shadows billowing out all around her. She heard Gaitlan yelling her name, but it sounded strange, like her head was underwater. Perhaps it was, in a way.

Another wave of power left her gasping for air, clawing the sandy riverbed.

"Mirra!"

Strong arms slid around her, sending fresh waves of pain rippling across her skin. Gaitlan cradled her gently to his chest, heedless of his wound or the red stain forming at his shoulder.

"Mirra, what's happening! What can I do?"

Tears streaming and body aflame, she only managed to whisper a single word. "Run."

Before Gaitlan could ask what he was supposed to run from, another wave of magic tore through Mirra, running through her like lightning. Her back arched, her mouth opened in a silent scream. A bit of her magic seeped into Gaitlan, igniting a fire deep within his bones.

He bit back the scream building in the back of his throat, maintaining his hold on Mirra as she convulsed in his arms. Sweat ran down the sides of his face when her magic finally released its torment of his body. Gasping, Gaitlan gently turned Mirra's face toward him.

"Mirra, stay with me," he pleaded, gently pushing a sweat-soaked strand of hair from her face.

Mirra was beyond hearing, beyond feeling, beyond anything that bound her to the corporeal world. The only thing that existed was the gaping void before her and the rivers of fire contained within her skin. She reached out for the void, pleading with it to end her suffering, to end her torment.

She felt it chuckle rather than hearing it. A gentle touch cooled her cheek; it was like a balm. Mirra leaned into the touch, holding it tightly to her face with both hands. The coolness spread from her cheek to the rest of her body, quelling the inferno within. The void in front of her faded away, and for some reason, it left her feeling sad.

The sounds of a crackling fire and thunder welcomed her back to the physical world, followed quickly by pain. She hissed, slowly pushing herself up to take note of her surroundings. She was in a cave. It was small and a bit shallow but able to keep the wind and rain from coming in. That and the blanket strung up over the entrance.

For the moment, she was alone; no sign of Gaitlan, save for the packs thrown against one wall. A small pot simmered over the fire, reminding her body that it needed sustenance to recover from its most recent ordeal. She wanted it, but every movement she made sent fresh waves of pain throughout her body, causing her stomach to clench and roll.

The blanket pulled back, revealing a drenched Gaitlan, water streaming down his face. His eyes brightened like the first leaves of spring upon seeing Mirra awake and sitting up. He dropped the bundle of branches near the door, his long legs gobbling the distance between them.

"Thank the gods," he whispered, his hand reaching out to cup her cheek. Realizing the dirt and dampness of his hand, he dropped it, choosing instead to ladle a small portion of the pot into a cup for her.

"It's not much, but I didn't know what else to do."

Mirra accepted the cup, blinking. "You did all this?"

"Yeah," Gaitlan said, rubbing the back of his neck. "Once you stopped seizing, I realized a storm was coming. I carried you away from the river and stumbled across this cave."

No words came to mind, so Mirra blew into her mug before taking a sip. Whatever it was—stew, soup—it was warm. The taste wasn't half bad either.

Gaitlan stared intently at Mirra, his eyes falling to watch the bob of her throat as she swallowed. Mirra's cheeks burned. "It's good."

Gaitlan beamed, causing a strange fluttering inside her

chest. He turned his back to her and started to shuck his soaked clothing. She couldn't tear her eyes away from the planes of his back. The broad shoulders that undoubtedly carried her to safety to be tended to by large, gentle hands.

Mirra shook her head and turned it, suddenly finding the cave wall interesting.

Something carved into the side of the cave caught her eye. It shimmered in the firelight. Mirra painfully rose to her feet, wrapping her blanket around her shoulders. She shuffled over to the cave wall and traced the carving with her fingers. There was something about the familiar marks, but she couldn't quite place it until she closed her eyes and focused only on the marks.

"Runes," she breathed, turning around, amazed. Nearly every inch of the cave was covered in markings. Back in dry clothes, Gaitlan turned, his eyes going to wherever Mirra indicated.

"I recognize some of them. This one here is for peace," she patted the one under her hand. "That one is for hiding from one's enemies. There's one for peaceful sleep, and that one ... that one is the mark of the Mystics."

She delicately traced the rune with the tips of her fingers, marveling. "This must have been one of their hideouts back in the day."

Gaitlan frowned up at the runes. "How do you know what they are?"

"I learned them from a book in the palace library."

Gaitlan shook his head. "There's no such books."

Mirra rolled her eyes. "Not explicitly, but there are hints and illustrations written in the legends. They're useless to anyone else."

"Save those who have magic."

Mirra's smile fell. Her elation turning to stone. "Yes. People like me ... and people like Julian."

"How?"

"I don't know," Mirra said with a shrug. "Perhaps we have Mystic blood running through us? But that's not what's important right now."

"And what is?"

"Legends speak of a lost city in the heart of Mystic Woods. It was the last stronghold for them before they were completely whipped out." She looked at Gaitlan expectedly, but his face was blank.

"We can hide out there," she said with an exasperated sigh. "No one will look for us there. And maybe I can learn some more runes that we can use to take down Lord Julian."

At the sound of Julian's name, Gaitlan's face darkened.

"Fine," Gaitlan said with a grumble. "We find this long-lost city, hide there, and figure things out ... together."

Warmth pooled in Mirra's core. Her mouth spread into an easy smile. "Together."

The storm lasted two more days. Mirra and Gaitlan occupied their time tending to their injuries and gear. Mirra practiced the runes carved on the walls repeatedly until she could draw them in her mind's eye.

Gaitlan watched her with unabashed wonder and envy. If he had her abilities, he wouldn't need to rely on anyone else to reclaim his birthright.

On their third day in the cave, sunlight woke them from their slumber. They broke camp, heading back to the river in search of a safe place to cross. That took the better part of the morning, and even then, it was only marginally safe. The water came up to their knees with plenty of opportunities to lose their footing in the sandy soil, fall, and be swept away in the rushing waters.

They trudged into the forest, stopping only to catch their supper, often falling asleep curled up beneath the branches of bracken, curled around one another for warmth. Gaitlan never complained, though Mirra could tell that he still carried many worries. He didn't question her as she took the lead, following some innate instinct that urged her forward.

She wanted to believe that her ever western trek was nothing more than simple logic, but deep down, she knew different. Perhaps the closer they got to the ancient city, the more the Mystic blood inside of her grew.

"Are we any closer, you think?" Gaitlan asked.

They had stopped near a small stream to refill their skins and to rest. Gaitlan lay on his back, using his pack as a pillow, throwing his mostly healed arm over his eyes, shielding them from the midday sun.

"It depends on what you're looking for."

Mirra and Gaitlan jumped at the sound of the unfamiliar voice, blades drawn. A young woman with coppery skin and shiny black hair smiled sharply at them from a branch of a tree. Her clothing, various shades of brown and green, with bits of bright beadwork and animal fur for embellishments. She held a recurve bow in her hand, with the other hand resting carelessly near a quiver full of arrows.

"We mean you no harm," Gaitlan said, stepping forward.

The woman's face twisted with disgust, and she spat. "No one was talking to you, Oathbreaker." She turned her attention to Mirra, her face full of concern right down to her ice-blue eyes, the exact same shade as Mirra's.

"Are you safe, Mashta?

CHAPTER
SEVEN

THE WOMAN TOOK A STEP FORWARD. "MASHTA?"

"I don't ... who are ... what?"

The woman frowned, firing an arrow at Gaitlan in the blink of an eye. Acting on instinct, Mirra extended her hand. A wall of velvety darkness encased Gaitlan, whose startled expression would have been humorous under different circumstances.

The woman's eyes narrowed to slits. She turned her attention solely to Mirra. The air hummed with constrained violence so thick that even the birds had fallen silent, lest it be turned on them. Mirra's hand slowly went to her belt, wrapping around the hilt of her dagger. The leather creaked beneath her white-knuckled grip. The woman's stony face and stance relaxed, and the world breathed a sigh of relief. She unstrung her bow, stashing it in her quiver before waving Mirra onward.

"Come, follow me. She will want to see you." She frowned at Gaitlan. "Leave him here."

Gaitlan stepped forward, scattering Mirra's barrier into dust. "Where she goes, I go."

The woman lashed out. This time, Mirra was too slow to

respond. A trio of knives cut thin lines across Gaitlan's face before embedding in the tree behind him. "You do not own her! She is a free woman, no matter what your people say."

Gaitlan raised a hand to his face, turning pale at the sight of scarlet fingers. His face soured, and his other hand tightened around the hilt of his sword.

"He's my friend," Mirra said, stepping in between Gaitlan and the woman. "It is like he says; where I go, he goes."

The woman gave Mirra a look of disgust before turning around without a sound. She marched through the woods, seemingly indifferent to whether or not they followed after her.

Gaitlan looked displeased at the prospect of following after the woman who attacked him twice without provocation. He looked at Mirra, silently urging they head in the opposite direction. Mirra shook her head. The woman had eyes like hers, and Mirra's instincts told her she could trust the woman. She followed after the woman, letting Gaitlan make up his own mind.

Gaitlan groaned and trudged after the women, making more noise than necessary.

They followed after the woman for several miles, every last one silent and tense. Questions bubbled inside Mirra until she felt like a kettle set to boil over the fire.

"My name is Mirra," she said when she couldn't take the silence a moment longer. She cringed at the slight twinge of desperation in her voice. "And this is Gaitlan."

"I do not care what his name is," the woman snapped, not bothering to turn around. "But you may call me Rux."

Terse silence fell over the trio again. Mirra chewed her

lip until it bled, worrying over her next words. Seeing no other way around it, she took a steadying breath and asked the question that would tear her world asunder.

"Are you a Mystic?"

Rux spun around, snarling, her eyes ablaze with white-hot anger. "That is not our name! That is what his kind calls us. We are the Ilmarrion, children of the stars, born at the beginning of all things. When their kingdoms fall and turn to dust, we will still endure, returning to the stars at the end of all things."

Mirra raised her hands in pacification.

The fire in Rux's eyes dimmed to be replaced by sorrow and regret. She turned and continued down the path only she could see.

The warmth from Gaitlan's body chased away the shiver that ran down Mirra's spine. "So it seems that all ... what did she say ... Ilmarrion ... have short tempers."

Mirra grunted, not trusting her voice. She flashed him a grateful smile over her shoulder before moving on. Gaitlan's attempt at humor for her sake comforted her more than she liked to admit.

The density of the woods began to give way, hinting at some sort of clearing on the horizon. Mirra stumbled over a loose stone and cursed. When she glared at the offending rock and stopped short, it looked similar to the cobblestones that lined the streets of Verance.

"Where are you taking us?"

Rux remained silent, a stoic figure treading through the outskirts of a lifeless city.

"Are you all right?" Gaitlan asked, coming abreast with

Mirra.

"I think she's taking us to the Mystic city I told you about. Look," she said, gesturing to the crumbling ancient road. "I think this used to be a road."

Gaitlan studied the stones in their path. Mirra watched his expression shift from realization, excitement, and guilt before becoming as calm and unreadable as a still lake. He stood silently, straightening his tunic before taking a step on a road that hadn't been touched by humans for thousands of years.

Trees became bushes and other small bits of foliage, but in denser woodland rose stone structures. Most were nothing more than short, crumbling walls covered in bracken. A few retained most of their original shape, indicating several tiny houses along the forgotten road.

A cold wind kissed Mirra's sweat-soaked skin, even though the air beneath the trees was as still as the crypt. The cool breeze sent shivers down her spine, raising the hairs on her skin. Whispers danced around her, pressing on her like water. She shivered again, wrapping her arms around herself. As suddenly as the voices appeared, they vanished, though the chill lingered.

"Mirra?"

Mirra shook her head. "I don't know."

Rux turned, her dark brow arched. "You hear them?"

Mirra nodded. Rux's hand went to the cord around her neck, pulling a small leather pouch from beneath her shirt. She fingered the bundle, lost in thought. Her gaze pierced Mirra, laying her soul bare.

"So that is what you are."

"And what is that supposed to mean?"

Rux shook her head, tucking the bundle under her shirt again. She placed a hand over her heart and inclined her head before resuming their trek.

Gaitlan halted, grabbing ahold of Mirra to make her stop as well. He urged her behind him. "You know what? I've just about had enough of this. Either tell us where we're going and who you're taking us to, or we leave."

A lilting, musical voice answered instead. "Then you will miss out much, I'm afraid."

Mirra's first impression was of light, pure white light that could only come from a god. The wind rustled the trees, causing their canopies to dance and sway, scattering shadows below. The brightness of the speaker flickered with the rolling shadows. Mirra peered through her fingers, seeing only a woman clothed in white and not a goddess come to earth.

The woman was dressed in a white robe with a sheer overlay that glittered in the sunlight. A mass of twisted fabric sat on top of her head, concealing her hair. She had painted patterns Mirra couldn't discern across one cheek and on her hands, up to her elbows.

Rux went to her knees, head bowed. "I found them on the outskirts of the Old Road. The girl wouldn't come without the Oathbreaker."

The woman smiled, deep lines forming at the corners of her crystalline eyes so stark against the darkness of her skin. "It is all right, Rux. If they were found, it is because the Ileing willed it so."

Rux stood, placed her hand over her heart before stepping off the path, disappearing into the forest. "You must forgive her," the woman said with a sad smile. "She's suffered much at the hands of man."

"What do you mean?" Mirra asked.

The woman came closer. It was then that Mirra realized what she'd mistaken for paint was the woman's natural skin. Mirra could only stare at the way the darker portions of the woman's skin faded and blended into the near-white tips of her fingers. The corners of her mouth pulled up into a bemused smile. "The Ileing couldn't decide what color suited me best, so I was blessed with both."

Heat spread across Mirra's cheeks. The woman didn't appear to mind her staring. "Who are your people?"

"My people?"

The woman cocked her head, studying Mirra intently. Power glowed behind her eyes. Mirra threw a light shield between the woman and herself.

The woman frowned. "That cannot be ... unless ..."

She cut a quick glance toward Gaitlan, her eyes pulsing.

Gaitlan's face paled, and he took a solitary step backward.

The power in the woman's eyes faded, returning back to their unnatural shade. "I am the High Priestess of Moakwyd, Usoa. Please come with me. I feel you have quite a story to tell."

Mirra moved forward, but Gaitlan stopped her. "Wait," he whispered.

Mirra jerked her arm free. "Come on, Gaitlan. This is why we came here."

She walked toward High Priestess Usoa like a woman possessed, and perhaps she was. The high priestess looked at her like she knew everything about Mirra. Her past, present, and future.

"Do not fret, your highness," Usoa said. "I am nothing like Lord Julian."

Gaitlan reared back. "What do you know of him."

"Not much, but I can promise you, he will never find you here. And if he does, we are not completely defenseless. Nor will we fall victims to his wiles like you."

Gaitlan's face turned a vibrant shade of purple as he rushed forward, spinning the high priestess around.

Three lightly armored guards emerged seemingly from thin air, circling around the prince, the tips of their spears at his throat.

Usoa sighed and waved the guards back. The guards stepped back but watched the prince with sharp eyes.

"I will warn you only once, prince. You are not amongst your people anymore. The reverence and tolerance you've grown accustomed to will not be found here. Take care of your actions."

Gone was Usoa's gentle expression. She regarded Gaitlan with a look that would have frozen steel. Mirra recognized it immediately; she'd received it most of her life.

Gaitlan stood as silently as the ancient stones around them, quivering with thinly restrained rage. Mirra moved to break the tension, but Gaitlan broke first. He lowered his gaze, seeming to shrink before the numerous eyes that bore down on him. Mirra felt a twinge of sympathy toward the prince. Yet, much to her shame, she remained silent, following after Usoa with a heavy feeling in the pit of her stomach.

Black lace settled across her face, obscuring her reflection in the mirror, but Braelyn didn't mind. If she couldn't see the world, then the world couldn't see her. It made it easy to forget the crushing weight of her loneliness that grew with each passing day. It kept the outside world from seeing the looks of disgust that contorted her face whenever she heard someone spreading poisonous lies. Her only solace was her daily visits to the Dark Mother's temple to 'pray' for her parents. As long as she kept in line, she was allotted a single measure of peace.

"Greetings, Your Highness."

Braelyn groaned behind her veil. Lord Tolin was persistent. He hadn't stopped hounding her every step since the day he cornered her in the temple.

"What can I do for you today, Lord Tolin?"

Lord Tolin walked by her side, his hands clasped behind him. "I know that the court is still in mourning, but a few members of the council of lords are having a small dinner in memorandum of your parents. I was hoping that you would join us. Though I fully understand if you would rather not."

Braelyn stopped short, turning slowly to face Lord Tolin.

Lord Tolin's face flushed as if he could see her disdain through her veil. "I'm sorry," he quickly said. "It's just ... some of us feel as if Lord Julian is purposely keeping everyone in the dark about what is truly happening in this kingdom, the nobles, and with you."

Braelyn stood perfectly still, barely even breathing. "I know what is happening in my kingdom. No one is keeping me from anything. I wish that people would respect my wish to be alone."

Lord Tolin bowed. Braelyn went on her way, her footsteps echoing sharply across the cold stone floors. Her heart beating wildly against her chest, her mouth sour.

What was that? Was it a test to see if I would play along? But what if he really meant what he said? Do I have allies? Do I dare to hope?

A large black carriage stood, waiting for her in the courtyard. She accepted the footman's hand out but felt none of its warmth or its strength. She sat, staring blankly at the blank wall in front of her. The world outside her carriage disappeared as she worried the knots of her life.

Lord Julian waited for her when she returned. She bit the inside of her cheek to keep her face neutral. "True beauty is a flower that blooms in the middle of winter." He took her hand and placed a delicate kiss on the top. Braelyn barely kept her shudder in check.

"I have no need for such flattery," she said coldly. "What do you want?"

Lord Julian flashed her a dazzling smile that undoubtedly fooled many people, but she knew his true face. She knew him for what he was, a viper ready to strike at any moment.

"I need your help in a small matter." He held his arm out for her to take. She hesitantly reached out and took it. He placed his hand on top of hers, gently led her back inside the castle.

Courtiers bowed deeply before whispering behind their hands as the pair passed by. Braelyn did her best to ignore them, but the hairs on the back of her neck still rose in ire. Her frustration turned to ice when she realized where he was taking her.

"No," she said, ripping her hand out of his grasp, ripping the veil from her face. "Not here, please."

His stayed the same, but a cruel light shone behind his two-toned eyes. "But princess, you are the only one who can choose the items for the royal archives. You are the only one who would know what the former king and queen treasured most in life."

Braelyn shook her head. Her nails cut tiny half-moons into her palms. Meanwhile, Lord Julian stood with his hand outstretched, looking at her as if she were a willful child throwing a small tantrum.

A small cluster of servants entered the hallway, stopping short when they spotted the princess and regent. One of the servants, a middle-aged woman with streaks of gray running through her dark hair, took note of Braelyn's panicked expression.

"My lady, is everything all right?"

Lord Julian's smile stayed true, but his eyes clouded over with violence. He turned those unnerving eyes from Braelyn to the servant. The servant's face paled, but she stood her ground with a defiant chin.

Bit by bit, Braelyn willed her pulse to slow, her body to relax. She plastered an empty smile across her face. "Everything is fine. Thank you for your concern." It took every ounce of her will and inner strength to move a single step closer to the last place she wanted to see. The servants curtseyed before continuing on their way.

Julian smirked down at Braelyn. "I know it will be hard for you to handle your parents' belongings, and I loathe to ask you, but there is no one else."

Because you chased them away, you sanctimonious bastard, Braelyn thought rebelliously. She allowed her rage to fuel her limbs, stopping only when she reached the threshold of her parents' chambers. The one place where they could drop their courtly personas and simply be a family is nothing more, nothing less.

The room was somehow less, knowing her parents would never enter again. She wrapped her arms around herself as if they could protect her from the emptiness that had taken over. Her throat and eyes burned the deeper she walked into her parents' room.

Nothing had been disturbed since their death as tradition dictated. Only the heirs or regents were allowed to enter the royal chambers during the mourning period. Not even servants were allowed in.

Braelyn's feet carried her toward the empty hearth. The exact path she'd taken countless times before. Twin chairs sat in front of the empty hearth. Her parents' chairs. How many times had she found them sitting together in front of a fire, reading a book or letter, or playing games of strategy? Her fingers reached out to touch a snow-white fur lap blanket draped over the back of one of the chairs. Her father's last anniversary present to her mother. The white fur belonged to arctic foxes that could only be found in Cemont and Vilnia.

Braelyn picked the blanket up, holding it to her face. Linger traces of her mother's perfume filled her nose. The dam of her emotions broke free; hot tears streamed down her face. She buried her face into the blanket, inhaling deeply to commit the scent to memory. She would never smell her mother's perfume again after this day. He would make sure of that.

"An unusual choice," Lord Julian commented as he plucked the blanket out of Braelyn's hands.

"Give that back to me," she growled.

A mild widening of his two-toned eyes was the only indication of surprise he showed. He handed the blanket over before retreating to her father's desk. He sat in her father's chair and opened her father's letters, reading each one carefully before responding, using her father's paper and quill.

Fire surged through Braelyn's blood, and for the first time in her life, violent images flashed through her mind. All the bloody and dark things she wanted to do to Lord Julian, to the people who helped him, to those who saw what was happening and did nothing. She'd been a fool; kindness and patience were the ideals of children. It was high time she faced the truth that the world was nothing more than a cruel place that wouldn't hesitate to crush the weak. She would no longer be vulnerable. She would no longer wait for someone to save her. She'd handle it herself. She would become a survivor.

Julian watched the princess walk about the room, picking up one item or another, playing with them before setting them back down. She clung to the fur blanket, keeping it close to her body like some kind of talisman against him.

Julian frowned. It wasn't like him to relinquish dominance. What was it about the princess in that moment that moved him to act uncustomary? She is beautiful when her eyes are filled with fire, he thought, tapping the end of the quill to his lips. In his mind, he replayed the scene over again, taking time to savor the color rising at her cheeks and neck, the firm yet subtle line of her lips. The way her eyes seared into the depths of his being.

Two heavy items thudded into his line of sight, breaking his line of thought. "Here," Braelyn said, her voice dripping with contempt. "Two items for the royal archives. Are we done here?"

Julian blinked slowly, the half-formed thoughts drifting back into the dark waters of his mind. His hand went out the closest item, a rose gold locket encrusted with chocolate diamonds. He wove its delicate chain in between his fingers, giving Mirra a look.

"Father gave that to mother the day Gaitlan was born. Inside is a miniature portrait of my brother and myself as babies. It was her most cherished possession, and this is," Braelyn paused, swallowing, "was my father's favorite game to play when we were together."

Julian looked at the small board of the world as they knew it and the accompanying ornate box that held the pieces used to play the game. He looked up at Braelyn standing as tall and imposing as any queen and spied a small leather journal tucked alongside the fur blanket.

"And what about those?"

Her grip tightened around the items. "They are for me. Do what you will with the rest; sell it, give it away, burn it for all I care." She turned and walked away from him before he could formulate a cutting remark.

Very well, princess, I'll allow you your trinkets, but just know, they come at a price.

Long after the princess returned to her gilded cage, Julian still lingered at the former king's desk. He opened the ornate box and removed one of the game pieces. There was a fair amount of detail for something so small. His fingers traced over the curves of the piece before pricking his finger on some sharp edge. Cursing, he stuck his finger into his mouth and scowled at the figure with a black smear across its face.

Mystics. Bah. Nothing more than a bunch of pacifists.

With all the power they wielded, they still managed to get overthrown in the end. Julian frowned; that may not be true.

Mirra had their eyes and their strange magic. She shouldn't exist, and yet she did. What did that mean for the rest of her kind? Julian's frown deepened into a scowl. It had taken decades of careful planning and cultivation to achieve his first of many victories. His appetite wouldn't be slated by a single kingdom on the ass end of the continent.

Julian rolled the game piece between his fingers before setting it down on the board.

Gaitlan.

He drew another and another until one side of the board was nearly complete.

Mirra.

Mystics.

The Council of Lords.

Braelyn.

One by one, he would have to tend to the potential obstacles in his way. Some would be more challenging than others, but they would all be dealt with in due time. Julian stood, gathering his letters, leaving the board on the desk. When building a new future, it was best practice to ensure that one had a firm foundation. And the only way to achieve that was to clear out what no longer served a purpose.

CHAPTER EIGHT

MIRRA COULD NOT STOP HERSELF FROM OPENLY STARING. The people she walked past, who were staring as openly as she was, could have come from anywhere in the known world. Pale skinned, olive-skinned, dark as the night sky and every shade in between. Hair of every color, texture, and styling made her realize just how narrow her view of the world indeed was. The old itch to flee over the horizon reared its ugly head in full force for the first time in years. And yet, she felt like she'd come home at last.

Gaitlan's reception was far more hostile than Mirra's. When eyes shifted to him, they turned hard and cold as frozen steel. He tried to ignore the hot whispers no one bothered to hide. From somewhere in the gathering crowd, a glob of spit sailed through the air, landing just shy of his boots. Gaitlan clenched his jaw so tight that Mirra was surprised that his teeth hadn't shattered.

High priestess Usoa strode through the city, greeting and waving at the people as she walked past.

They reached a cluster of large buildings in what looked to be the center of the city. Priestess Usoa walked toward the most prominent structures, walking up half-crumbled steps covered in moss.

Mirra froze in the shadow of the building, her eyes fixated on the broken dome green with age, the scent of charred flesh and smoke mingling with the sweet air of the forest.

"Mirra?" Gaitlan placed a gentle hand on her shoulder, bringing her back to reality. He gave her a questioning look.

"I'm fine. Let's go."

Gaitlan studied her too pale face a little longer before removing his hand, taking a supporting position directly behind her. His eyes turned from Mirra to the temple. Outwardly, there was nothing special about it. It looked similar to a dozen ancient temples he'd seen in the history books. And yet, the sight of it sent Mirra into a panic. Mirra, the one person who never allowed their emotions to get the better of them. Gaitlan wiped his sweaty palms against his thighs before following after.

When she reached the top of the stairs, Priestess Usoa turned, folding her hands in front. "You undoubtedly have questions. I will answer them, but for now, rest. The acolytes will see to your needs. Might I recommend a hot bath, followed by a warm meal and some undisturbed sleep?"

Mirra opened her mouth and was silenced by a raised hand.

"I have duties that I must attend to before tonight. We will speak then."

As if on cue, the great doors of the temple opened with a loud groan. Light spilled into the temple, chasing away most of the darkness. Peering deeper, Mirra spied beams of buttery light from the holes in the dome overhead.

Her hand went to her knife as six people appeared out of

the shadows. Every person wore a different colored robe, ranging from a muted gray to the night sky's black-blue hue. Mirra gave them a timid smile that wasn't returned. Most had blank faces, but one acolyte's face was twisted by surprise and repulsion.

Mirra blinked slowly when she realized that the woman's hatred was not directed at Gaitlan but at her.

High priestess Usoa guided the scowling acolyte to her side. The acolyte's face softened when she looked at the high priestess. A cloud shifted overhead, casting a shadow over the high priestess and her acolyte. When the sun shone on them again, Mirra's breath caught in her throat.

Where the high priestess was light, her acolyte was dark. She stood tall next to the high priestess, with stars in her hair, and the fire of the sun in her eyes.

"This is Oya," Priestess Usoa said. "She will serve as your guide to the city and help you with anything you might need."

Oya turned her head sharply, bits of metal catching the light, her mouth open. Remembering who watched her, Oya buried her emotions beneath an aloof mask.

The remaining acolytes quickly scurried back within the safety of the temple, condolences evident on faces, but for who? Mirra couldn't be sure.

"Follow me to your rooms, or is it room?"

Mirra and Gaitlan made twin faces of alarm, sputtering "No, thank you" and "Two rooms is fine" simultaneously.

The corner of Oya's full mouth creased slightly, softening her hardened exterior. She raised her hand, and a young boy in a white robe came forward.

"This novice will show you to your room," she said to

Gaitlan.

Elation swelled inside Mirra's chest. Something was captivating about the priestess, and she found herself wanting to spend more time with her.

"Come along, Kivuli."

Mirra blinked. "My name is Mirra."

Oya's expressionless face bore into Mirra's, the silence stretching on. Blinking once, Oya turned and said, "Follow me."

Mirra starred at Oya's retreating back for a moment before coming to her senses and hurried after. Frustration trailed behind Oya like a bitter perfume, sending Mirra's head spinning. Mirra tried to keep track of what corridors Oya led her through, but the only thing she could focus on was the priestess in front of her.

"Here you are," Oya said, her voice sharp, bringing Mirra back to herself.

The door was nondescript, and so was the hallway. She cursed her thoughtlessness, knowing that she'd have to traipse through the maze of corridors until she had the route memorized.

"What's the matter, Kivuli? Not as grand as what the prince gave you?"

Anger surged through Mirra. Shadows gathered around her clenched fists. "What did you call me?"

"Kivuli. It's what you are."

"Yeah, you're gonna have to explain it."

"Didn't your parents or tila teach you anything?"

Mirra closed the distance between them. "Making

assumptions about people is dangerous."

Oya's face darkened. "Are you breaking hospitality?"

Mirra snorted. "I'm not that ignorant." She sighed, rubbing her face. "I don't have parents or a tila. I grew up in an orphanage in the capital, surviving by my wits and a lot of dumb luck."

Oya's eyes went wide for only a moment before they bore into Mirra's, searching.

"You really know nothing?"

"I didn't know that I had magic until a few months ago, let alone that I was an Ilmarrion. The prince and I were only coming here to lay low and hopefully find something in the ruins that would help us defeat Julian."

Something akin to pity rolled across Oya's face. "You are right. I shouldn't make decisions about people before I know them."

"What's the meaning of the word you called me?" Mirra asked.

Oya paused. "The full phrase is Umbezi ä Kivuli. The rough translation is 'Traveler of the Void.' It's what Ilmarrions with your abilities are called."

Mirra closed her eyes and let the word settle in her consciousness. It didn't quite feel right, but it was nice to finally have a name to put on what she could do.

"How do you know? Did Rux tell you?"

Oya shook her head, her braids clicking. "It's not exact, but we can sense the aura of another Ilmarrion. To me, you're dark, quiet, and filled with secrets. I read that's what most Ilmarrions felt when meeting one of your kind."

A crease formed in between Mirra's brow. "Are there others? Others like me?"

Oya shook her head. "No, they died out long before the Purge. But nothing stays gone forever. It simply hides away until it's needed again."

"Oh!" was all that Mirra said. "Well, I'm tired. I should rest."

Oya watched Mirra struggle with the door, concern in her eyes. "I'm sorry."

"Me too." Mirra closed the door behind her and slid to the floor.

They died out a long time ago. They died out a long time ago. They died out ... They died ...

White-hot tears spilled over, carving out a path through the dirt on her face. Her throat tightened, keeping back the soul-retching scream that rose from the darkest pits of herself. The fragmented pieces of her buried hope rained down, tearing her tender soul asunder.

Grief turned to hatred. She hated Oya for smashing her unspoken desire. She hated Gaitlan for carrying the blood of the people responsible for the desolation of her people. But she hated herself more for all the years she waisted, too stubborn to speak the truth of her heart. Mirra's nails dug into her palm, drawing blood as she swore to never do that again.

A knock at the door pulled Mirra back from the depths of despair. Using the end of her sleeve, she hastily whipped away any lingering signs of her tears.

"Yes," she called out in a hoarse voice.

"I have snacks!"

Mirra rubbed her face one more time before opening the door. On the other side stood a young girl of fourteen, dressed in a simple white robe cinched at the waist by a red sash. Her round face was bright and cheerful, framed by two long strands of hair. The rest was gathered into a long braid that jingled when she swayed on her feet.

"I'm Kasumi. It is so nice to meet you. The whole temple has been buzzing since Rux brought you into the city."

Kasumi skipped into Mirra's room like a playful breeze, setting an earthen plate and mug on a small table before taking a seat on a small chest at the foot of the narrow, unmade bed.

"I bet you're tired. I'll make your bed for you." She paused, pointing at the table, urging Mirra to sit and eat.

Mirra sat down heavily on the other end of the trunk.

Kasumi bustled about the room, the end of her braid chiming with each step.

"And to have come with the Undorsian prince!" Mirra blinked slowly. She hadn't realized Kasumi still spoke to her.

"He isn't what I pictured, you know? I thought he would be cruel, evil-looking, with eyes as black as sin. Maybe even a wart or two, but he's not. He's kind, hurting but still so kind. I mean, anyone who was betrayed as he was, witnessing the horrors he witnessed ..." Kasumi closed her eyes and shuddered.

A slow blink. "He told you?"

Kasumi paused twin patches of scarlet on her moon-shaped face. "Not exactly. I stopped by his room first with snacks. Sometimes I accidentally see things I shouldn't, ya know?"

Mirra cocked her head. "What type of magic do you have?"

Kasumi's blush grew as uncertainty crept into her almond-shaped eyes.

"I grew up away from other people like us," she told Kasumi, whose mouth fell open in surprise. "I don't know anything about ... our people. Could you tell me more if it's not too much to ask?"

Kasumi started to make Mirra's bed again. When she spoke, it was to the bed, and not Mirra.

"We don't ask a person to explain their affinity. It's like asking a person to talk about how they relieve themselves. But I am a priestess, even though I'm still in training, so I'll tell you."

Kasumi sat on the edge of the bed, her hands folded in her lap. Her playful face suddenly serious, she took a few moments to gather her thoughts before speaking. "What we can do, our abilities, are different person to person. But they're all rooted into the Five Pillars of Isalie; Harvor, Dunning, Fasht, Sa'la, Nexi. Isalie is the source of all life in the world."

She placed her hand over her chest. "My clan is tied to the Sa'la. This power allows us to see what's in a person's heart. Our connection is not the same. Some people are closer to their pillar than others. On the lighter end, you only get a sense of their emotions. Strong affinities can take a person's memories and make them their own. If I focus, I can sense the emotions of everyone around me."

"That sounds exhausting. I think I would go mad," Mirra said with a shudder.

Kasumi laughed. "It was in the beginning. I had to learn how to shield myself at a young age. When my training with my clan's priestess went as far as she could go, it was clear that my connection to the Sa'la was strong. My parents sent me here so I could learn to master my gifts and serve our people."

"Where is your clan from?"

"Lorcea. We share the northern plains with the horse lords. They don't mind too much, as long as we stay away from their herding grounds."

Mirra frowned. "I had to learn about Lorcea when I was younger. I never heard about another group of nomads on the northern plains."

Kasumi threw her head back and laughed. "That's the whole point." Her mirth fell, and she pulled the end of her long braid into her lap. "Many of the laws that allow people to hunt us down like animals are still in place. My brother was killed after he exposed himself by soothing a panicked horse."

Mirra reached out, placing her filthy hand over Kasumi's pristine one. She made a face, quickly withdrawing her hand.

Kasumi's smile returned, though not as bright as before. "When you're ready, I'll take you to the baths. They're actually pretty nice if I do say so myself."

At Kasumi's urging, she left the dishes on the table with the promise that they would be gone by the time she returned. Kasumi chatted the entire way, answering as many of Mirra's questions as she could.

According to Kasumi, most Ilmarrions made out of Undros during the Purge and split into small roving groups that traveled all over the continent. As hatred of the Ilmarrion's spread, many of the great cities and holy sites were destroyed.

"If it wasn't for Usoa, much of our history would have been lost."

Mirra cocked her head. "What do you mean?"

"Usoa is the oldest Ilmarrion by most accounts." Kasumi tapped her finger against her chin. "I think she's earned her position as high priestess shortly after the Purge. But I don't know if that's true. All that I know is that she was here when my grandmother's grandmother came to the temple."

"Aren't we supposed to have long life spans?" Mirra asked. "At least that's what I read in the books I was able to find."

"Not anymore," Kasumi said. "Since the loss of so many holy cities, our connection to the Ileing is hanging on by a thread. We still have our connections to the five pillars, but not much else. There are a few of the old ones left, but the rest of us age like humans."

Kasumi's face turned pensive as if she could pierce through the veil of time and see a future where her people were nothing more than ghosts singing through the grasses of the great plains.

Mirra wanted to comfort the young priestess but couldn't find the words.

Heaviness clung to the pair until they walked through a half-crumbled arch, entering an open space filled with steaming stone-lined pits. Kasumi smiled and gestured to the pits with a bow. "Enjoy your bath."

"What about clothes?"

Kasumi smiled again. "Just ask Grandmother." She turned and left Mirra alone in a world half consumed by steam, the bell at the end of her braid jingling merrily with each step.

"Grandmother?"

She walked through the baths on light feet, keeping

close to the collapsed wall where most of the steam collected. She walked the entire perimeter of the space to only confirm that she was utterly alone. Placing her hands on her hips, Mirra wondered if Kasumi had played a joke on her.

Sighing, she peeled off her road-worn clothes, placing them in a heap beside the furthermost bathing pit. She didn't relish the prospect of putting filthy clothes back onto a clean body. Still, she had no other choice unless the illusive Grandmother decided to show herself.

Steam curled off the calm water. Just beneath the water, stone benches ran along three of the sides. Mirra carefully put a foot into the water. A heavy sigh, nearly a groan, escaped her mouth as the heat from the water caressed the pains in her foot. Mirra slid into the water, finding a nice groove in the stone bench. Up close, the water had a faint scent of sulfur, but nothing too off-putting. Once the heat from the water eased away most of her stiffness, Mirra slid off the bench and fully submerged her body. She scrubbed her scalp, wishing she had soap or something to get more of the dirt, sweat, and gods-know-what-else off her.

Mirra rose from the water with a gasp, raking her hair back. "What can I get for you, youngling?"

Mirra heaved herself out of the bathing pool, rolling into a fighting stance. A translucent woman stood across from her, a bemused smile on her face.

"Who the hel are you?"

The woman cocked her head at Mirra's question. "They call me Grandmother is an honorific title since I'm not related to anyone here."

"All right," Mirra said, easing back into the water, eyeing Grandmother with suspicion.

A crease formed in between Grandmother's brows. "You are not one Clans. You are one of the lost."

A breeze caressed Mirra's damp skin, raising the hair on her arms. Grandmother's form rippled and faded, though her words lingered in the air, pressing against something deep within Mirra. When the breeze faded, Grandmother returned.

"What are you?"

Grandmother's smile returned. "I belong to the Idüing."

"Idüing?"

"It is Usoa's task to tend to the mind. It is mine to tend to the body." Grandmother waved her hand. More people emerged from the mists. In their hands, they carried everything that Mirra needed for her bath.

Mirra watched them put everything down before fading away into the steam. She eased back into the waters before her legs gave out beneath her. Her breathing became erratic, making it feel like she couldn't draw enough air into her lungs. She heard the heavy, rapid beating of her blood inside her head.

"Be at peace, cousin," Grandmother urged, placing a small black bundle by the edge of the pit. "Let the Ileing enter and soothe the storm inside."

Grandmother's features grew more distinct the closer she knelt to the water. Her eyes shone with power as she touched the water with the tip of her finger. Shimmering ripples rolled across the water, breaking against the sides of the bath and Mirra's body.

When the first ripple touched her, Mirra felt a cool wave crash against the heat of her blood. Another hit, causing the same sensation. Mirra's heart and breathing slowed with each cooling wave, and a sense of peace washed over her. When she felt herself, the ripples vanished as if they'd never existed. Mirra stared up at Grandmother with a mix of awe and gratitude.

Grandmother straightened, her body already fading back into the mists. "If you need anything else or if the clothes aren't to your liking, simply think my name, and I will appear."

Mirra watched Grandmother fade away until she was alone in the baths once more. Suppressing a shudder, she quickly washed, letting the mundane task center and ground her.

Once clean and dry, she reached for the bundle to see what Grandmother thought she should wear. She frowned, expecting to find a dress, but when she finished unwrapping her new clothes, she found herself smiling.

She donned the simple homespun breeches and a dove gray tunic that fell to her thighs. The wrappings that the clothing came in turned out to be a new traveling cloak. When she unfurled the cloak, a pair of sturdy but straightforward leather shoes fell to the ground. Mirra would have preferred boots, but the shoes were lined with some type of fleece that made her toes curl in delight.

Mirra ran a comb through her hair and frowned at the uneven strands that fell in her face, no matter what she did. I could use a haircut, Grandmother.

In the steam, or from it, Mirra couldn't be entirely sure, a body took shape. It wasn't Grandmother but one of her attendants. The attendant held shears in her hand and motioned for Mirra to sit on the edge of a window.

"I need it short enough to manage on the road but long enough to pull it out of my face."

The attendant nodded and went to work, gently twisting a section of Mirra's hair on top of her head before making her first snip.

Mirra made it back to her room with only two wrong turns. After her bath, her body felt heavy and sluggish. Her eyes burned with exhaustion, and her yawns grew more frequent. She threw herself onto the bed with a heavy sigh, scrunching the pillow before burying her face into it. It smelled lightly of soap and fresh air. Mirra took one last deep breath, drawing the comforting scent deep into herself before fading away into a dreamless sleep.

Kasumi woke Mirra sometime later. Mirra rubbed the sleep from her eyes and grumbled, "What time is it?"

"It's time for the evening meal."

Mirra rose, straightening her tunic. She ran her fingers through her freshly cut hair, savoring its new lightness.

Kasumi said nothing as she waited for Mirra, with her hands clasped in front. "Did you sleep well?"

"Well enough. Where's Gaitlan?"

Kasumi blushed. "He, well … had a bit of a fiasco in the baths. It took us quite some time to convince him that Grandmother wasn't a ghost."

Mirra chuckled, shaking her head. "Poor princeling. I probably should check in on him just so he knows that I'm alive. It might help him calm down a bit."

"He'll be joining us for the evening meal."

"Then let's get going, shall we?"

Mirra heard the music before she saw the people. It floated in the evening air, drawing her forward like a bee to a flower. When they reached the courtyard where the evening meal was held, Mirra could only stare in wonder.

Torches encircled the open courtyard, casting dancing shadows on the buildings that enclosed the yard. In the middle, a great fire crackled, occasionally sending sparks high into the night sky. A large table stood near the fire, covered from end to end with food. Mirra breathed deeply, her stomach rumbling and mouth watering.

Kasumi nudged Mirra forward with a gentle but well-placed poke to the ribs. Mirra shot Kasumi a withering glance, but the girl had already disappeared into the growing crowd. Alone, unease stirred in the pit of her belly. Unfamiliar faces turned to stare at her.

Whispers in strange languages filled her ears, their tones wary. Mirra swallowed, willing her face to remain blank. The table became her anchor, giving her something to focus on other than the sea of whispers around her.

She reached the table but didn't pick up the plate or any of the food. She didn't want to be the first one. Instead, she scanned the courtyard, desperate to see a familiar or friendly face. Through the flickering flames, she spied one familiar face. Gaitlan stood stiffly against a wall. His arms crossed tightly against his chest, eyes rapidly scanning the crowd. When his eyes settled on her, his entire body sagged with relief.

He moved to her but stilled when she held up a single finger. She made her way to him, keenly aware of the eyes that tracked her every move.

"Hey, princeling," she said.

"Where have you been?" he whispered hotly.

"The same as you, enjoying the hospitality of the Ilmarrions."

Gaitlan scowled, opening his mouth a couple of times before pressing it into a thin line. They fell into silence. Mirra leaned against the wall and pretended to watch the crowd with Gaitlan, when she was watching him in all actuality.

He had been given clothes similar to hers, except for the color of his tunic. The burnt orange suited him the way black and gray worked her.

"So, how does it feel," Gaitlan asked, "knowing the truth?"

Mirra shrugged. "I don't really know. It never really crossed my mind that they were alive."

"I can't even imagine."

Mirra sighed. "Honestly, it's a bit overwhelming." She studied Gaitlan from the corner of her eye. He seemed defeated. "How are you feeling?"

A hush fell over the crowd. Usoa, her acolytes, and novices filed into the courtyard. Oya's eyes briefly met Mirra's before focusing on the high priestess' back. Mirra heard a familiar jingle and waved to Kasumi, breaking her stoic expression. Kasumi smiled, waving back before an acolyte nudged her.

Gaitlan stiffened at her side, going for a weapon he didn't have. Curious, she leaned around him to see what set him on edge. A single acolyte carried a large bowl filled with steaming water. Through the steam, Mirra caught a glimpse of Grandmother's face. She pressed her lips together in a tight smile to keep from laughing.

When the procession reached the fire, the novices separated, standing off to the side. The acolytes took up positions around the fire and raised their arms. It was then that Usoa began to walk around the circle of acolytes. With closed eyes, she sang a song in a language unfamiliar to Mirra and Gaitlan. She sang for a time, then paused as if waiting for a reply. The acolytes shouted a reply, then Usoa took up the song again. She walked around the fire nine times before the song was over.

As the acolytes' last reply faded away, Usoa turned and smiled at the gathered people.

"Blessing of Ileing and Sohä'la be upon you tonight and all nights to come. Tonight, we have reason to celebrate because one of our lost has finally found her way home."

Usoa beckoned Mirra to stand by her side. Mirra pushed off the wall, brushing the dirt from the back of her tunic.

"Welcome home, Mirra."

Cheers and applause rolled through the crowd, though it carried an undercurrent of suspicion. Usoa carried on.

"As many of you may know, Mirra did not come here alone. She traveled with Prince Gaitlan of Undros." She gestured for Gaitlan to join her.

To his credit, Gaitlan's face showed none of his early distress. Instead, he smiled and waved, nonplussed by hostility swarming around him. He stopped in front of Usoa and bowed deeply to her.

"No thanks are needed, High Priestess Usoa. I was more than happy to assist Mirra to find her people."

Usoa's smile was chilled. She let the silence stretch to an uncomfortable level before clapping her hands together. "Let the feast begin!"

The acolytes and novices left their positions, either mingling with the crowd or heading toward the food. Music started again, and a few dancing circles formed.

Mirra let out a breath. "Not bad, princeling."

Gaitlan pinched the bridge of his nose. "Stop calling me that, and this isn't the first time I've been introduced to a hostile court."

"I would hardly call us a court, your highness," Usoa said. "I know you're most likely famished, but I would like to speak to the both of you in private for a moment."

Gaitlan and Mirra trailed after Usoa. She led them to a massive, gnarled oak tree. Usoa sat on a stone bench, folded her hands neatly in her lap, and stared at Mirra and Gaitlan.

Gaitlan met Usoa's gaze for a few minutes before he shifted on his feet, rubbing the nervous energy from his fingers.

"You may stay here while you figure out your next steps." Gaitlan's shoulders sagged in relief. He opened his mouth to thank the priestess, but she held up her hand and continued. "While you are here, Prince of the Oathbreakers, you must follow our rules and customs. It would be best if you stayed either in the temple or the training grounds. You will not make many friends here. Other than that, whatever we have is yours. Use it well."

Gaitlan nodded to the priestess, who then turned her attention to Mirra.

"While the prince figures out how to save his people, you will learn about yours. You will learn our history, our customs, and how to better use your gifts."

Mirra bowed. "Thank you, High Priestess."

"I wouldn't thank me yet. Oya will be your teacher, and from what I hear, she's quite the taskmaster."

"I've had worse," Mirra said with a smirk.

"You'll learn to regret those words, Kivuli." Oya stood behind Mirra, with her arms crossed, a deep frown carved into her face. Her eyes promised pain and exhaustion for Mirra. "Be at the training grounds at dawn. A novice will show you the way. Don't be late."

Oya turned and strode toward the temple, undoubtedly planning a multitude of ways to make Mirra's life a living hell.

Gaitlan chortled. "Good luck."

Mirra stuck out her tongue and stormed off to the feast, determined to stuff her face until she fell into a coma.

CHAPTER NINE

BRAELYN FUNNELED HER GRIEF INTO LEARNING WHAT IT meant to be the ruler of a country. From sunup to sundown, with a slight reprieve to Yulla's temple, she poured over books on the running of the state. She read books about diplomacy, strategy, and economics. At least, that's what it looked like on the surface. Over several weeks, Braelyn came to a simple conclusion —she needed to break free from Lord Julian's grip. Braelyn's quill snapped between her fingers, scattering ink across her notes.

Swearing softly to herself, Braelyn used the blotting rag to clean most of the ink from her hands. She only succeeded in smearing more ink across her hands. At this rate, her hands would be stained black.

Just like his.

No, she thought vehemently, shaking her head. She was nothing like him.

"You should wash your hands with some milk before the ink fully sets in, your highness."

Braelyn jolted in her seat. One of the priestesses that

worked in the library stood behind her desk, hands clasped, the perfect picture of demure grace.

"Thank you," Braelyn said, standing. "Just leave everything where it is. I'll be back later."

The priestess bowed before disappearing down a darkened row of shelves.

Braelyn sighed, shuffling the scattered notes into a semi-organized pile. When she was sure that she was alone, she slipped a small nondescript book into her pocket. She strode out of the library, the book burning against her leg.

The kitchen staff was all too eager to provide a small bowl of warm milk for her to wash the ink off her fingers. Braelyn didn't bother to hide the pleasant surprise from her face. The cook sent another bowl filled with rose water to rinse the milk off her hands to prevent a sour smell later and a couple of secret sweet buns wrapped up.

Braelyn tried to thank the cook for the sweet buns, but she waved the princess off with tears in her eyes. Guilt twinged in her gut. She needed to escape so her brother could have a real chance to save their home, but how many innocent people would be hurt when she fled? Perhaps her hands will end up stained, after all.

The sound of chiming bells sent Braelyn scurrying back to her room. She only had one hour before the evening meal. She had tried in the beginning to avoid the great hall and, by proxy, Lord Julian. He tolerated her mild disobedience in the beginning, but not anymore. Lord Julian made sure she knew that through thinly veiled threats and small displays of power.

In normal circumstances, an hour would hardly be enough time for her attendants to get her ready. Depending on the event and attendees, it could take three hours to prepare Braelyn for the evening meal. But with a kingdom in mourning, opulent clothing and flashy jewels were forbidden, freeing up more of her time. She intended to use the remaining time to add to her escape plan.

Braelyn removed the book she'd taken from the library, her fingers tracing over the cover with a level of reverence that was typically reserved for holy items. To her, the book was. Outwardly, there wasn't anything special about it. It was barely bigger than a diary, but it was its contents that caused her fingers to tremble.

She gently opened the book, its spine cracking from disuse. She held her breath as she turned the cover page, equal parts hopeful and fearful.

Strange letters stared back at her from the page. Braelyn's brows furrowed deeply as cold dread pooled at the bottom of her stomach. She flipped through every page, her anxiety growing until she threw the book across her room. It struck the floor, bounced, and slid under her bed.

Braelyn threw herself into a chair, both palms pressed hard against her eyes. Her breath came out in great gasping gulps. She pressed her palms into her eyes. Twin trails of tears ran down her face, carving a path through the makeup on her face.

THE MUSIC THAT FILTERED THROUGH THE TORCH-LINED hallway was at odds with the somber dress of the people gathered inside. Musicians played a merry tune that would have stirred several people to form dancing circles under normal circumstances, but the floor remained vacant.

Nobles clustered together in small intimate clusters, their fervent whispering barely concealed by the music.

"Princess Braelyn!"

All eyes turned to the top of the stairs where Braelyn stood, a dark pillar of grief and anguish. With a single steadying breath, Braelyn descended.

Down, down, down.

The silent mantra played over and over with each step. Down to the viper pit. Down with the ever-growing desire to burn everything to the ground and down with howling darkness that dwelled where her heart should be.

At the bottom of the stairs, the court bowed as one to the princess. She walked through them as if they were nothing but the demons of her nightmares, eyes trained on the dais at the other end of the room. Braelyn clenched her fists, the only outward display of emotion she allowed, at the sight of Lord Julian sitting in her father's chair.

Her father had sat in his chair straight back and regal. Lord Julian disgraced the former king's chair by lounging in it with no more reverence than a man choosing a woman for the night.

His sadistic smile grew the closer Braelyn drew to him. Instead of halting at the end of the dais, Braelyn strode straight for him, stopping just before the toes of their shoes touched.

"You're in my seat," she said with a bright smile that didn't reach her eyes.

Lord Julian's smile faltered a fraction before returning. He made a great show of pushing himself off the chair, straightening his tunic.

"By all means, your highness."

She bristled at the condescending undertone of his voice but reclaimed her father's seat. With a wave of her hand, the evening's entertainment began. Braelyn leaned back in her father's chair, grateful for the dark gloves that hid her white-knuckled grip on the arms. She settled in for a long evening, pretending not to be wounded while surrounded by blood-thirsty jackals.

THE CLOCK TOWER STRUCK TWO HOURS PAST MIDNIGHT when Braelyn trudged back into her room, her bones transfigured from airy bone to cumbersome lead. She slouched off her dress and accessories, letting them fall to the floor in careless heaps before she pulled on a soft nightdress. Her eyes burned, and her brain screamed for sleep, but she forced herself to sit down to work through the pile of missives she'd neglected over the past week.

Her vision was blurred, and her fingers cramped by the time she signed her name on the last letter. She read the same empty, meaningless condolences from people who'd hardly even looked her way while her parents had lived. They now spoke to her as if they were her deepest confidant and one true friend. Her jaw hurt from the many hours she spent clenching her teeth together over the audacity of the noble class.

Braelyn stood from her chair and stretched, her back popping from sitting hunched over her small writing table. If her volume of correspondences continued to grow, she'd have to invest in a proper writing desk. A massive yawn pushed its way through, stretching her jaw to its limit. That was another problem for another day.

The sound of chirping birds drew her attention toward the window. Dawn's soft rosy glow had already started to creep up through the glass. Braelyn groaned, snatched a scrap of paper, scribbling a note for the maidservants that would arrive a few hours later.

Utterly spent, Braelyn threw herself into bed, wrapping her mother's fur around her before falling into a soundless slumber.

An incessant knocking at her door drew Braelyn from her bed. Her blankets clung to her, making every movement a fight for freedom, eyes burning from exhaustion. She'd left specific orders to not be disturbed until the evening meal.

She threw her door open wide, not caring who was on the other side or that her hair was a mess, and she was only clad in a nightdress.

"What?" she growled at the soon-to-be-dead person that was foolish enough to disturb her.

Lord Tolin stood frozen on the other side, his hand raised to knock again. His eyes swept over Braelyn's sleep-addled appearance, a faint blush creeping up his neck. "I ... um ... you weren't at the morning meal or in the library. I thought ... well, I feared."

His blush now crept up to his face, staining his cheeks a violent shade of red. He awkwardly rubbed the back of his neck, his sputtering dying underneath Braelyn's murderous gaze.

"Well, you can clearly see that I'm alive and unharmed. Now, if you'll excuse me." Braelyn moved to slam the door in his face. Lord Tolin moved, sensing his closing window of opportunity. He moved forward, blocking the door with his foot.

Braelyn's eyes widened with shock briefly before narrowing to slits. "You're too bold. All it will take is one yell from me, and you'll find yourself a guest of the dungeons."

Lord Tolin's face paled. He swallowed before speaking. "I am well aware, your highness. But my boldness is derived from a noble reason. A reason I need to explain to you fully before you make your decision."

Braelyn relented with a sigh, backing up so the impertinent young lord could enter her chambers.

Lord Tolin visibly sagged. "Thank you, your highness. I know this is highly irregular, but I am ..."

Whatever else he was about to say was cut off by Braelyn's swift strike to his nose. Stars danced across his vision, and the sudden warm wetness running down his face told him that his nose had been broken. He fell to his knees, biting back the string of curses he wanted to hurl at the stubborn princess. He pinched the bridge of his nose to staunch the bleeding and stared up into the coldest eyes he'd ever seen.

"This is your last warning, Tolin. I don't know what game you're trying to play, but I want no part in it. I will allow you the remainder of the day to gather your things and leave the castle. If I find that you're still here by the evening meal, I will have you thrown into the dungeons."

Lord Tolin stared up at the princess, his rebuttal dying before it ever had a chance to fully form. He bowed his head, ignoring the throbbing around his nose. "As you wish, your highness. I am sorry for any harm my actions have caused you. I wish you peace going forward."

Braelyn scoffed. Peace; she'd never know peace again until the man responsible for her parents' death lay bleeding at her feet. She turned her back to Tolin to pull on the rope that would summon her maids. If she was awake, she might as well get to work.

Striking Lord Tolin in the face made one thing startling clear for her. The longer she stayed in Verance, the more of a pawn she'd become. An instrument to keep her brother in line and to rule over her people. And as far as she was aware, there were already two opposing factions vying for control over her.

Braelyn clenched her fists, pulling her lips back into a silent snarl. She was done being another person's plaything. She was strong. Mirra knew that. That was why she let Braelyn sacrifice herself so she and Gaitlan could escape. Mirra knew that Braelyn had the strength to not only endure but survive.

First things first, Braelyn needed to escape the city and head to K'aski, the capital of Nealet. Her mother and Empress Elipie had a longstanding friendship from the time they were young girls. If there was anyone in the world who'd help her, it was Empress Elipie.

She would have to travel light and under a false name. A disguise was something else she would have to procure, and money. Braelyn ran her hands through her tangled locks. Swords were out of the question, and she didn't even know where to begin getting one. She couldn't fight with daggers like Mirra and would most likely hurt herself if she tried. But the road was dangerous to travel without some type of weapon.

Braelyn stood in front of her window, staring out without seeing, chewing her nail. She loathed putting her people in danger, but at least this way, there was a slight chance for things to right themselves. Braelyn nodded. It would be worth the risk. She would make restitution to those who suffered the most after she and her brother returned. Braelyn turned her thoughts toward making her escape. It would take time for her to gather what she needed without drawing attention. To add another element of difficulty, she had no idea how many spies Lord Julian or Tolin had watch her. She would have to take the utmost care to appear as innocent as possible while looking for openings.

Her first opening came a few days later. While pretending to pray to Yulla, the Dark Mother, one of the priestesses beseeched an audience with her.

"My deepest apologies, your highness," the priestess said with a deep bow. "I hate to bother you, but I have a small request to make, if I may?"

"Not at all. How can I help?"

"There is a sickness that is running through the Merchant and Divine Districts. It hasn't reached the homes of the nobles or the castle, but I fear it's only a matter of time."

Braelyn cocked her head. "What do you need from me? We have some resources in the castle, but I don't think we have enough to be of any help here."

The priestess waved her hands. "No, please keep the resources meant for the castle. The only thing we ask for is a donation of money and hands. We have some money from offerings, but most of that is taken up by the temple upkeep. We hope to stock up and prepare healing kits to give to local apothecaries and healers to stem the path of the illness. We will need extra hands to make and distribute these kits."

Braelyn schooled her face. Thank you, Great Mother

Yulla, keeper of shadows and secrets, for showing me the way to my salvation.

"I think that can be achieved. Send a list of estimated costs and laborers needed. I will get them to you as quickly as I am able."

The priestess bowed deeply. "Thank you, your highness."

"Not at all," Braelyn said, bowing in return. "The royal family must tend to the temples as well as the people."

Her mind swirled with ideas the entire way back to the castle. It wouldn't take much for her to sneak a small bag of coins, as long as she was the one to handle the ledgers. The priestess' request also gave her an excuse to spend more time away from the castle. With any luck, she'd even be able to acquire a commoner's garb and a safe place to store her pilfered items until she was ready to flee.

As soon as she returned to the castle, Braelyn met with the court treasurer. She filled him in on the situation. Together, they calculated a rough estimate of funds to send to the temple. It would take some time to draw up the funds, so the earlier they started, the better.

For the first time since her parents' death, Braelyn's steps were light. The shadows of her pain had dissipated, just for a moment. Lord Julian saddled next to her, grabbing her arm with more force than necessary.

"Tell me why Lord Tolin was seen leaving your chambers with a bloody nose three days ago?"

Braelyn plastered a vacant smile on her face. "Lord Tolin? I'm afraid I can't quite place a face to the name? Are you positive that it was my room he was seen leaving?"

Wicked delight danced along Lord Julian's eyes. "Yes, my dear princess. I am quite certain. It is my responsibility to safeguard your virtue as well as your life."

Braelyn couldn't stop herself. She threw her head back and laughed. "My life. Without my life, you wouldn't be enjoying the power you do right now. I pray you always manage to keep it."

Lord Julian released her arm, surprise written across his face.

Braelyn regretted her boastful words but kept her smile rooted. She let some of her ever-present anger shine through her eyes. Perhaps that would be enough to fool him into thinking her words were nothing more than thinly-veiled barbs, the only weapon she had to hurl at him.

Worry clawed at her stomach. Braelyn carried out her evening performance as perfectly as she could, keenly aware of the real and imagined eyes that tracked her every step.

WE CAN'T THANK YOU ENOUGH FOR ALL YOUR HELP, YOUR highness." The High Priest of Ydris and the High Priestess of Yulla bowed deeply to Braelyn.

"It is an honor to serve," Braelyn said, returning the bow. "Please let me know if there's anything else you require, no matter how trivial it may seem."

"We will."

Braelyn stood back and surveyed her work. Three wagons stood in front of the temple of Yulla, waiting to be unloaded. In addition to the funds and workers requested, Braelyn also procured additional herbs, wax, containers, and bandages. Even though she was using the sudden illness to mask her movements, she took a small measure of pride in what she could accomplish in a short period of time. The joy quickly became tainted with guilt, knowing she'd be leaving as soon as she was able.

Needing something to keep her hands and mind busy, Braelyn strode down the temple steps to the first wagon, whose cargo was already in the process of being divided.

"There's no need for you to help with the unloading, your highness," sputtered a young priest when he nearly handed her a box of clanking jars.

Braelyn flashed him a genuine pleading smile. "Please let me be useful. I've spent too much time lost to grief. Allow me the blessing of an honest day's labor."

The jars in the box clinked together loudly, betraying the young priest's nerves. Braelyn felt the smile on her face becoming strained. Thankfully, one of the elder priestesses saved them both.

"Let the princess help." The young priest nearly threw the box at Braelyn, eager to move past the awkward exchange. The priestess shook her head, causing Braelyn to press her lips tightly together to keep back the laughter that threatened to bubble out.

"If it's a distraction you require, then I think I can find something more fighting for you."

Heat rushed to her cheeks. "I can do more than you think."

"Undoubtedly," the priestess said with a slight inclination of her head. "But you are the crown princess, the next ruler of our country. And we must treat you as such."

Braelyn sighed, passing the box off to another. "As you wish."

As it turned out, helping to care for those recovering from the illness was the only task deemed fitting for her station. She wasn't at risk of catching the sickness herself, as long as she kept her face covered, and the only tasks required of her were the retrieval of water and listening.

At first, many of the patients were too scared to open their mouths, but they began to open up to Braelyn as the days went on. She sat back and marveled at the lives of the everyday citizen. She learned about their joys, their suffering, and more importantly their dreams.

Her daily ministrations drew a few other court members, all eager to earn her favor, to join in the effort to stem the sickness' path and the caring of the ill. Braelyn could only sit back and shake her head.

The temple's main chamber was always quiet, yet a noticeable hush had fallen over the patrons and priestesses.

A small procession solemnly made its way through the room. A senior priestess led the way, swinging a censer. Plumes of blue-gray smoke billowed with each swing to flow like water behind her, enveloping the cart pushed by two junior priestesses.

Braelyn's eyes widened at the jumbled array of something her mind refused to recognize. Ice water filled her veins, stealing her breath and the strength in her limbs. Stumbling backward, she flung her hand out, desperate for anything to root her to the corporeal world. The scent of smoke and blood filled her senses, sending her crumbling to the floor, coughing and choking.

She felt a presence at her back and the pressure of hands

under her arm. Braelyn silently screamed, clawing against the black bonds that threatened to pull her into the gaping abyss, never to be seen again.

"Princess, princess! Braelyn!"

Braelyn opened her eyes, blinking against the bright light of the afternoon sun filtering in through a stained glass window. The smell of smoke and blood was replaced with a god-awful aroma that caused her stomach to heave and clench. Only her iron kept the contents of her stomach where they belonged.

"What happened?"

The same priestess who sent her to the recovery room sat next to Braelyn. She picked at her nails. "I'm so sorry, your highness. We have to remove the deceased quickly. I didn't think what the sight would do to you."

"Oh," Braelyn said, shifting. Her palms pressed into a straw-stuffed mattress. She stared at the simple bed she'd been placed in, blinking slowly. Her head felt fuzzy and stuffed with cotton. "Why do I feel like this?"

"It's the wakeflower," the priestess said. She stood and poured some water into an earthen cup. "The effects should wear off shortly. Here, some water will help."

Braelyn accepted the cup, holding it with both hands. She stared at it for a few moments, struggling to remember what she was supposed to do with it. Bringing the cup to her lips, she tipped the cool water down her raw throat. Perhaps her screams had been real.

A light knock drew Braelyn's attention to the doorway. The High Priestess of Yulla smiled kindly at her. "Thank you, Sasha, for tending to the princess. I can take over from here."

Sasha stood and bowed before walking out.

Braelyn felt a surge of protectiveness rise in her over the retreating priestess' back. "Don't punish her, please."

The high priestess's brows furrowed. "I had no intention of punishing her or anyone. No one can predict how someone who's suffered like you have will act. You could have had no reaction today, tomorrow, or ever. We are trained to help in such occasions."

Braelyn looked down at the cup, still clasped tightly in her hands. The high priestess said nothing as she took the seat Sasha vacated. As the minutes ticked by, Braelyn sensed that the priestess was giving her the space to leech off some of the darkness she harbored in her soul since her parents died.

"I don't really remember much. Only the smell of smoke and blood."

The high priestess reached out and placed a gentle hand on Braelyn's arm. "I've watched you come here every day. I don't think you're praying for your parents all the time. But I think you come here because you're looking for something."

Braelyn's heart froze.

"You may not yet know what it is, but know that we are here for you. Our dark mother is equal parts cruel and gentle. However, do not linger too long in her darkness. All too quickly can it turn from comfort to a prison you can never escape from."

Braelyn swallowed and nodded, keeping her eyes trained down so the high priestess couldn't see the panicked relief in her eyes.

The high priestess stood. "Rest here as long as you need." She bowed to Braelyn briefly before making to walk out of the room. She lingered in the doorway, turning to speak once more. "I would urge you to remain at the palace for a few days, but I know that's asking the impossible. Especially since we're nearly ready to distribute the healing kits you so graciously dedicated your time to."

Braelyn's head shot up. "So soon?"

"Yes. They should be ready by the new moon. My priestesses will hand out the first batches, with more to follow. Thank you again for your help, your highness."

"Not at all," Braelyn responded automatically.

The new moon.

That only gave her four days to gather her resources and secure passage. She chewed the end of her thumb. She could wait and sneak in during another round of distribution. Braelyn chewed her nail and wondered if she'd be able to keep her plans a secret for much longer.

She swung her feet off the bed, surging to her feet. The room spun, sending her careening into a small trunk along the wall. Braelyn opened the trunk and smiled. Inside sat a mass of black robes worn by all the priestesses. The final stages of a plan clicked into place. Quickly, she bundled up the robe into her cloak. She had much to do during the next four days.

THE ONLY LIGHT IN THE CASTLE CAME FROM THE TORCHES that ran along the parapets. Not even the stars were designed to make an appearance. For the first time ever in her life, Braelyn smiled at the darkness. Huddled against a stone pillar in a stolen robe, she sent another grateful prayer to Yulla for the small blessing.

Overhead, two members of the roving nightwatch lingered, chatting about trivial matters. Braelyn gritted her teeth, silently cursing the men. After an eternity of mindless chatter, they carried on with their patrol route.

Braelyn painfully waited long minutes to ensure that no other watchmen lingered before stepping out into the pitch-black courtyard. She kept to the border of the open-aired walkway, not fully trusting her senses. Light may be limited, but there was enough for a keen eye to detect movement.

Her heart pounded so loud that she was sure that any passerby would hear it. Every sound, real or imagined, sent her scurrying for cover, with every ounce of her senses strained to determine the source.

It took her twice as long to reach one of the lesser manned side gates than her previous attempts. Sweat already beaded across her forehead and the small of her back. This was the most dangerous part of the plan. If she was caught here, she'd never get the chance again.

Like every other night, a single guard was on post. Young and inexperienced, he leaned against the wall, yawning. Braelyn settled down into the hollow of a bush and waited.

The bell tower chimed the hour, and Braelyn was still crouched in the bush. She shifted as much as she dared to keep her blood flowing. She'd just started to fret when a sharp whistle cut through the silence. She nearly collapsed in relief as the guard peeled off the wall to walk over to the kitchen maid with a seductive smile on her face. The guard returned the smile, already working on the ties of his breeches.

Braelyn waited a few more moments before slowly rising

from her hiding place. Poised like a deer entering the glen, her eyes zeroed on the last door between her and freedom. Her entire body tensed, ready for the sprint of her life.

She loosened her breath and emerged from her hiding place.

A set of solid hands collapsed around her arm and mouth, pulling her back into a warm body. Primal instincts woven into every woman in existence flared to life, fueling every kick of her legs and swing of her arms. Sadly, it wasn't enough to free her from her captor. Hot tears streamed down her face as images of her horrible future played out in her mind. What would Lord Julian do to her? How would he take out his anger on her? Flogging, beating, rape?

Her captor dragged her into a small, dark room before he released her from his grasp. Braelyn ran forward, hoping to find another door, only to run into another person.

"Peace, princess; we mean you know harm."

Braelyn jerked back, recognizing the voice. "Lord Hamal?"

From behind her, a match was struck. In the flare of light, she stared up into a kind face.

Too many emotions to be named welled up inside Braelyn, constricting her throat and burning her eyes. She threw her arms around Lord Hamal as if he were a lifeline.

"What are you doing here?"

"I could ask you the same thing, my lady."

More light filled the small room from the small lantern held by another familiar face, Lord Tolin.

"I thought I told you to leave my city."

Lord Tolin's smile held a hint of sadness. "I'm afraid it's not your city anymore, your highness. I think this time, you will listen to what I have to say."

Braelyn opened her mouth to argue, but Lord Hamal placed a firm hand on her shoulder. "No, my dear; you will listen." He gestured for her to take a seat on a crate. She did, arranging her stolen robe around, taking her time to look at the faces of the ones responsible for foiling her escape.

In addition to Lord Tolin and Hamal, there was another man. His face was the only one not familiar to her. He was older than Tolin but younger than Hamal.

Tolin took note of her stare. "Ah, yes, I suppose a small introduction is in order. May I present Lord Prenn? His lands are to the southeast along the coast."

Lord Prenn bowed his head. "I don't make it to court too often. I only came now because Tolin reached out to me."

Braelyn turned her attention back to Lord Tolin.

Tolin coughed lightly, adjusting his clothing before speaking. "We all know the story that Lord Julian is spouting about the night the king and queen died. We also know that it's a load of horse shit."

Lord Hamal coughed pointedly. "What Tolin is trying to say is that we and others like us don't completely believe Lord Julian's version of events. That, coupled with the fact that he's been keeping you from us, has only added to our suspicions."

"So that's led a number of us to work toward the truth of the matter."

Braelyn blinked slowly. "The truth of the matter? The truth of the matter is that the bastard manipulated my brother, killed my parents, and nearly had me killed. And if I hadn't sacrificed myself, I would be with my brother and Mirra right now!"

Lord Hamal breathed a heavy sigh of relief. "So your brother did make it out after all."

Braelyn pressed her traitorous lips together before she could spill any more secrets. She didn't trust this gathering of nobles any more than she did Lord Julian.

Lord Hamal saw the distrust in her eyes, took a small step back, hurt flashing across his face. On the other hand, Lord Tolin seemed pleased with her reluctance to accept their words at face value.

"I know you have no reason to trust us," he said, "but I hope that now you're at least willing to allow us to prove ourselves to you."

The bell tower struck the hour. Braelyn sighed; her one and only window had closed. "I guess I have no other choice, do I?"

Lord Tolin shook his head. "No, not really."

CHAPTER TEN

A SOFT KNOCKING AT HER DOOR WOKE MIRRA FROM HER slumber. She peeled herself from the warmth of her bed, blurry-eyed and yawning. It felt like she'd just fallen asleep, though the light streaming from the window was the soft glow of dawn.

"What?" she growled, rubbing the sleep from her eyes.

"Acolyte Oya sent me to wake you. If you don't hurry, you'll be late and have to risk her wrath." Kasumi pushed past Mirra, carrying a small picture of water and a stack of clothes. "I brought you some clothes to change into. They aren't much, but it won't matter if you get them dirty or bloody."

Mirra blinked slowly, staring at the pile of heavily patched clothes sitting on the bed.

"Let's go, sleepy bones. You're the one that said Oya wasn't 'that bad.' She's planning on making you eat those words. You don't want to give her another reason to make ya suffer?"

Mirra stood, pulling her nightshirt over her head. "I don't think anything I do will sway her one way or the other."

Kasumi shrugged. "True, but let's not put that to the test."

Mirra was left with no choice but to follow Kasumi's directions and get ready for her ungodly early training session with Oya. After dressing, Kasumi led Mirra down a series of corridors.

"Is she that bad?"

"Not really. She's just ... intense. She's Usoa's successor, and sometimes the stress of it all gets to her."

Mirra made a noise in the back of her throat, unsure of what to say. She couldn't truly begin to understand the type of pressure Oya lived with daily. But if it was anything like the stress Mirra felt for the past week hauling the prince around to keep him from either falling into Julian's clutches or dying, she'd had a small inkling.

Kasumi left Mirra at an open-air pavilion. "If you follow the path, you'll find the training yard. My guess is that Oya is already there, waiting for you." Before Mirra could offer her thanks, the young priestess had already scampered away.

Shaking her head, Mirra stepped out onto the cobblestone path and headed toward the painful lesson her mouth earned her.

Stone pillars lined the path. Many had crumbled into stumps, their corpses covered by moss and vines. Mirra ran a hand down the length of a half-crumbled pillar with a sorrowful expression. So much lost, whether to the Purge or to time.

The path led to a large open space of land. A low, stone wall ringed the entirety of the area. At the far end of the training space stood two weapon racks. One held wooden training swords and spears. The other had deadlier options.

Curious, Mirra strode toward the racks. She ignored the

training weapons and went straight for a spear with a large curved blade. She took it off the rack, giving it a few slashes, testing its weight and balance. It was heavier than she'd expected. Mirra tried to wield it single-handedly and dropped it. She picked it up again and tried a few staff-wielding moves to see if she could even wield such a weapon. It took her a few tries, but she managed to get through a single movement without dropping the strange weapon or nearly cutting a limb off. Mirra held the weapon in front and ran her hands down the length of the staff.

"It's called a glaive."

Mirra jumped, spinning around. Oya sat on the wall, her arms braced on her knees, dressed in the same fashion as Mirra. She arched a single brow at the weapon pointed in her direction, nonplussed.

"If you're done ogling the weaponry, let's get started."

Mirra snorted, tossing the glaive across her shoulder. "You're the boss."

Oya narrowed her eyes, sliding off the wall to meet Mirra in the middle of the field. Mirra smirked, twirling the glaive around her body before resettling it at her side.

Mirra stood to the side, giving Oya access to the weapon racks.

"I will not need them," she said, moving into a fighting stance.

Mirra eyed the priestess, alarm bells ringing in the back of her mind. Widening her stance, Mirra pointed the tip of the glaive at Oya.

Oya charged forward, the corner of her mouth twisted

into a feral smirk.

As soon as Oya came within range, Mirra swung it at her head. Instead of ducking or dodging like she expected, the blade crashed into an invisible wall, sending sparks into the air.

Oya's eyes burned with power. "Pathetic," she said.

Mirra bared her teeth. "Now, don't count me out yet, priestess. I'm just getting started."

Mirra swung the glaive again in a wide arch toward Oya's left side. Golden light rippled when the glaive made contact with the invisible wall. Mirra stepped, using her momentum to increase the force of her blows. Again and again, she struck Oya's wall of power, searching for any kink in her armor.

She had to admit that Oya was a skilled fighter. The priestess countered every one of Mirra's attacks with a grace that only came from years of training and practice. Mirra realized she preferred this version of the priestess rather than her uptight, formal one. This Oya had just the right amount of mischief that sent ripples of excitement through Mirra's body.

Oya deflected another one of Mirra's attacks. Mirra used the force of Oya's strike to swing the glaive around her shoulders and head to come down on her exposed neck.

Mirra retched up with her other hand to grab the staff of the glaive, halting its trajectory, but it slipped through her fingertips. Oya's and Mirra's eyes went wide.

Oya was the first to react, knocking Mirra to the ground while creating a small circular shield of golden light.

The glaive struck the shield and ricocheted to the far side of the training yard, its blade plunging into the ground.

"You've been trained well," Oya admitted. "But you fight like a human, not an Ilmarrion. We do not need blades or staffs to take down our foe. Show me your magic, Mirra. Release your shadows, and let's see how much you need to learn."

Rising to her feet, Mirra called on her magic. The gentle light of dawn dimmed, swallowed up by the darkness that rippled and pooled around Mirra's body like some primordial river. The only light still lingering around Mirra was the iridescent glow of her eyes.

Oya smiled and nodded her head. "Good. Now let's see how long you can keep it up."

Sunlight pooled into Oya's hands as she rushed forward. She swung at Mirra with the same ferocity and grace as a desert cat. Mirra could barely keep up, often having to release the hold on her magic to deflect strikes with her bare hands. Patches of scorched skin soon took over her hands and arms.

"How have you managed to stay alive this long?" Oya teased as she waited for Mirra to get back on her feet after being thrown from a blast aimed at her gut. "It appears that the only time you can remotely do anything with your power is when your life's on the line. Let's test that theory."

Oya resumed her attacks with vigor, pressing on Mirra with each step.

Unable to do anything against the onslaught, Mirra held her hands up, palms blistering, and clothing smoldering. The scent of burning hair filled her nostrils, taking her back to the burning city of her dreams. To the strange woman with the knife that consumed everything around it. To the darkest pit of herself, where the core of her magic dwelled. Mirra reached out into the void, and the void reached back.

"Mirra," Oya said, her voice tight. She stepped toward Mirra, her hands raised in placentation, her mouth open to speak.

Mirra didn't give her the chance.

With a flick of her wrist, she sent rolling black waves at Oya.

Oya rolled to the side with practiced ease. Jumping to her feet, her eyes shone with a mixture of power and frustration. Power flowed along her body like tiny rivers of sunlight.

"Enough, Mirra!"

But Mirra was beyond reaching. Never before had she truly let go, giving herself entirely to the force that slumbered inside her.

The dark wave surged toward Oya, crashing against a barrier of golden light. Oya stood her ground, the first two fingers of both hands crossed in front of her face. She muttered under her breath rapidly. A ball of light grew in the crux of her crossed fingers until a massive rune hung in the air.

Seeing the rune, Mirra roared, launching herself at Oya, dark talons forming on the tips of her fingers.

"I'm sorry," Oya said softly before uttering the final words of her spell. "Cruth. Õ'at. Baas."

Light as bright as the sun exploded from a single point. Mirra cried out in pain, her consciousness rising from the void. She fell to the ground, shielding her eyes from the blinding light.

Even when the light dimmed, she remained on the ground, curled up like a child. It was only when she heard the sound of approaching footsteps did she risk a quick glance from behind her fingers.

Oya walked through the fading light like a goddess

descending from the heavens. The sunshine highlighted the curve of her shoulders and the gentle planes of her face. She held her hands in an odd position, with another rune hovering in the air in front of her.

Oya's face was contorted with guilt. "Rest," she commanded, sending the rune at Mirra with a slight push.

Mirra tried to scramble away, but her limbs had no strength left in them. As the rune neared, she threw her arms up in defense.

Oya's soft sorry was the last thing Mirra heard before falling into a gentler version of darkness.

MIRRA'S CONSCIOUSNESS STRUGGLED AGAINST THE glittering chains that kept it from merging with her body. She strained against the chains, banging her limbs and joints on objects she couldn't make out in the dark. The world she was trapped in was void of any signs of life. No light, no smells, no sounds, not even her own struggles. Mirra knew she should have felt panic, fear, or anything, yet she felt nothing. It was as if the darkness that surrounded her swallowed up everything until there was nothing left. It was only the most primal portions of her mind that lingered, urging her to fight. To not give in to the darkness, not yet.

"But I'm so tired. My entire life's been one fight after another."

"Then let go," said a voice that she heard, yet not heard. "All things come from here, and all things must return here when their time is over. Stay. Let go of your worldly tethers to join the Sohäla and be at peace."

A small smile broke out across Mirra's face. "That doesn't sound too bad."

Mirra stopped fighting. A sense of weightlessness and peace filled her. The golden chains around her went slack, allowing her to float away.

"Yes, this isn't so bad. This is where I belong. I am home at last."

Light burned through the void, scattering the recesses of the strange world. With the light, life came crashing like a storm. Mirra cried out, shielding her eyes and curling up as small as she could to protect her senses from the sudden onslaught.

"Mirra! Mirra!"

Mirra spied the shadow of a hand reaching out for her in the brightness. She wanted to turn away, but the sound of her name spoken by that person brought tears to her eyes and the warmth back to her limbs.

Surrendering to the nothingness was an option. Mirra felt its eyes watching her on her back. If she still wanted, she could turn from the light and find peace in nothingness. But her heart ached to rejoin the person that called for her to return to the light. Torn between two worlds, Mirra stood on the threshold, with one foot rooted in both worlds.

From the side of the nothingness, Mirra felt a sigh. "The call of Ileing is still strong in you. Farewell, daughter. We will meet again, at another time."

The world of nothingness faded away, causing Mirra to lose her footing. She stumbled, throwing her hands out to break her fall. The person in the light surged forward, latching onto

Mirra, pulling her back to the corporeal world.

"Mirra, can you hear me? Mirra, answer me, please."

Everything hurt. Mirra groaned and turned her head in the direction of the person who was calling out to her.

Oya breathed a sigh of relief, reaching out to take one of Mirra's hands into her own. "Thank the stars. I was afraid that I killed you."

"Wasn't for lack of trying."

Oya let go of Mirra's hand. She looked down at her lap, hiding her face behind her hair. "You're right. This is all my fault. I should have handled the situation differently."

"Yeah, you were a bit of a bitch."

Oya's head shot up, a look of surprised indignation painted across her face. Mirra started to laugh, but it quickly turned into a coughing fit. A cup of sweet, cool water appeared in front of her.

Mirra drank the entire contents of the cup, feeling life returning to her body. "Where did you send me?"

Oya's brows furrowed. "I didn't send you anywhere. I simply ..."

Gaitlan burst through the door, cutting Oya off. His eyes landed on Mirra lying in bed. Her deathly pale face, the dark circles under her eyes. His lips pulled back into a silent snarl as he turned his attention on Oya.

"What the hel did you do to her? You were supposed to train her, not nearly kill her!"

"Be still, prince," Oya said, rising to her feet. "As you can see, Mirra is fine; nothing that a few days rest won't cure."

It took Gaitlan three long strides to cross the room. He loomed a full head and shoulders over Oya, yet she still managed to look down at him.

"Take heed, princeling. It is only by our good graces that you are allowed to stay. You are an outsider. More importantly, you carry the blood of the people responsible for the suffering of my people. Do not test our patience."

Gaitlan's knuckles went white.

Mirra pushed herself into a seated position. "Enough the two of you. Gaitlan, if you want to help, then get me something to eat. I'm starving."

Gaitlan cut his eyes at Mirra briefly before turning, slamming the door behind him as he went.

Mirra sighed, leaning her head back against the headboard. "Wanna explain to me what happened?"

"Not in particular."

Mirra patted the edge of her bed. Oya sighed again and retook her seat.

"Our people have certain affinities that allow us to wield magic."

"I know; Kasumi already filled me in."

Surprise flashed across Oya's face briefly before settling again. "Your kind of affinity hasn't been seen in many ages, not since the days of the Lost Court."

Mirra cocked her head.

"It's an ancient story," Oya said with a wave of her hand. "You can read it later. But the takeaway is that people like you, with an affinity with the Nexi, are not only rare but essentially wild cards. If the other four pillars are life, the Nexi is the opposite."

"Death?"

"Not really; it's just ... nothing, a void, an absence of living essence. It's the place of secrets and mysteries. Lies and loss. Those who wield the Nexi also don't follow normal structures. Their abilities and affinities fluctuate greatly, even in a single person."

Mirra picked the skin around her thumbnail. "What does that mean for me?"

"It means," Oya said slowly, "that there is only so much that we can teach you."

Mirra's face fell, her hopes crushed.

"We can teach you our history, our costumes, and some practices. You can be taught the basics of our magic and ways to wield it, but the finer aspects of your affinity—those will have to be gleaned from what remains of our history."

Mirra leaned back, closing her eyes. "Great, back to square one."

Oya huffed, a corner of her mouth pulling. "Not quite. But like I told the prince, you need a few days' rest."

"Fine." Mirra scooted down into her bed. "One last thing."

Oya nodded her head.

"Did you mean to send me to it?"

"To what?"

Sleep tugged Mirra back down. Her eyelids were already closed. "To the place where the Nexi thing lives. It said I could come with it, but then you showed up, and it went away. It called me daughter."

Oya's mouth fell open, but Mirra had already fallen asleep. A great sense of dread filled her stomach, and for the first time, she questioned if Usoa made the right choice letting Mirra in. She stared at the sleeping Mirra for several minutes afterward before reaching out to gently brush back a stray strand of hair from her face. Mirra shifted in her sleep, turning her face toward Oya's hand, a small smile on her face.

Oya's heart danced wildly, sending her swiftly to her feet and out the room.

MIRRA WOKE TWO DAYS LATER WITH NO LINGERING EFFECT from either her fight with Oya or the other world. She rose early, making her way to the training yard. It was as empty as the first day she walked onto it, but that's how she wanted it.

She made a beeline to the weapon rack and picked up the glaive, twirling it around in her hands with a half-smile on her face. She'd adapted relatively quickly to it the other day.

The image of Oya's eyes going wide as the blade of the glaive swung down at her flashed across Mirra's memory. She still had a long way to go before she'd be considered proficient.

Sliding into a fighting stance, Mirra went through a series of movements, blending staff fighting and swordplay together. She turned off her mind, ignoring the questions that brewed and bubbled just beneath the surface. She pushed them away until there was nothing left but the weight of the glaive in her hands and the sweet ache of her muscles as they shifted through the movements.

With one last strong swing, Mirra stood in the center of the training yard, breathing hard, covered in a fine sheen of sweat. She relaxed her form, tilting her face toward the sky. Both her body and lungs were on fire, but it didn't matter. She was clean, purged of all harsh shadows and twisted truths. It was as if that golden light had burned away whatever was holding her back from reaching her true potential.

A pointed cough drew her back to her surroundings. Gaitlan stood at the entrance to the training yard with his arms crossed tightly across his chest and a deep scowl.

"You should still be in bed."

Mirra bristled at his tone, her ire chasing away exhaustion. She pointed over her shoulder with her thumb. "Take your pick, and let's see who needs to rest."

"If that's what you want," Gaitlan said, his expression turning hard.

Gaitlan stopped across the yard. Mirra pressed her lips together to keep from laughing. She understood his anger toward Oya; she felt the same. But there was no reason for him to be angry for her being out of bed after a couple of days.

Snatching a sword from the rack, Gaitlan swirled it around, testing its balance and weight, disgruntled approval painted across every inch of his body.

Mirra schooled her face into polite blandness when he turned around and stomped to the middle of the yard.

"Don't you want to warm up first?" Mirra asked.

Gaitlan's mouth set into a firm line as he shifted into a fighting stance.

Mirra shrugged and followed suit.

The two faced each other, poised to attack. Gaitlan moved first, feinting to the right before following through with a low crescent sweep.

Using the benefit of her weapon's reach, Mirra deftly blocked his attack, using her momentum to carry over to one of her own.

Gaitlan ducked and weaved, avoiding her swing with surprising ease.

Gaitlan growled and pressed Mirra with a series of rapid strikes and slashes. Mirra spun her spear around, blocking and deflecting.

Sweat ran down the sides of her face, stinging when it got in her eyes. Her arms shook with each block and swing. Gaitlan was fresh, whereas she was already tired from her training session earlier. If she didn't end the fight soon, she'd lose, and Gaitlan would win, sending her back to bed.

Calling on her magic, Mirra sent it spiraling down her spear, focusing it at the blunt end. As the power built, she looked for weaknesses she could exploit. Gaitlan tripped over a loose stone, losing his balance, giving Mirra the opening she needed. With a quick twist of the blade, she sent his sword flying, and in the next move, she slammed the end of her spear into the ground, sending a wave of shadows in all directions.

Gaitlan was thrown to the ground, with the air knocked out of his lungs. When he opened his eyes again, Mirra stood over him, the tip of the spear pointed at his throat.

"You cheated," he spat.

Mirra smirked. "No, I didn't."

"Yes, you did. You would have lost if you hadn't used

magic."

"And how is that cheating?"

"She's right, princeling."

Oya sat on the low wall with a slight smile on her face. Today, she wore the robes of her order. Oya moved, the dark shadow of her leg visible in one long graceful line.

Mirra's heart jumped into her throat. She turned and walked over to the weapon rack, taking her time, securing a leather bag over the glaive's blade. She blinked as she fumbled with the ties. Her mind replaying the swing of Oya's leg and how the sunlight made her midnight skin shine.

"Magic is nothing more than an ability that some have, and some don't. It's no different than being stronger, faster, or a natural with a blade. The fighter that uses all their abilities is the one that will walk away."

Oya extended her hand to the prince.

Gaitlan rolled to his feet, ignoring Oya. He spared Mirra a passing glance before stalking away. "Don't push yourself too hard. You're fresh out of bed," he growled.

"He's right too," Oya said, inclining her head in the prince's direction. She eyed Mirra's sweat-soaked shirt and flushed face. "Wash up and eat something hearty. I'm to take you to the Citadel today."

Mirra perked up. "The Citadel? What's that?"

Oya flashed Mirra a knowing smile before sliding back over the wall, calling out over her shoulder, "Clean up and eat."

Mirra stood in the training yard long after Oya left, her brain struggling to remember how to move. Snapping out of her daze, Mirra banged the heel of her palm against her forehead several times.

"I must have pushed myself too hard," she said to the open air that couldn't say anything to the contrary before disappearing into the darkened corridors.

IT TOOK EVERY OUNCE OF RESTRAINT INGRAINED INTO HER since coming to Moakwyd for Oya to not laugh at the open wonderment painted on Mirra's face. The Citadel was one of the few buildings that weren't a crumbling ruin or haphazardly maintained. Rising over the shattered glass top of the greenhouses, the Citadel stood like a proud sentinel pointing to the heavens.

"There are six floors inside," Oya explained. "The first five are named after the pillars of our magic."

"And the last one?"

Oya held a finger up her mouth, her eyes sparkling with mischief. "It's a secret. Only those who have made it to the top and pass the final test can hear its name."

"How hard is it to make it to the top?"

"It depends on the person. Some only need the first level to control their magic. Some, a little bit more. For those of us training to be priests and priestesses, we have to master all six levels."

Oya stared up at the pinnacle of the tower and sighed. "But that's not why we're here today. Today, you face the key test."

"Key test?"

Oya nodded but didn't elaborate. She led Mirra to a

small door at the base of the tower. "This is the only way into the Citadel."

Mirra stared at the door. "Where's the handle?"

"That's the test," Oya said. "You must find a way to gain entrance. You must do this on your own. I cannot help you. Kasumi cannot help you. And I don't think the princeling would even know where to begin to help."

Oya clasped Mirra on the shoulder. They were so close that Mirra caught a whiff of the sweet oil rubbed into Oya's skin. Heat crept up Mirra's neck and spine as she worried about what she smelled like after two intense training sessions, even after a long bath.

"Well, then," Oya said. "I'll leave you to it. You have until the next new moon to enter. If you fail, then the Citadel will forever be closed to you."

A deep line furrowed in between Mirra's brows.

"That is how it has been since the beginning. The magic used to create the Citadel and the challenges are older than any living being on this earth. We cannot undo them, nor can we defy them. Good luck, Kuvili."

Oya left Mirra at the foot of the towering building without a backward glance. Mirra watched her walk away, her gaze captured by the swaying of her robes and the light caught by the embellishments in her hair.

Shaking her head, Mirra turned and stared at the door again. She stepped closer, running both her hands and eyes over every inch of it. The door appeared to be made out of wood. It felt and sounded like every other wooden door she'd come across, yet she saw no way to pry it open.

She then walked around the tower to see if she could spy another door or perhaps a window that she could climb through. Nothing. Standing back in front of the door, Mirra placed her hands on her hips, chewing her bottom lip.

Oya said that the door was the only way 'in.' Did that mean there was another way out? If there was another out, that meant it could be a way in. She could wait in the shadows for another priest or priestess to come by, then wait for them to leave. She shook her head. The new moon was only a fortnight away. She didn't have the time for people to become complacent and forget about her. There was only one option left for her. Mirra put her hand against the door and slammed her magic into it.

When Mirra regained her senses, she found herself several feet away from the tower. Every inch of her screamed in pain, and black stars danced across her vision. The only thing she heard was a high-pitched ringing that didn't go away, no matter how hard she rubbed her ears.

Someone grabbed her by both her shoulders and spun her around. That sent her world spiraling, forcing her to clutch to the other person like a lifeline. Once the world stopped spinning, she looked up into the face of an extremely worried Gaitlan. He gave her another shake, and it was then that Mirra realized his mouth was moving, but she couldn't hear the words, only the ringing.

She rubbed her ears again, allowing Gaitlan to lead her away from the tower to the shade of a small oak tree. The more she moved, the better she felt.

"I think I can hear again," she said after slapping her hands against her ears.

"Good," Gaitlan said. "Now, care to explain what that explosion was?"

"What explosion?"

"The one that I felt all the way back inside the temple!"

Mirra's temples throbbed in tandem with her heartbeat. She squinted against the growing pain. "I don't know about any explosion. The last thing I remember is trying to open the door to the Citadel with magic."

"Well, I think it backfired," Gaitlan said, moving out of the way so Mirra could see the Citadel looming in the distance. The ground in front of the tower was scorched black; even some of the stones had been turned black. But the door, the god's forsaken door, was completely untouched.

CHAPTER ELEVEN

THE SUN SHONE BRIGHTLY IN A ROBIN'S EGG SKY. THE breeze in the gardens was warm and fragrant. Bees buzzed merrily from rose to rose, sipping at the sweet nectar nestled at the bottom of silky petals. Braelyn sat at an ironwork table with a pot of herbal tea while reading a book about a hero fighting against demons to save his kingdom. She sighed, setting the book aside.

"Is it that bad?"

Lord Tolin bowed slightly to Braelyn, producing a bouquet of wildflowers before sliding into the vacant seat across from her.

Braelyn hid her blushing face in flowers, taking in their delicate scents as she quelled the thrumming in her blood.

"Is everything all right, princess?"

"Sorry, it's just been a long time since anyone's gotten me flowers."

Tolin rubbed the back of his neck. "They're just some wildflowers I found on the way here."

"But you took the time to get them for me," Braelyn

said, unable to keep the smile off her face. She placed the bouquet on the table and folded her hands in her lap. "If we speak softly, we can speak freely here."

Tolin cast suspicious glances around the garden. "Are you certain?"

Braelyn chuckled. "I am sure. My mother designed this garden herself. We are sitting too far away from any walkway or parapet for anyone to hear. And the roses are too dense for anyone to crawl into. My mother claimed she loved their wildness, but in reality, she used their thorns and some plain bramble to create a sanctuary."

"Impressive."

"And useful. Now, what do the other lords have in mind? I'd hate to learn that you thwarted my one chance for freedom for some foolish ideal."

"No, princess; although that is the ruse that we need to maintain."

Braelyn waved an impatient hand.

"To be frank, we don't know who supports Lord Julian, who opposes him, or who is watching from the sidelines to see which way the winds of favor blow. That makes the matter of what to do with you a highly delicate situation."

"If you had let me go when I had planned, the matter wouldn't have been so delicate, as I recall. I found a way to escape and nearly did so on my own."

Tolin nodded his head. "That you did, yet we discovered your plans easily enough. Who's to say that Lord Julian didn't either and was letting you escape to have you killed off in some accident?"

Braelyn blanched, her stomach souring.

"Where would you have run to, princess? Nealet? Lorcea? Zallino? Bardon? Lord Julian could have spies in every single court in the known world. That was his job before he decided he'd be a better ruler than your parents."

Braelyn took a swallow of her now cool drink to mask her emotions.

Lord Tolin leaned forward, his eyes filled with a stern yet kind gleam. "And forgive me, but you don't look like you have any wilderness skills."

"And so what if I don't?" Braelyn shot back. "It's not like anyone knew this would happen, so why should I have learned those things?"

Tolin leaned back in his seat, his hands up in placation. "Fair point, but I think we may have a solution, if only for a little while."

Braelyn leaned forward, her expression schooled into polite interest.

"The Holy Isle."

"The Holy Isle?"

"Yes. Kingdoms around the world send people to study from the masters. So, that makes the island neutral territory. It's well understood that any kingdom that dares to attack the holy island will find the entire world against them."

"That won't stop Lord Julian. He'll send assassins after me."

"He might, or he may leave you there cut from the only resources you've ever known. However, it does give us time. Time to garner allies. Time to sow seeds of doubt amongst Lord

Julian's followers and time for your brother to rejoin you. Together, you will have a stronger voice."

Braelyn picked a tiny white flower off the bouquet, ripping the delicate petals from their seats. "It is a sound plan. Thank you. When do I leave?"

"A fortnight from today. Lord Hammal is garnering your passage out of Undros with a few misleading routes as well. The other lords are doing the same."

"What about you? What's your role in all this?"

Lord Tolin blushed, his hand going to his neck once again. "I am to pretend to court you, my lady. The other lords will pass information to me, then I pass it along to you."

"That's rather bold of you, Lord Tolin."

"It wasn't my idea."

Braelyn raised a brow.

"Not that you wouldn't make a fine wife one day," Tolin stammered, his face bright red. "It's just that I'm closest to you in age, and the whole court knows that I've tried to get in your good graces."

Braelyn's composure evaporated. She threw her head back and laughed. "By all means, my dear Lord Tolin. Fake woo away."

CHAPTER
TWELVE

MIRRA'S BREATH CAME OUT IN GREAT, GASPING GULPS, sweat running down her face. Though the sun was nowhere near its zenith, she'd already stripped down to loose britches and a breast band. Mirra narrowed her eyes and shifted into a fighting stance. "This time, I will beat you!"

Squaring to her target, a pitch-black cloud swarmed around her clawed hands. With a yell, Mirra rushed forward, tossing fists full of darkness ahead.

Each ball struck the door to the tower, dissipating like smoke in the wind, just like every other time.

Her deadline was fast approaching, yet she was nowhere nearer to gaining access to the tower than she had been when she first started. She tried using the few runes she knew to no avail. Then she fell back on her training from Lord Julian by lying in wait for someone to enter or exit the tower. That approach failed as well. No matter how long she waited, not a single person entered or left the building.

Mirra stared at the pristine door and crumpled to her knees. She wanted to believe that the constriction in her throat and stinging eyes were the results of her efforts and not the weight of defeat.

The sound of heavy footsteps approached. Mirra paid them no mind. If they belonged to an attacker, she welcomed them. Death was preferable to failure.

"Still no luck?"

Her jaw popped from how suddenly she clenched. Wordlessly, Mirra pushed herself to her feet, storming over the tree where she tossed her things.

The shade was pleasantly cool to her flushed, exposed skin, though it did nothing to cool her frustrations. Mirra ignored Gaitlan's calls, focusing only on uncorking her water skin and pouring the water over herself after taking a long swig.

"That bad?"

Mirra continued to ignore him, throwing herself to the ground, staring blankly up at the shifting limbs overhead.

Gaitlan rubbed the back of his neck, casting a wary look from Mirra to the tower. With a heavy sigh, he lowered himself next to Mirra. She tensed, turning away from him. He picked at the grass by his feet, his brow furrowed.

"Perhaps you're going about it the wrong way?"

Mirra's tightly controlled anger snapped, sending her spiraling to her feet. She loomed over Gaitlan, legs wide, fits tightly clenched at her sides.

"Shut up! What would you know about this! You've had everything given to you, and I can't get this one thing!"

Gaitlan rose to his feet. "That's not fair."

Mirra scoffed. "Oh, excuse me, your majesty, but I only speak the truth."

Gaitlan snapped back. "I didn't do anything!"

"That's right! You did nothing! You did nothing but hunt, drink, and fuck while enemies gathered at your back. Your father was wise to deny you the crown. You'd destroyed the kingdom!"

Gaitlan and Mirra froze, the hateful words hanging in the air between them. Shame overtook Mirra's anger. She opened her mouth to apologize but was stopped by a sudden blow to the side of her face. Stars danced behind her eyes, and a light coppery tang filled her mouth. When the world shifted back into clarity, it was Gaitlan who loomed over Mirra, his fists clenched tightly. His face is white with rage as he stared down at Mirra with nothing but contempt in his gaze.

Mirra raised her hand, gently touching the side of her face he struck. A small bump had already formed, tender to her touch. She turned and spat red. She didn't attempt to rise. She bowed her head and waited for the next blow that never came.

When she lifted her head, Gaitlan had already stormed off, leaving her alone with her guilt.

WHAT IN THE WORLD HAPPENED TO YOU?" OYA REACHED out and touched the swollen side of Mirra's face. "This couldn't have been from the tower ..."

Mirra turned her face away. "I don't want to talk about it."

Oya lowered her hand and turned back to the table she'd been working at before Mirra shuffled into the apothecary. She worked quietly, humming softly to herself as she ground dried

189

herbs into a fine powder. Occasionally, she'd refer back to a small, simple bound book.

Other Ilmarrions worked in the apothecary as well. Some in simple garb; others clad in robes of the priesthood. Before Mirra entered, the room had been filled with quiet but continuous conversations. But now, silence fell, and those who labored did so quickly to get away before the growing tension came to a head. She had searched out the apothecary to ease some of the pain and swelling in her face. Still, now her stomach twisted and burned as the memories of a similar room took hold of her.

Kasumi bounced into the room. "Gaitlan really did hit you good."

Mirra's brows shot up in surprise.

The bell at the end of her braid danced merrily as she skipped over to one of the many shelves that lined the space. She dug around, eventually pulling a small clay pot from the shelf. She opened the lid, sniffed, then scraped the inside with her pinky. She rubbed the contents between her pinky and thumb, nodding in approval.

"This should do the trick."

She next walked over to a small box, unlatching the lid. Mirra's mouth fell open as she spied the ice that filled the box, sending tendrils of cold vapor into the air. Kasumi broke a small piece of ice off, then closed the lid. She snagged a thin rag as she passed a table, much to the table owner's protest.

Kasumi placed her things on the table near Mirra. She wrapped the ice in the cloth before handing it over. "Keep this in place until the swelling goes down a bit. Then apply this ointment to the inside of your mouth. Two or three days should suffice."

Mirra stared down at the wrapped ice for a moment before pressing it against her face with a sigh. The cold pushed back the pulsing heat and numbed the pain.

Kasumi flashed a bright smile before skipping out of the apothecary without another word.

Half of the people working at the tables shook their heads with laughter in their eyes before returning to their tasks. Mirra chewed her bottom lip before wincing in pain.

"Drink this before you apply the ointment." Oya sat a small steaming cup of tea next to the jar. "It's willow bark tea. It should help with the pain a better than ice."

Mirra picked up the tea and took a sip. It was bitter and acrid. Warm and cold warred against one another inside her mouth. She placed the cup back down. "Thanks," she said.

Oya smiled softly, setting every nerve in Mirra's body aflame. "No problem. Let me look at that for you."

Oya gently took away the ice and stepped close to examine Mirra's jaw. Mirra closed her eyes against Oya's sudden closeness. Heat crept back into her face, and it had nothing to do with the absence of ice.

The scent of sweet oil wafted through the pungent aromas of herbal remedies. Mirra peeked, her breath stolen from the magnificence in front of her. Sunlight danced along the soft planes of her face, drawing Mirra's eyes to the curve of Oya's cheek, the swell of her lips. It tore all thoughts from her mind, changing the rhythm in her blood. It pulsed in tandem to the song that moved Oya's life force through her.

Mirra's throat constricted as her eyes welled up with an

emotion she couldn't quite place. Oya broke contact with Mirra's swollen face, putting space between them. The sudden loss of connection sent Mirra whirling, breaking the dam that held back her tears.

"Does it hurt that badly?" Oya asked, already turning to fetch more medicine.

"No!" Her reply came out as a shout, drawing the attention of everyone in the room, but Mirra didn't care. All that mattered was that Oya stayed by her side.

"Mirra?"

She looked down and saw that she'd latched onto Oya's wrist, clinging to it as if it were a lifeline. Oya's delicate wrist was the only thing that kept Mirra tethered to the corporeal world, that kept the foreign emotions from completely taking over. She shuddered at the thought of what they could drive her to do when she let go.

Under her fingers, Mirra felt Oya's pulse race. Mirra released her wrist, snatched the jar of ointment, and ran from the apothecary.

She shook her head as she ran, hoping to resettle her thoughts to no avail. She threw herself into bed, not bothering to undress or wash, and fell into a fitful slumber.

The following day when she woke, she felt a bit like her old self. Though the lingering remnants of her dreams hinted that they had been far from ordinary. Her entire body felt hot and uncomfortable, almost as if her skin had shrunk through the night.

Seeking release, she headed to the training field. Much to her dismay, it seemed like Gaitlan had the same idea.

The prince was already covered in a fine sheen of sweat as he shifted through his stances. Guilt from the previous day washed over Mirra. In her haste to retreat, she stepped on a twig, its snap reverberating unnaturally through the air.

"Mirra, wait!"

Her shoulders bowed inward, but she forced herself to turn and face the prince. She lifted her head and schooled her face into an empty mask. Gaitlan sheathed his sword, setting it down on a stone bench before crossing the distance.

His eyes were wholly focused on the bruised side of her face. The shame and guilt she felt over her harsh words were mirrored in his face.

"I shouldn't have said what I said," Mirra said, her words coming out louder than she intended.

Gaitlan's face softened a fraction. "And I shouldn't have struck you."

With no more words, the pair stood, facing each other awkwardly, unsure of how to proceed.

"I can leave if you want to be alone."

"No, it's all right. It's better when I have an opponent."

Gaitlan nodded and retrieved his sword, his stance alert but relaxed.

Mirra retrieved the glaive and took her position across from him. Gaitlan was the first to move, faster than before, but not as quickly as one would move in an actual match. Mirra countered smoothly, stepping around to strike his exposed side with the end of the glaive. And so, their dance began, neither one putting much effort into gaining an advantage over the other.

Near noon, they halted. Gaitlan took a swig from a

waterskin before tossing it to Mirra. She took great gulps, with small trickles escaping from the corners of her mouth. Gaitlan watched the twin streams race each other down her neck until they disappeared beyond the collar of her shirt.

Flushing crimson, he uttered the first words that came to his mind—that had been on his mind since he saw Mirra struggling to open the door.

"Don't force it."

"What?"

Gaitlan made a face before explaining further. "Don't force your power into the door."

Mirra tilted her head, swallowing the irritation that rose instinctively. Seeing her willingness to listen, Gaitlan continued.

"I don't have magic, nor do I fully understand how your people's abilities work. But from what I've gathered since arriving, your abilities aren't something you have to force. You're born with them. The effectiveness of your abilities is something you have to work on, but without it, you'd still be able to wield it."

His words made sense. Without any training, she'd been able to tap into her magic from an early age. It was only recently she'd learned how to focus it into something other than instinct-based.

"Interesting theory; wanna see if it works?"

She was rewarded by the smile that broke across his face. "Led the way."

She flashed him a half-smile and went to face her opponent one last time.

MIRRA SHOOK THE NERVOUSNESS FROM HER LIMBS,
bouncing from one foot to the other. She rolled her head on her
shoulders, pondering just how she was going to 'open herself' to
the door. She glanced over her shoulder. Gaitlan lingered beneath
the tree where their frustrations came to a head. He gave her a
reassuring gesture. She closed her eyes, taking three deep breaths.

Mirra drew up her magic until it rolled beneath her skin.
Rippling strands of darkness danced across her body, ruffling her
hair and clothing. Once settled, she strode toward the door as if
she had no doubt in her mind that this time, it would open for
her. She placed her hand on the sun-warmed wood. Her shadows
gently rolled into the door, dissipating as they always did. Her
heart sank. She was going to fail the first test she actually wanted
to pass.

With sorrow growing in her chest, Mirra pressed her
hand harder into the wood, the grain pressing into her palm. She
did the one thing left to her, the only thing she'd never done in
her entire life—beg.

"Look here, door; I need to get inside. I need to ... I've
never felt like I belonged anywhere. When I was a child, I would
spend hours looking for people who looked like me. I searched
countless faces for any sign of belonging. I never found that until
now. Please. Please. Please. Let me in. I ...want ... to come ...
home."

Silence only answered her plea. Defeated, Mirra pressed
her forehead against the door. She would have to leave with more
questions than answers. Perhaps high priestess Usoa would let
her borrow a few tomes to study on her own while she wandered
the world with the prince. "Oya ..."

Letting go of all her disappointment in one long breath, Mirra struggled to will her face into a nonchalant mask until she could grieve in private. As her fingers trailed away, she heard the unmistakable click of a lock giving way. The door swung open, revealing gaping darkness.

Mirra lingered at the threshold. Not quite believing what she saw, Mirra glanced over her shoulder to see if Gaitlan saw the same thing she did. His eyes were as wide as hers.

"What are you waiting for!"

Mirra smiled and took the first step toward discovering her full potential.

GAITLAN STARED AT THE TOWER LONG AFTER MIRRA HAD disappeared inside. That smile. He'd never seen her look so unbridled and open before. He'd seen her smile as brightly a hundred times before back in Verance, but there had always been a wary edge to her smiles, laughs, everything.

At the sight of her true self, his heart stopped cold. He still struggled to remember how to breathe correctly. He couldn't deny it any longer. Mirra was beautiful, and somewhere between losing everything, going on the run, and fighting black-eyed demons, he had fallen for her.

"Shit."

MIRRA STUMBLED ALONG IN THE DARK, ARMS SPREAD WIDE. There was no sound inside the tower, save for her own rapid breaths. She should have run into something or someone by now.

Not keen on sitting alone in the dark, she trudged forward, stretched to the breaking point for any indication that she hadn't fallen into a void, forever lost.

In the distance, a tiny pinprick of light flickered into existence. Mirra surged toward the light, gaining speed with each step. The light stung her eyes, but she continued on in a dead sprint. With one final spurt of speed, Mirra crossed the threshold of light, stumbling blindly into a new room. She tripped over something and fell hard on the stone floor.

Applause erupted around her. Blinking against the harsh light, Mirra pushed herself to her feet, keeping her body poised to either attack or defend.

"Peace, young one," Usoa beamed. "Welcome home."

Home.

The word ripped through Mirra, shattering the walls she'd built to protect herself and soothed hurts she'd never been aware of until that moment. Her throat tightened, eyes burning from more than the shift from dark to light. Swallowing, she pressed her lips tightly together. She chose a spot over Usoa's shoulder to focus on until she gained control over her emotions.

Usoa continued to smile at Mirra, though something about her face hinted she understood what Mirra tried to hide.

Behind Usoa, Oya stood. Her face unreadable. She inclined her head slightly before turning to leave.

Mirra watched her go, ignoring the sharp pain that arose in her chest. Soon, she was surrounded by a mass of Ilmarrions that she didn't know. They congratulated her and welcomed her into their numbers. Still, Mirra could detect an undercurrent of suspicion and unease behind the bright smiles.

She was an outsider, raised amongst the people who had destroyed their civilization by breaking treaties and promises. Mirra knew that she would feel the same if she were in their shoes, yet that didn't erase the hurt. But those emotions weren't helpful, so she pushed them down, burying them under the guise of inference.

"Tonight, we shall have a feast," Usoa said, her voice ringing out across the room. "Everyone should attend to welcome Mirra's induction into our ancient arts."

The crowd dispersed, chatting amongst themselves as they went, equally excited and curious about the change in Mirra's status, until only Usoa and Mirra remained.

Usoa motioned for Mirra to follow, leading her down a half-crumbled hallway.

"I hope that you're enjoying your time amongst your own kind."

Mirra shrugged. "Well enough. Kasumi has been the most kind, and I think Oya and I have reached an understanding."

Usoa chuckled. "I'm glad. She was most anxious that you wouldn't find a way in."

Mirra's smile faltered when she remembered who was responsible for helping her pass the test.

"What is it?"

"I can't stay long," Mirra said, her shoulders sinking. "I only ever intended to lean enough to help Gaitlan reclaim his throne from Julian."

Usoa waved a careless hand. "Why should you care for human kings and their intrigues? You can finally connect to your heritage. Though we live here, there are still many nomadic bands roaming the world. Inquiries will be made as to why you ended up in a human orphanage. "

Mirra shook her head. "Maybe one day, but Julian is a problem for everyone, not just Gaitlan. He has magic. It's like mine but not."

Usoa stilled her eyes hard. "What do you mean?"

"His magic is like black serpents or eels, slithering and cold. We were attacked by mercenaries with black eyes. I think ... I think he's controlling them somehow. Normal weapons couldn't stop them. I was only able to kill one when I pushed my magic into my blade."

Usoa's eyes turned distant, looking at something beyond where they stood. "What else can you tell me about this man?"

"He has one eye like mine. I don't know anything about his past. But he somehow imbued the tattoo he uses to mark his agents with some sort of binding spell. I was barely able to break it."

"Show me this mark."

Mirra held out her wrist, pulling back her sleeve to expose her tattoo. Usoa gently took hold of her forearm with one hand and traced the snake with a glowing finger.

Usoa shuddered and released Mirra's arm. "What he uses doesn't come from the same source as yours or our people's."

Mirra rubbed her wrist. "Then where does it come from?"

"I'm not sure," Usoa said.

Mirra could taste the lie that hung in the space between them. She peered into the high priestess's face, but the woman was adept at shielding her thoughts. Mirra knew Usoa wouldn't divulge her suspicions. But she was willing to give the high priestess a chance before extracting them herself.

Usoa sent Mirra along, promising to speak with her more later, after the feast. She walked back to her room, relying on her feet to remember the way. She played her conversation with Usoa over and over in her mind, analyzing the high priestess's every move, facial expression, and tone. She was so consumed by her thoughts that she ended up running into something warm and firm that smelled slightly of soap and sweat.

"There you are," Gaitlan said, grabbing her by the shoulders.

"Oh hey," she replied, rubbing her nose. "I made it through."

Gaitlan hung his head and laughed. "I can see that. Where did you end up?"

"Somewhere inside the main temple. The high priestess and a bunch of others were there to greet me. They're holding a feast tonight to celebrate."

A look flashed across Gaitlan's face too fast for her to read. He straightened, dropping his hands to the side. "I'm happy for you."

Mirra arched her brow. "Okay," she said slowly. "Well, I'm going to take a bath and then take a nap. You should probably do the same. I have a feeling tonight's celebrations will last until dawn."

Gaitlan didn't respond. He remained rooted to the ground, staring at Mirra as if she were something not of this world. Mirra shuffled past him and walked as fast as she could to her room.

Why was he looking at me like that?

There was something about Gaitlan's face that drew up a heavy feeling in her chest. Three words crept from the corners of her mind. She shoved them back down before they could sink their claws into her mind, adding one more complication to her life. Despite many of his failings, Gaitlan was an attractive man. And spending weeks on the road only strengthened their connection. Perhaps, one day, they could be friends, but nothing more. She wouldn't bind herself to another's will ever again.

CHAPTER THIRTEEN

THERE WAS SOMETHING TO BE SAID ABOUT THE ROUGH and wild beauty of the world beyond the cities. Braelyn stared out the window of her carriage, drinking in the looming trees that lined the deeply rutted road that took her further and further away from her gilded cage. Her heart ached when thoughts of never being able to return home danced across her mind. And yet, for the first time in weeks, she breathed freely without a worry.

Lord Tolin muttered something in his sleep, shifting to find a more comfortable position, drawing her back to her surroundings. Braelyn studied the young lord who she'd slowly come to think of as her only friend in the capital. The other lords who helped her did so out of respect for her parents. Behind their kind smiles, she felt their aversion to her ascension to the throne with every glance.

Lord Tolin was different in more ways than one. He was tremendously kind and selfless. He told Braelyn during one of their fake courtship outings that he came to the capitol solely to help her. She laughed in his face, causing his cheeks to flush, but now, after two days on the road with him, she had started to believe his intentions. After all, it was his clever lie that got them out of the city, to begin with.

I DON'T THINK IT WISE," LORD JULIAN SAID WITH A DEEP frown, "for the princess to leave the safety of the palace, let alone the city."

"It's not a matter of what's wise," Lord Prenn interjected. "It's a matter of what's necessary. Prince Gaitlan spent his entire life learning how to govern the kingdom. He traveled with his father and other crown representatives, developing and fostering strong relations with the other lords and kingdoms. The princess's education was to prepare her for a life of support to the crown. She has only the barest understanding of what it means to wear the crown. She will need the support of the nobles if she's to keep control, preventing civil war."

With the other lords in agreement, there was nothing Lord Julian could do to keep the princess under his direct control without raising suspicion.

"Very well, my lords," he said with a heavy sigh. "But her safety should be the utmost concern. I would feel more at ease if she started with a quick trip. To test the waters as it were."

"Excellent," Lord Tolin beamed. "I volunteer my lands as her first venture into the wider world."

One of the older lords shook his head at Lord Tolin's eagerness. "I don't think seeing half-developed lands is the fastest way to a woman's heart, young man."

Lord Tolin blushed as other lords chuckled softly. He titled his chin in defiance and said, "Who knows, my lord, perhaps the princess would prefer a bit of underdevelopment in the face of being surrounded by lands plucked within an inch of its life."

The gathered lords' chuckle turned into bawdy laughter. The lord who intended to embarrass Lord Tolin turned a brilliant shade of red before storming away.

Lord Tolin flashed a cocky half-smile at the retreating lord's back before turning to join Braelyn for their weekly tea date in her mother's garden. A large, heavy hand landed on his shoulder with enough force to tip him slightly to the right. He spun, coming face to face with Lord Julian. Though his face was calm, the fire blazing in his eyes burned hotter than the deepest pits of hel.

"Smile all you want, lordling, but do not forget who the true power of this land lies with."

Lord Tolin pulled his shoulder free.

"It resides with her," he said, his voice like tempered steel.

Lord Julian glowered at Lord Tolin with rising furry. Lord Tolin stood his ground, not backing down, not even blinking until something odd happened to Lord Julian's ice-blue eye. A writing tendril of black spiraled out from the pupil, encircling the vibrant blue before slithering back from whence it came. He blinked rapidly, conceding a single step.

Lord Julian also took a step back, a small knowing smile that lasted less than a breath. The image of that blackness swirling around Lord Julian's eye would haunt Lord Tolin's dreams for several nights to follow. The sooner he and Braelyn were out of the city, the better.

THE CARRIAGE WHEELS HIT A LARGE DIVOT, CAUSING LORD Tolin to hit his head against the carriage's wall.

"Gods above," he cursed, rubbing the side of his head. "Your first major task should be fixing these roads, princess."

Braelyn hid her laugh behind her gloved hand. "I'll get right on that, my lord, right after I avenge my parents, reconnect with my brother, and see the traitor hanged for his crimes."

Lord Tolin shot her an incredulous look before chuckling at his own folly. "I understand; priorities."

He looked out the window, inhaled deeply, then smiled.

Perhaps it was the gentle expression on his face or the way the setting sun's light bathed him in golden light. Either way, Braelyn's breath halted.

Lord Tolin turned, his face going from carefree to concerned in a matter of seconds. "Is everything all right, princess?"

Air returned to Braelyn's lungs. "Yes, I must be getting tired."

"We should reach my home by nightfall." He regarded her a bit. "I think you might like it there. It is a bit rough, but being sandwiched between the mountains and Mystic Woods, my people don't have much in the way of arable land."

"What do your people do?"

"We raise sheep for their wool, tend orchards full of apples, and fish in the rivers."

"And do these enterprises serve your people well?"

Lord Tolin chuckled. "I wouldn't say they serve us well, but they do keep most of us well fed with simple but fulfilling lives."

"Not all?"

"It's impossible for everyone to have everything they need all the time. There are good years and lean years. Times of peace and times of war. The only thing we can do is our best and keep trudging forward until the sun shines on our face again."

Braelyn clamped her lips together to keep the bitter retort building on her tongue from lashing out. She knew that he meant well, and his words did hold a small measure of truth. But it's hard to keep moving forward when someone has ripped out your heart, lungs, and bones.

True to his word, their carriage rolled up to Lord Tolin's home just as the sun disappeared behind the tree line. Chickens roamed freely about, screeching their displeasure over the disruption of their evening routines. Smoke billowed from nearly every chimney, scenting the brisk air with woodsmoke and charring meat.

Already, servants lit candles in many windows, turning them into beacons of safety in the encroaching darkness. A plum man and woman burst through the doors with broad smiles on their faces.

Braelyn watched with bemused delight as they ran straight to Lord Tolin and embraced him.

"It's so good to see you again, my lord," the man said, releasing Lord Tolin. "I got your message, and everything has been taken care of."

"Thank you, Ulessis."

"That's enough jabbering out here, my lord. I bet ye are hungry. What did they feed ya in the capitol? Ya look like a twig, boy."

Lord Tolin laughed. "May I present Princess Braelyn."

Braelyn inclined her head with a shy smile on her face as the pair turned, some of the mirth falling from their faces.

The woman swept Braelyn up in her ample arms before she could react.

"Oh ya poor dearie," she cried. "Ye've been put the fires of hel and more." She loosened her embrace but did not let go of the princess. "Now, don't ya worry yer pretty little head about any of that while yer here. If you need anything, and I mean anything, child, you send for Misses Thatcher, ya hear me?"

"Yes ... of course," Braelyn sputtered, taken completely aback by the woman's behavior.

Lord Tolin rescued her from Misses Thatcher with a gentle but firm hand.

"I'm sure she will, Ms. Thatcher, but for now, I think a hot meal and a soft bed are in order."

"Right ya are, my boy." Ms. Thatcher turned and bustled back into the manor, hollering commands to the gathering servants as she went.

"She's been with my family for as long as I can remember. When I was little, I thought she was my second mother. It wasn't until I was much older that I realized we had a special relationship not often seen outside these lands."

Braelyn swallowed against the sudden tightness in her throat. "It is special. I don't think my own parents were as warm as Ms. Thatcher." Braelyn walked forward, putting space between her and Tolin's pitiful look.

She loved her parents and looked back on her memories of them with fondness. But she couldn't deny that there always had been a layer of formality that kept her parents separate.

Seeing the warm greeting Tolin received from his servants and how everyone smiled brightly and openly made her realize just how guarded her entire life was. There wasn't a single place or person that she could be her true self with. She didn't even know who her true self was.

"My family isn't big on formality if you can't tell," Tolin said, rubbing the back of his neck.

"That's not a bad thing," Braelyn said.

"Tell that to the lords back there," he said, gesturing over his shoulder.

"I can imagine all the trouble you got in when you first arrived.

"Loads. I can regale you with my early tales of utter failure in court over dinner."

Braelyn found herself laughing, her sorrow melting away like winter snows on a sunny day.

Dinner was a simple fare that warmed her to the core. Ms. Thatcher, it appeared, deemed it her mission to make Braelyn as comfortable as possible, slipping her extra sweets after dinner and escorting Braelyn to her room.

"Ye'll have a nice view of the sunrise over the mountains tomorrow morning," she informed Braelyn as she scooped hot coals into a bed warmer. "Summer might be just around the corner, but these mountains keep us cool well all the way to the summer solstice. Is there anything else ye need, dearie?"

Braelyn slid into the bed, sinking into its softness. The mattress cradled her body, easing the pains from being cooped up in the carriage for so long. The comforter was thick and smelled slightly of heather. Braelyn buried her face into it, hiding the tears that rimmed her eyes. "It's lovely."

Ms. Thatcher gently stroked the top of Braelyn's head. Braelyn pretended that the gentle touch belonged to her mother, soothing away the remnants of a nightmare. Hot tears fell silently down her face, dampening her pillow. Ms. Thatcher stayed, a silent pillar of support, with the promise of secrecy unspoken between them.

OVER THE NEXT TWO DAYS, TOLIN MAINTAINED THE pretense OF showing Braelyn around his lands. They visited numerous villages, meeting with officials and locals alike. They dined with minor nobles who served under Tolin's family, their evenings filled with easy conversations, laughter, and dances.

Braelyn smiled and played her part as the shy yet determined soon-to-be ruler, using her time to make as positive an impression as possible. All too soon, she would be whisked away, cloistered amongst priests and scholars, cut off from her people. She chewed her nails down to nubs, with worry about what would happen to her people should she fail, should some part of the plan go awry.

"Relax, princess," Tolin urged.

Braelyn jumped in her saddle, a slight blush spreading across her face. "I am calm, Tolin."

"If you say so."

Braelyn bristled slightly at his mocking tone. Tolin threw his head back and laughed. Braelyn's frown struggled to keep its position but eventually lost to the laughter bubbling inside. How long had it been since she laughed freely and unfettered? Only a season had passed since the murder of her parents and the ascension of Lord Julian. Still, to her, it felt like she had been suffering for a lifetime. She smiled softly at Tolin's back as he rode ahead, chatting with one of their armed escorts. She could live a thousand lifetimes and never be able to repay him or the others for what they've done for her. In another life, she might have even considered him a good marriage match.

Shaking her head to scatter useless thoughts, Braelyn urged her horse into a mild trot to catch up. Her desire to flee seeped its way into her steed, turning its trot into a gallop. Braelyn ignored the calls for her to slow down, shifting to maintain her seat, blending her spirit and the horse into one. The horse's muscular legs were hers. Its powerful heart beating with a rapid but steady beat mirrored the heart in her chest. By the time Tolin's home came into view, both she and her horse were breathing heavily, a fine sheen of sweat glistening along their bodies.

Tolin came thundering up the road, pulling on the reins rough to stop his horse next to her. The rest of their party came staggering in, concern etched on every face. Tolin reached out and lifted Braelyn's chin. He stared into her eyes, reading the words she didn't dare speak, lest they come true.

Braelyn found herself leaning into Tolin's touch, drawn to it like a drowning sailor to a bit of wreckage. Surprise lit in his eyes, and he, too, leaned in until they were close enough for their breath to mingle.

"Shall I take your horse, my lord?"

Tolin and Braelyn pulled back sharply. A young hostler stood before them, bowing deeply. Tolin coughed, dismounted, handing his horse over to the boy. He helped Braelyn off her horse.

"I have some business to attend to this afternoon. Please feel free to use my home however you need."

Before Braelyn could muster a reply, Tolin had already released her and started heading toward the house. She watched Tolin walk away from her with a sharp pain in her chest.

"Your highness?"

Braelyn ignored the guard's worried expression, picking up her riding skirts to head inside. "I am going to my chambers. Please inform Ms. Thatcher that I would like something cool to drink; thank you."

The guard bowed before scurrying to carry out her request.

As Braelyn walked to her room, she kept replaying her near kiss with Tolin. What would have happened if she crossed the remaining distance? She liked Tolin, and if his actions were any indication, he wanted her as well.

A maidservant already waited in her room to assist in getting out of her riding skirts and into a warm, loose-fitting dressing gown. Sitting before the vanity, she let her mind wander while the maidservant unpinned her hair and brushed away any tangles.

She could easily picture life here, nestled between the mountains and forests. Living a simple life amongst simple people who were honest and open. Greeting Tolin as he returned from visiting their people, small children clamoring for his attention. The way he smiled at her before encircling her in his arms, kissing her deeply.

A black-gloved hand entered her vision, pulling her away from Tolin and their children. Her once happy fantasy quickly turned into one of horror, filled with smoke and blood-soaked floors.

The hands holding her wretched her around, bringing her face to face with the orchestrator of her destruction, Lord Julian. Black serpents slithered in and out of his clothing, dripping venom from their stark white fangs.

"Did you honestly think you could escape me, princess? You belong to me. Your home belongs to me. Your blood belongs to me. And there's no one to save you."

"No, no, no!"

"Do you not want to leave your hair free, your highness?"

Braelyn blinked rapidly, bringing the real world into stark focus. Lord Julian wasn't there. No one lay bleeding at her feet because she foolishly dared to live a simple life.

"No," Braelyn sputtered, struggling to regain her composure. "I think I need to lie down."

The maidservant inclined her head, swiftly braiding Braelyn's golden locks. "I'll return before the evening meal."

Braelyn gave no sign that she heard the girl, too focused on the horror reflected back at her in the mirror.

After several long minutes, Braelyn rose from her seat and curled up on her bed. She grabbed a pillow, holding it close to her body. She buried her face and cried, pulling the pillow closer to muffle the sounds.

Isn't this dress too formal?"

Two maidservants held a gorgeous dove gray dress between them. Braelyn reached out to trace the delicate embroidered charcoal gray flowers stitched along the bodice.

"I canna tell ya, dearie," Ms. Thatcher beamed. "It'll ruin the surprise."

Braelyn arched a brow but allowed the maidservants to complete their task. Technically, she was still in mourning, and the dress reflected that but in a less stark and dreary way. For some reason, the dress brought to mind a sense of hope. Yes, her world was still in darkness and disarray, but the light had started to return. A light lit by Lord Tolin.

Tolin stood at the bottom of the stairs, waiting. He caught sight of Braelyn and smiled, his eyes alight with approval.

A half-smile splayed across Braelyn's face as she descended the stairs to take Tolin's offered arm.

"I must say, that dress looks absolutely ravishing on you, your highness."

"I agree."

Tolin inclined his head. "I hope you can hold onto that once you see the hall."

Braelyn's smile faltered. She kept her grip on Tolin's arm light to not betray the torrent of emotions coursing through her.

A pair of footmen bowed, pulling the doors to the hall wide.

Music and laughter came pouring out. The room was

awash in light from the thousands of candles burning overhead and in holders along the wall and tables. Faces turned toward Braelyn and Tolin. Several people raised a glass in greeting before turning back to their conversations. A small band played a merry tune at the far end of the hall that several couples danced to.

"This is what you were doing all afternoon?" Braelyn asked, unable to keep the surprise from her face.

Tolin nodded. "This is your last night here before you move onto your next destination. Unfortunately, I won't be able to join you. I am needed here." Tolin gave her hand a gentle squeeze.

Braelyn grinned, giving his hand a slight squeeze in return. "I understand, Lord Tolin. I am grateful for everything you've done for me during my stay. I hope to see you in court upon my return."

Tolin bowed over her hand, placing a small kiss on the back of it. "Until then, please enjoy yourself tonight."

Braelyn dispersed into the crowd, falling right into her crown princess persona. She didn't bother to keep the excitement and happiness from her face, knowing that everyone would attribute it to the evening's festivities. She drank, feasted, and danced like a woman rediscovering the joys of life after a great upheaval.

She stood, talking to one of the minor nobles she met during her visit, when Tolin tapped her on the shoulder.

"If you'll pardon me, your highness, but would you like to dance?"

"I'd be honored, Lord Tolin."

Tolin led her to the dance floor, where the musicians had

just started a new song. It was slow and romantic, providing an excellent excuse for Tolin to pull Braelyn in close.

"After this song, wait five minutes, then head to the small door in the right corner."

He twirled her around so she could spy the door over his shoulder.

"It will lead you outside. Look to the distance for a small light. That is where you will meet your escort to Eastport. From there, Lord Hamal has booked your passage to the Holy Isle."

"What about you?"

"I'll see you off, but I have to stay to pretend to send you off in the morning. After that, I have to remain here for a while so Lord Julian's spies can't tie me to your 'disappearance.'"

"Please be safe," Braelyn urged, the bloody images of her nightmare flashing across her mind.

Tolin leaned in, pressing his forehead against hers. They stopped moving; the world stopped moving. "When you look at me like that, I want to keep you."

Heat crept up from somewhere deep within her core. The song ended, and applause rippled around them. Braelyn blinked against the sudden realization of others. Tolin sighed, releasing his hold on her.

"Remember, princess, five minutes, then slip away. I will be waiting for you in the clearing."

Tolin slipped into the crowd, disappearing from her sight. Braelyn remained on the dance floor until the next song started. A dapper young man approached and asked for the next dance.

"I'm afraid I must decline," she replied. "I need a bit of a breather."

The boy's face fell.

"Perhaps the one afterward?" She'd be long gone by then, but she didn't want one of her last acts in her kingdom to be letting one of her people down. Granted, she was, in a way, but the youth would recover quickly, seeing how he had already moved on to a small cloister of ladies in brightly colored dresses.

Braelyn watched the exchange between the young man and the ladies, feeling older than her years. Turning away from youthful ignorance, she maneuvered through the crowd until she was in a place to slip out without anyone noticing her departure.

The corridor was dark, utterly void of candlelight or moonlight. Braelyn briskly walked, keeping one hand against the wall to ensure she stayed on track. That proved to be useless when the corridor ended without making a single turn or intersection.

Pressing her body against the door, she placed her ear to listen. The wood was either too thick, or the outside too quiet for her to pick out anything. She whispered a quick prayer to the Dark Mother to shield her from unfriendly eyes before turning the handle to the door and walking out into the night.

Darkness enveloped her, stealing away her sight. Braelyn froze, stretching her senses to their breaking point for any sign of danger in the night. Only the sound of crickets singing in their nocturnal songs greeted her. She released a breath, closing the door behind her. Scanning the tree line, she searched for the single candle flame that was her beacon to freedom.

After several minutes and some wild stumbling around in the dark, she spied it not too far in the distance. Picking up her skirts, she hurried into the brush, aware of the time she waisted by moving slowly. She tried to not cringe as sticks and brambles cracked and snapped in her wake, ringing out like sentry alarms.

She stumbled into the clearing, nearly falling to her knees. Thankfully, a sturdy sapling was within reach. Her palm came away wet and sticky. She cringed against the sap, wishing she had something to wipe it off before she ruined the dress Tolin got for her.

Looking around the clearing, she couldn't see much beyond the single candle burning in a lantern and some nondescript black lumps at the edges of the clearing. Tolin had said he'd be there to see her off. Where was her escort?

"H-hello?"

"Lord Hamal? Tolin?"

Braelyn walked beyond the safety of the candlelight toward the dark masses in the dark.

The ground beneath her feet squelched, and something wet and warm oozed through the thin fabric of her shoes.

The sound of a branch snapping sent her spinning, heart in her throat. Bright lights flooded into the clearing, blinding Braelyn.

She cried out, shielding her eyes as she took a reflective step backward. Her foot hit something large, sending her tumbling over it to the ground. More wetness from the ground seeped into her dress, coating her face and neck.

Her stomach heaved as she recognized an all too familiar scent. A scent that she would never forget all the days of her life —the scent of fresh blood.

Braelyn's eyes shot open, forcing her to come face to face

with another sight that would never leave her.

Tolin's head lay on the ground scant centimeters from her blood-stained fingertips. She stared into his lifeless eyes, eyes she'd come to cherish, eyes she hoped to spend the rest of her life staring into gone forever.

"What ... how ... why?"

"Did you honestly think you could escape me, princess?"

Her blood turned to ice. Slowly, she turned and peered over her shoulders. Lord Julian emerged, cut from the darkest pits of hel. A cruel smile splayed across his face.

"Truth be told, I had wondered if my sources were misinformed, but then I had a lovely evening with Lord Shoot, and he ... spilled the beans, as it were, about the whole affair. Honestly, I'm a bit disappointed in you, princess. I thought we were finally past all these little acts of rebellion."

Lord Julian shook his head like she was a child lashing out against their parents.

Braelyn scrambled to her feet. Something primal urging her to claw at her enemy, to bite, to kick, to rip his throat out.

Two large goons caught her by the arms before she could get any closer. Braelyn thrashed in their arms, screaming until her throat turned raw, kicking and spitting like a wild cat.

Lord Julian tutted. "Now, now, princess. That is no way for a lady of court to behave. I thought your mother taught you better than that."

"You lying, soulless bastard! I'll rip that rotted piece of a heart right from your chest."

Lord Julian leaned in closer, his smile taking on a devilish edge. "I might end your miserable existence right here, right beside your lover." He toed Tolin's head with the tip of his boot.

"Do that," Braelyn growled, "and the throne will be forever beyond your reach. There's no way the sitting lords or the people will accept you as their king. They're only biding their time until they tear you down."

Something dark shifted behind Lord Julian's eyes. He stood, milling over her words. "You have a point there." He tapped a long finger against his chin, thinking. "One option would be to drug you and keep you locked away somewhere, but that won't work for long. Oh, I know ..."

Lord Julian's eyes turned completely black, as black as the day he killed her parents. Rolling up his sleeve, the pale skin of his arm shone in the moonlight. A dagger flashed in his other hand. He winked at Braelyn, who hung limply between her captors, and slashed his arm.

Braelyn gasped as a black, oily substance oozed from the wound instead of bright blood. Lord Julian mumbled words too softly for her to make out. The oily substance rolled back onto itself until it resembled a black slug. He tossed the slug on the ground before rolling his sleeve back down, the cut already healed.

"Leave the bodies, but ensure it finds its home." Julian turned, extinguishing the light with a careless wave of his hand. The clearing plunged into darkness. In the distance, Braelyn heard the sounds of people. Someone must have heard her screams and come to investigate. Hope swelled until she felt the cold touch of the thing Lord Julian created.

She tried to free herself from her captors, but they were trained soldiers with more muscle than she could ever hope to gain.

"Quit your fussing, you prissy bitch," one of the men snarled, backhanding Braelyn.

"Cut it out, Gary. I don't think our boss wants her all bruised."

"Who fuckin cares, Shan? She's already covered in blood. A bit of bruising on her pretty face will help sell the story he's spinnin right now."

Shan shook his head. "I don't like any of this. Where's that weird worm thing?"

"The hel if I know. Stop being such a pussy and hold her down so it can crawl inside her, lucky thing."

"You have some serious problems, mate."

Braelyn's head slammed into the blood-soaked ground. Dirt mixed with blood found its way inside her mouth. She struggled to spit it out. One of the goons laughed.

"I think I might want to have a bit of fun tonight."

"Don't even think about it."

"And what are you going to do about it?" Gary heaved Shan up by his collar, releasing his hold on Braelyn. "Not a gods damned thing. You've been a thorn in my side since day one. I should kill ya and be done with it."

"Fuck off, Gary. The only reason why you're still walking free is because of me. A meathead like you wouldn't last a day without someone like me. Now, stop fucking around, and let's finish the job."

Gary bared his teeth but let Shan go. The men turned their attention back on Braelyn, who nearly made it to the treeline.

The men lunged, cursing. Braelyn flung herself into the trees, not caring about the noise in her wake. Branches and brambles snagged her dress and tore at her hair. She ignored the rips and twinges of pain. She could hear her assailants thrashing behind her. Fear lent strength to her legs, carrying her onward through the bramble.

A raised root proved to be her undoing. She crashed to the ground once more, crying out when her face struck against a stone.

Gary and Shan were on her before she could scramble to her feet, hoisting her up with more force than necessary.

"Don't try that again, you bitch," Gary snarled.

"If you're going to insult me," Braelyn gasped, "at least come up with a more original word."

Behind Gary, Shan chuckled. Gary's eyes flashed, slamming Braelyn repeatedly into a tree until she gasped for air. She slid to the forest floor when he released her. Shan reprimanded his partner again. As the two quarreled, a small glittering light in the underbrush caught Braelyn's blurry gaze. Braelyn reached out toward the light.

She reached and reached, her body too beaten and exhausted to do much else but crawl along the forest floor. Just as Gary yelled at her to stop moving, she touched the light. It faded away, leaving her at the mercy of her captors.

Hot, bitter tears ran down her face as she was led back to the clearing, her arm twisted painfully behind her back. Shan relit the candle to search for the creature Lord Julian created. "Bring her here, Gary. Put her head right here and try to not screw this up anymore tonight."

Gary cursed under his breath but followed his partner's orders. With one meaty hand, he held her head to the ground.

Braelyn could only stare in horror as the black slug slithered its way toward her. A renewed urge for escape filled her bones. Gary cursed and called for Shan to help him hold her in place.

Braelyn struggled in vain against the two men, her panic rising. Just as the abomination slithered up her face, she screamed in rage and fear. The weight holding her down ripped away by some unseen force, sending the men into the surrounding trees hard enough to snap their spines.

The black slug was not deterred, making its way toward Braelyn's ear. She clawed against the thing attempting to violate her, drawing blood with her nails until she lost all control of her limbs. A terrifying force entered her body.

Arching against the flow of that force, Braelyn opened her mouth wide in a silent scream. Every part of her body burned and froze until she could no longer maintain her consciousness and fell into the dark oblivion of her mind.

It was there that Lord Julian found her, along with his dead men, when he'd come to find out why they hadn't returned. Kneeling, he turned Braelyn's head from one side to the other before peeling back her eyelids. He pursed his lips before gathering her into his arms. Something had stopped his agent from entering and taking control. He didn't know what, but he'd find out one way or another.

In the woods behind Lord Tolin's home, a stone stained with fresh blood shimmered in the night. Silver light ran through the near-invisible engravings on the rock. The trees near the blood-soaked trembled, their leaves cascading down like snow.

CHAPTER FOURTEEN

A SOFT RAPPING AT THE DOOR STIRRED MIRRA FROM HER slumber. Rubbing the sleep from her eyes, she shuffled across the room.

"Are you ready to get dressed?"

Mirra blinked rapidly as Oya pushed her way into the room, followed by a trio of white-robed apprentices. With the ease of a general directing their troops, Oya issued one command after another until everything was to her liking. She sent the apprentices away with a small nod of thanks, turning to face Mirra with a bemused expression.

"What? Did you think I was going to let you go like that?"

Mirra ran a hand through her tangled hair while looking down at her crumpled tunic.

"Well ... I planned on brushing my hair."

Oya laughed, shaking her long braids. Mirra's stomach fluttered at the sound.

"I figured as much. You don't seem like the kind of

person who likes to get dressed up."

Mirra shrugged. "I dressed up when I studied the ways of the court with Lady Nora, and then when I was in court, pretending to be Julian's niece."

A strange look rippled across Oya's face. "Then, at least I don't have to start from square one." She laughed again, though it sounded strained.

Oya sat Mirra down on the edge of the bed before getting to work. She picked up a small glass vial, lifted the stopper, and sniffed. Nodding, she poured a portion of the contents into her hand, rubbing them together before raking her hands through Mirra's tangled locks.

The scent of a heady flower soon filled the air. "What is that?"

"Magnolia oil. It's a special tree that only grows along the southern Nealitian coast near the capital."

"Have you ever been there?"

Oya paused, picking up a wide-tooth comb. "The Council of Kings sometimes sends out soldiers to 'rescue' magic wielders from the dangers of the world. What they actually do is enslave them, using their gifts to turn the seawater into river water so they can keep their gardens lush and green."

Mirra turned, looking at Oya over her shoulder. Though Oya's hands continued their task, her eyes saw something only she could see.

"Did you lose someone?"

Oya shook her head. "You hear stories." She shook her head. "Now is not the time for sad stories." She placed the comb down, walked around to face Mirra, and held out her and. "Pick one."

Three brightly colored beads were nestled in the center of Oya's outstretched palm. Mirra glanced over the beads, each one beautiful in its own way. She raised a brow.

"In my homeland, we braid adornments into our hair for each major event in our life. Surviving to three, learning the stories of the tribe, first bleeding, things like that."

"Okay."

A faint blush darkened Oya's cheeks. "Even though we're all Ilmarrion, our traditions come from the lands of our birth, our clans, tribes, families. Seeing as how you have none of those things, I thought ... you might like to commemorate connecting to your heritage this way."

Mirra swallowed against the tightness in her throat, turning her attention back to the beads. One was the color of blood with white swirls. The next was a deep purple with a small gemstone inlaid in the center. The last one was made from beaten copper.

"I think the copper one fits me better than the others. They're a bit flashy."

Oya chuckled, pocketing the other two. Wordlessly, she gathered a section of hair from behind Mirra's ear. With deft fingers, she braided the lock, using the copper bead to secure the end.

Mirra swished her hair, feeling the slight difference between the braid and the rest of her hair.

"When you put your hair up, it shouldn't be too noticeable, and when it's down, nearly invisible. I know you might have to remain unseen at times."

Mirra fingered the braid. "Thank you truly."

Oya smiled shyly, reaching out to touch the braid. Their fingers met, sending sparks into the air.

The women stared at each other, eyes locked, as the tether between them tightened until Mirra rose to her feet.

With a level of tenderness never displayed before, Mirra reached up to cup Oya's cheek. She marveled at the difference between their coloring and how they seemed to go together as if they were opposite sides of the same coin.

"Mirra," Oya breathed, her hand reaching up to clap Mirra's.

Mirra stayed silent, letting her body do what it wanted, closing the space between them until their bodies pressed tightly against each other.

Oya licked her lips, drawing Mirra's attention to them. The corner of Mirra's mouth tugged upwards, promising all sorts of mischief. Oya returned a shy smile, bringing her head closer.

"Why don't you find out for yourself."

Mirra let out a throaty chuckle, reaching up to cup Oya's other cheek. She let a silent question rise in her eyes, a brief moment for Oya to reconsider. Oya nodded, closing her eyes. Mirra licked her own lips before bringing her face to meet Oya's.

"Usoa's looking for you, Oya," Kasumi said, crashing into Mirra's room, breaking the spell.

Oya and Mirra lept back from each other, twin blushing rising. Though Mirra's was more noticeable.

Kasumi cocked her head, her eyes darting between the pair.

"I leave her in your hands." Oya walked out as if nothing

had happened, leaving Mirra deflated.

"Do you want your hair up or down?"

Mirra's fingers fiddled with the copper bead. "How about half up?"

Kasumi smiled, urging Mirra to take a seat. She chatted away merrily about the preparations for the night's festivities, moving on to apply a bit of cosmetics to Mirra's face.

"You still have some time before everything starts. You shouldn't need any help dressing. Do you need anything else?"

"What do your people do for things like this?"

Kasumi's eyes cut to the copper bead, now visible. "We do something like this. We have a big party, full of food, music, and dancing. After the meal, but before all the fun starts, gifts are presented. Sometimes you'll get things to help you on our next stage, or sometimes it's something pretty."

"Thank you," Mirra said. "See you later?"

"Wouldn't miss it," Kasumi said, giving Mirra a friendly wave before bouncing out of the room.

Her hand went to the bead again, rolling it between her fingers. In her mind, she replayed her almost kiss with Oya over and over. What was it about Oya that drew Mirra to her? Never before in her life had she ever felt such a strong urge to connect with someone. To open herself up to them, exposing all her vulnerable parts.

Was it because Oya served as a direct line to a part of her life she never knew existed, or was it something more? Then there was Gaitlan. Over the course of a few weeks, something had blossomed between them as well. It wasn't as strong an emotion as Oya's, but when it did rear its head, it came crashing in like a wave.

Mirra made a pained face. She didn't know what to do, and furthermore, did she even have the luxury of fretting over relationships?

EVERYONE WAS SMILING AT THE BONFIRE. FROM somewhere in the throng, musicians played a lively tune that drew people to the writhing mass of dancers. Spectators clapped along the sidelines, pausing their conversations for food and drink. The tables where the food had been laid in such capacity that Mirra had no doubt that every citizen of Moakwyd contributed at least one dish. It was hard to not be swept up in excitement.

Mirra's outfit for the evening was a long overtunic that hung nearly down to her calves, with side slits at the side for easy movement. The tunic dark pewter color paired nicely with the fitted black pants underneath. She loved the way the ends of the tunic swished around her legs as she walked. If she ever ended up at another fancy party in the future, this was going to be her outfit. She was done with the tight-fitting corsets and heavy dresses.

As she made her way through the crowd, looking for familiar faces, numerous people stopped her to congratulate her success with the tower.

"Welcome home, sister!"

"I can't wait to see what affinity you have. I hope it's Su'la."

"I can't believe they only gave you fourteen days to get

through. I had a whole month!"

"Congratulations!"

"Congrats!"

"Cheers!"

"Sláka!"

Mirra smiled and nodded her head at each well-wisher.
She didn't offer more than a polite 'thank you' in return. It didn't
bother the party-goers to see how they turned back to their
original focus when they said their peace.

Mirra shook her head, silently laughing at the
similarities between the Ilmarrions and the Undorsean
courtesans.

"I don't even think I had this big a turnout for any of my
birthdays."

Gaitlan straightened, a coy smile on his face.

"You look nice."

And he was, dressed in a brown tunic trimmed with a
blue so deep it looked nearly black in the dark. His hair had been
cut, and his face shaved clean. He looked much like his old self
again, save for the pain lingering at the corner of his eyes and
mouth.

"Glad you approve since all this is in your honor. Try to
not let it get to your head."

Mirra snorted. "Fat chance of that ever happening. You
forget, princeling, I grew up poor and wild. Parties like these
were never part of my childhood. It's a bit awkward having so
much attention on me."

"Might as well get used to it," Gaitlan said, gently

shoving her with his shoulder. "Between your beauty, skill, and soon-to-be mastery of magic, men will lay everything they have at your feet for a single kiss."

Starlight danced around her heart. "Who in their right mind would ever want that?"

Gaitlan shrugged. "If Braelyn's to be believed, every woman in court. If you don't want that, what do you want?"

Mirra tilted her head back to stare at the stars. "I used to spend hours at the docks, watching the ships coming and going. I wanted nothing more than to get on one and sail over the horizon. I wanted to be unfettered and free, with no one to worry about but myself."

Gaitlan paused, a peculiar look on his face. "That sounds awfully lonely." Mirra shrugged. "I noticed you said 'wanted.' Do you not want that anymore?"

Mirra sighed. "I guess. I haven't given it much thought lately. Enough of this. Let's eat and dance, princeling."

Mirra took Gaitlan's hand, pulling him toward the food.

OYA STOOD IN HER TYPICAL POSITION NEXT TO USOA SINCE her arrival at Mirra's celebratory feast. Though she smiled and chatted politely with her fellow priests and citizens, her eyes scanned the gathering for Mirra's face.

Her mind went back to earlier when she almost kissed Mirra. Even the mere memory of the smolder in Mirra's eyes still sent ripples of excitement down her spine. Oya fingered the end of a braid, savoring the sweet burn of desire. None of the girls she knew from her village had ever made her feel this way.

Although everyone had given her family a wide berth. Even her years in the floating city in K'ashi, no one had ever made her feel the way Mirra did after a few short weeks.

Beside her, High Priestess Usoa made a disgruntled sound. "I wish she'd left him at the city gates."

Oya followed the high priestess's gaze, and what she saw caused her heart to leap into her throat. Mirra and Gaitlan were dancing together. They spun the other around, clumsily trying to mimic the steps of those around them.

Gaitlan tripped over his own feet, nearly taking another couple down with him. He managed to keep everyone on their feet but Mirra. Mirra had doubled over, arms wrapped around her middle, with the most carefree expression on her face as she laughed.

Even from where she stood, Oya saw Gaitlan's blush. He snapped something to Mirra, who only whipped away a tear, waving his indignation away.

A small flash near Mirra's neck drew Gaitlan's attention. He reached out to touch the bead Oya braided into Mirra's hair a few hours before. Jealousy surged through Oya, swelling beneath her skin like juices from overripe fruit.

Mirra took a quick step back, stopping Gaitlan. His hand lingered awkwardly in the air between them. Mirra's face turned guarded for a moment before she fashioned a smile. Gaitlan frowned, leaving Mirra near the dancing circle.

Quelled, Oya left her spot by Usoa's side, walking through the crowd with a singular purpose.

MIRRA WATCHED GAITLAN'S RETREATING BACK
with a heavy heart. Sighing, she turned back toward the music.
She wanted to rip her hair out. Why did she jerk away from
him? She'd seen the hurt on his face. He hadn't meant anything
by it, and the bead wasn't anything special.

The person who put it there is.

Mirra shook her head vigorously, scrunching her face in
frustration.

"Do you not like the music?"

Sweet hel.

Mirra slowly turned. Oya stood behind her, looking
slightly uncomfortable. "No, it's fine," she said, running a hand
through her hair. "It's just ... never mind."

Oya looked over her shoulder. Her face softened as she
watched her people. "It's been a long time since we've done
something this big. Families tend to celebrate passing the tower
test themselves."

"And I don't have one," Mirra said sadly.

Oya's head whipped around, the beads and hair cuffs
clacking against each other. "You may not know your bloodline,
but you do have a family." Oya placed her hand over her heart.
"We are your family. No matter where we were born, the regional
traditions we keep, we are Ilmarrions, first and foremost."

She reached out, taking Mirra's hands into her own.
"And so are you."

The corner of Mirra's mouth tugged up on its own
accord. Oya locked eyes with something over Mirra's shoulder.

"Come, I want to show you something."

Oya pulled Mirra after her, not bothering to wait for her

reply. Mirra stumbled after Oya, twisting to spy what had spurred Oya into action.

Gaitlan had returned to the spot where he left Mirra. She gave him a small wave that he didn't return.

Oya led Mirra down a series of open-air pathways until they halted in front of a small building Mirra hadn't seen before.

"I think you might like this," Oya said with a wide grin. She led Mirra up the stairs, then tugged on the battered door. It opened a few inches, showering the pair with debris.

Oya slid through the slight opening, not caring if her clothes got dirty or damaged.

Mirra watched her. Something sour nagged at the corners of her mind until she was tempted to run back to the bonfire. The way Gaitlan looked at her as she was led away made her think of her old gang from her childhood. How many times had she seen that look on Bao's face, Tull's, or Kril's? How many times had Em smiled, the same pained, when she pushed her away because getting close to people meant being hurt?

"I dunno," Mirra said. "I think we should head back. Besides, it's too dark to see anything."

A light chuckle drifted out between the crack in the door. "I don't think darkness can keep anything from you, Kivuli. But if you require light ..."

Golden light illuminated Oya's smiling face as she retreated into the shadows.

Mirra lingered at the entrance, her eyes wide. Something shifted in Oya's face, spurring fire along Mirra's bones. Carried forward by that fire, she wedged through the door, wincing slightly when the semi-rotten wood snagged on her tunic.

"So, what is it that you want to show me?"

"This." Oya lifted her hands into the air, releasing the small ball of light she summoned.

Much of Moakwyd was left to ruin, and the sight of crumbling buildings or parts of buildings was something that Mirra had become accustomed to, but the scene that Oya's light revealed stole the breath from her body.

A small grove of ash trees stood in the middle of the remnants of a library. There wasn't a single bookcase that wasn't tipped over, rotted, or blacked. Mirra walked over to the nearest pile of scattered books, her steps across the stone floor the only sound, and reached for one of the books.

"I'd be careful. Most of the books are centuries old and delicate."

"Then why are they here, tossed aside like nothing?"

Oya ran a hand against one of the ash trees. "During the Purge, there was only so much that our elders could do. They protected what they could and tried to not think about what they left behind."

Mirra released a breath, choosing to pick up one of the scattered pages that littered the floor. The side that faced the elements had been bleached clean, but faint lines of writing could still be seen on the other side. Mirra walked over to Oya, gently tucking the page into her tunic.

Oya gave her a tight-lipped smile. "Much of our history, our traditions were lost. But that's better than what happened to the rest."

"What happened?"

"They stole it, claiming it as their own. They took our

lands, our knowledge, and our relics, saying they were theirs all along."

"Relics?"

Oya nodded. "Our smiths used to be skilled enough to imbue artifacts with magic. They were mostly used as stores for when we reached our limits. Still, depending on the purpose the item was created for, they could be used offensively or defensively."

Mirra's heart fluttered wildly against her chest. She reached out, grabbing Oya by the shoulders. "Are there any left?" She leaned in closer, locking eyes with Oya, searching for any sign of deceit.

Oya blinked a few times. "No. What we had was used up long ago. The only relics with any power left in them were probably mistaken for divine artifacts by the human priests."

Mirra released Oya, rubbing her fingers against the memory of pain from when she touched that cursed mask all those years ago.

"Why did you bring me here?"

"Because you need to understand, truly understand, what it means to be one of us. I will spend the rest of my life scrounging around this library and dozens more like it, trying to piece back together with a culture that will never be the same. Destroyed and scattered by the very people you're so desperate to help."

Her spine snapped straight. Mirra slowly turned, her eyes narrowed. "It's not their fault. They didn't do anything to you."

"No, but they reap the benefits from the slaughter of our

kin."

"I thought we were past this," Mirra said, pain slowly seeping into her voice.

Oya chewed her bottom lip, not meeting Mirra's gaze. "We've lost so much. I don't want us to lose more. You're the first Ilmarrion touched by the Nexi in a thousand years. Your arrival could mean so many things to our people ... to me."

The end came out barely above a whisper. Oya kept her eyes trained to the ground, her hands fiddling with one of her braids.

Mirra's heart swelled, crying out. Clenching her fists to keep her emotions in check, she spoke. "The only reason why I'm standing here right now is because of Gaitlan's sister. She allowed herself to be captured, a prisoner of the man who killed her family. Gaitlan's an ass, or at least he used to be. But right now, he has no one to lean on but me. Trust me, I would love to drop him off somewhere and disappear, but I can't, not anymore."

Oya lifted her head, looking at Mirra from beneath her brows.

Mirra ran a filthy hand through her hair. "Look, I'm not so good at this whole friend thing, especially with you. Half the time, I want to hit you, and other times ..."

"Other times?"

The words stuck in her throat, threatening to choke her if she didn't release them into the world. She scrunched her face. She wouldn't speak the words.

Warm hands framed her face. Mirra's eyes shot open. Oya's open face filled her vision, her eyes dancing back and forth, searching.

Mirra pushed her emotions behind the wall she used to keep herself safe. She wanted to press her lips against Oya's, but she didn't, too afraid of how the simple act would irrevocably change the course of her future.

Whatever Oya saw drew a sad smile from her. With a sigh, she pressed her forehead against Mirra's.

"I've been selfish. The foundation of your life is crumbling beneath your feet, and here I am, trying to force you into something you're not ready for."

Mirra reached up, placing her hands on top of Oya's. Her hands shifted to cup Oya's face, running her thumbs over the arches of her cheeks. Words waged war against each other inside Mirra's heart.

All her life had been a fight. She fought to stay alive, running wild through the Merchant District. Then she fought to survive Lord Julian's training, always trying to stay three steps ahead. Now, she was stumbling through the dark, putting her neck out for a person who never gave two shits about her before, turning away from someone whose very presence threatened to tear down every last brick of the walls she built to protect herself.

"It is all right to take time for yourself. Figure out who you are and what you want. I will be here waiting when you do." Oya stepped back, releasing Mirra's face.

Panicked, Mirra tightened her grip and pulled. Oya's mouth crashed into hers. Oya opened her mouth in surprise, and Mirra took full advantage, deepening the kiss.

Electric fire coursed through her body, leaving trails of starlight in its wake. She pulled Oya closer, melding their bodies together. Oya was shocked no longer than a single heartbeat before she wrapped her arms around Mirra, kissing her back in earnest. Mirra reached up, tangling her fingers in Oya's braided locks.

All too soon, they were forced to break, both gasping for air. They remained silent, foreheads resting gently against each other.

"Thank you for everything," Mirra said, breaking the silence.

"Remember, I will always be here, no matter what you decide."

CHAPTER FIFTEEN

A BEAM OF SUNLIGHT MADE ITS HOME ACROSS MIRRA'S face, bathing her world in a painful crimson light. She threw her arm over her face, turning away from the offending light. A slender arm snaked around her middle, pulling her back. Mirra's body tensed as she peered over her shoulder.

Oya furrowed her brow, pulling Mirra in to nuzzle between her shoulder blades.

Memories from the night prior flooded in. Mirra dancing with Oya, Gaitlan, and others. Stuffing her face until her stomach felt ready to burst. And cup after cup of spiced wine. Most of her memories were of Oya's face, her lips, the scent of her skin and hair until they stumbled into her room in a tangle of limbs and kisses, to only end up falling asleep wrapped in each other's arms.

A section of Oya's braids had fallen across her face. Mirra reached out and gently moved it aside. Oya stirred slightly but didn't wake. She tightened her grip, drawing a smile from Mirra.

Strange, this feeling. Mirra still didn't quite know what

to make of it, but she knew that it terrified her as much as it exhilarated her.

A knock at the door forced Mirra to extract herself from Oya's grasp. Grabbing her tunic that lay in a crumpled heap on the floor, she pulled it on before opening the door.

"Good morning, Mirra."

High Priestess Usoa loomed in the doorway, a pensive look on her face.

"I hate to be the bearer of bad news at such an hour, but I'm afraid …" A look of surprise flashed across Usoa's face when she spied Oya asleep in Mirra's bed.

"I … uh … we didn't …"

High Priestess Usoa's surprise faded into a benign smile. "Please don't mistake my surprise for disapproval. This type of union is not taboo amongst our people."

Mirra's face burned red hot, her mouth opening and closing like a fish.

High Priestess Usoa pressed her lips tightly together to keep her laughter from bursting out of her. She peered over Mirra's shoulder, her face softening. "Oya has been through so much in her young life, though not as much as you. I'm glad she found someone to show the softer sides of herself."

High Priestess Usoa noticed the shift in Mirra's demeanor, a crease forming between her brows. Whatever questions she wanted to ask, she kept them to herself. She knew that if Mirra or Oya wished to come to her about their relationship, they would. Until then, she had more pressing things to discuss with the young woman in front of her.

"Follow me."

Mirra tugged on her breaches and followed after Usoa. She spared the sleeping Oya one last glance before gently closing the door.

They walked to a small garden with a tiny fountain covered in moss. The only water sat in the base, thick with algae. Mirra thought about the library Oya took her to the night before. How much longer would the Ilmarrions be able to survive like this? How long would they be able to hold onto their ways before they were lost to the passage of time?

"Death isn't something to fear," Usoa said, breaking Mirra's thoughts. "Without death, there cannot be life. The leaves from the trees rot along the forest floor, adding nutrients back into the soil. All living creatures kill and consume other life forms to survive. When a man and woman join, their essences blend and die so that a new life can be formed."

"Is this why you woke me up so early?"

Usoa chuckled. "No, but I know that look on your face. I see it often in others. Even on my own at times. What I'm trying to say is that there is a natural order to the world. Nothing can stay as it is forever."

Mirra pinched her lips together, turning away from Usoa and the fountain.

"And just as nothing can stay forever, nothing is gone forever."

The priestess's words sent slivers of power rippling along Mirra's bones.

Usoa sighed, taking a seat along the fountain's edge. "Our history is long. We lived in these lands long before humans clawed their way up out of the dirt. Some even believe that

243

humans are descended from Ilmarrions who carried no affinity for the Ileign. But that's not what I wanted to talk to you about."

She patted the edge of the fountain and waited for Mirra to take a seat before continuing.

"Just like the humans, we, too, had a ruling family once. Their seat of power was here in Moakwyd, but they ruled this entire continent."

"How could one family keep control over that many people?"

"Ilmarrions have never been as numerous as humans. Our lifespans once spanned centuries, and we produced offspring less frequently than we do now. The family was less like a family in the traditional sense and more like a single clan. A clan whose affinity was to the Nexi. Do you know what the Nexi is?"

"The void from where everything is born and the place it will return to."

A single brow arched in mild surprise. "Yes, that's right. Life and death keep the other in check, balanced. The Nexi clan was chosen to rule over the Ilmarrion people to balance our impact on the world. The other affinities are drawn from elements that encourage life."

"Over the years, the numbers of the Nexi clan dwindled until there were only a handful of families left. Then they, too, were gone. In the wake of their disappearance, a dark and terrible entity entered our world; The Eater. It ravaged our world, destroyed whole lands, swallowed people until we were able to defeat it with the help of the humans."

Apprehension twisted Mirra's stomach.

"The abilities of Lord Julian you described are

disturbingly similar to our records of The Eater. And then there's you. The first Nexian in over an age. Two forces thought gone from this world, arriving at the same time to only clash against the other."

Mirra swallowed the rising bile in her throat. "What does it mean?"

High Priestess Usoa closed her eyes, loosening a long breath. "I cannot tell you."

Mirra surged to her feet. "What! Why the hel would you dump all that on me without telling me what to do? How to fix it! Anything!"

"I can't tell you because I don't know." Usoa'a hand went to the red jewel at her neck. "I don't even know for sure. I can only offer you speculation. What I can do is send you to someone who knows more."

"Where is that? Isn't this the largest collection of our history in the world?"

Usoa slowly shook her head. "No, it's not."

HE NEEDED TO TALK TO HER, NEEDED TO TELL HER THE whole truth. Seeing Mirra dance with Oya, the way she smiled, the light in her eyes, was like a knife to the heart as much as it filled him with joy. Mirra had become precious to him throughout their journey. He'd seen sides of her that Lord Julian didn't even know. And the mere fact that she could smile and laugh showed just how strong she was.

It wasn't the best time for declarations of love. Their lives were too unstable with too much that took precedence, but there was never a suitable time if the past weeks taught him anything. He needed to make some changes in his life, and telling Mirra how he felt before losing her to another was a start.

Gaitlan straightened his clothing, quickly combing back his hair with his fingers when he reached her door. He plastered his best carefree smile on his face and knocked.

Oya answered the door, bleary-eyed, dressed only in a light shift that showed off the curves of her body, and the velvety darkness of her skin shone through.

"What are you doing here?" The words flew from his mouth before he could stop them.

Oya scowled up at him, crossing her arms over her chest.

Gaitlan's eyes locked onto Oya's instead of roaming her body, too afraid to see what had drawn Mirra to her.

"Did your parents fail to teach you manners, princeling?"

Gaitlan bristled, latching onto his anger. "Where's Mirra? I need to talk to her."

Oya stared at him for a moment. Her bright eyes, so like Mirra's, cutting him to the core. "She's not here," she said at last, turning her back on Gaitlan. She left the door open so he could see the disheveled bed and clothing scattered across the floor.

Oya picked up her dress from the floor, pulling it over her head. She picked up her shoes but didn't don them. She walked past Gaitlan, shifting so no part of her body, not even her dress, touched him.

"Why don't you leave? This is where she belongs, but your presence makes her feel obligated to stay tethered to you."

Gaitlan straightened, squaring up to his opponent. "If she truly wanted to stay, nothing I could say would ever change her mind." He took pleasure in the momentary doubt that flickered in Oya's eyes.

"Mirra has a loyal heart. If she leaves with you, it is only because she feels like she has to, not because she wants to."

Oya smirked over her shoulder, knowing she'd dealt the last blow, before sashaying down the hallway, leaving Gaitlan questioning in her wake.

MIRRA RETURNED TO HER ROOM, HER MIND REELING. TO think that her existence and Julian's were linked sent shivers down her spine. She shook her head, dispelling the connections forming in her mind. Nothing was finalized, not until she knew for sure. But to figure that out, she needed Gaitlan to be willing to take a slight detour; although it actually might work better for him in the long run.

The Holy Isle was neutral territory. Lords and potential priests from all over the world gathered there to learn and exchange knowledge. There Gaitlan would be safe from most of Julian's reach. That's not to say that an assassin couldn't make its way onto the island, but it would take some time for Julian to learn of Gaitlan's arrival on the island and to orchestrate the attack.

She might be able to leave him after that, confirming or disproving the high priestess's theory. Separate, there was a greater chance for their collective survival. She would be able to spend time connecting to her people.

And spend more time with Oya.

Mirra wondered what it would be like to be with Oya.

To walk with her in the light. To spend her days in study while her nights would be occupied by meaningful discussions and heated debates. To finally feel like she was in the place where she belonged, with her entire future open to her.

"Where were you?"

Mirra couldn't quite keep the cringe off her face.

Face painted a startling shade of crimson, Gaitlan loomed over Mirra.

"The high priestess needed me." That seemed to quell some of his hurt, but not all. She could only surmise that he found out that she and Oya spent the night together, not that they did anything worth note. "I actually need to talk to you."

She pushed past him, pulling her tunic off as she went. She felt Gaitlan tense behind her. "Don't get any fancy ideas, princeling. I just need a clean shirt."

From the trunk at the end of her bed, she pulled out a clean, undyed shirt. She closed the lid and took a seat before directing Gaitlan to enter her room and close the door behind him.

Mirra fiddled with the bead braided into her hair, mulling over her words carefully before speaking. "Have you ever heard of a being called The Eater?"

Gaitlan shook his head. He leaned against the door with his arms crossed.

"It's a dark entity that eats the world."

"Is that some Ilmarrion boogie man?"

Mirra scowled at his tone but couldn't really blame him. "Something like that. I told Usoa about Lord Julian's abilities, and she thinks that they align with The Eater's."

Gaitlan released his arms. "So, does she know how to defeat him?"

Mirra shook her head. "She won't say one way or the other. I think she's too afraid to say it aloud. We need to gain access to the archives on the Holy Isle."

"Why?"

Mirra chewed her bottom lip. "Because that's the last collection of pre-Purge Ilmarrion history in the world. Apparently, the Abbot and the High Priestess have an understanding. He keeps their existence secret, and she helps to translate text for him."

"When do we leave?" Gaitlan murmured, afraid of the answer he knew she'd say.

"In a couple of days," Mirra said. "Usoa said she needs to prepare something to help us get to the island. Meanwhile, I thought I should try to learn something before I go."

"You're coming with me?"

"Of course," Mirra answered with a chuckle. "You'd be dead a hundred times over if not for me."

At first, Gaitlan's heart swelled over Mirra's answer, but now Oya's words echoed through his mind.

If she leaves with you, it is only because she feels like she has to, not because she wants to.

Despair coated Gaitlan's tongue as he choked the following words out. "You can stay if you want to. I can make it to the Holy Isle. You've done enough for my family and me already."

He turned to leave but was stopped by Mirra latching onto his shoulder.

"What in the three realms are you getting at? I know I haven't been the best companion, but I can't leave you now."

"And why not! You don't owe anything to my sister or to me! You got me out of the city. That's enough to pay back for the betrayal you had a part in."

Dark fire danced at Mirra's fingertips. "You think that I'm doing this for you? What do you think Julian will do to me if he finds me? I lied to him, remember? I betrayed him! I have his mark permanently inked onto my skin!"

She thrust her tattooed wrist at Gaitlan, who blanched.

"I may be helping you, your highness, but it's only to serve my own ends. I like your sister but not you. You're self-centered, weak, incompetent. You'd be dead if not for your sister and me. So, how about you get off your high horse and stop thinking that the world revolves around you?" Mirra's breaths came in heavy gulps, her fists clenched tightly at her side.

"If I could leave you, I would. I can't leave the fate of the world in the hands of some pampered prince who wouldn't last a day in the life of a normal human being."

"But you're not a human, are you, Mirra?" Gaitlan snapped back. "You're Ilmarrion."

Mirra silenced him with a raised finger. "Don't speak again unless you want to meet your parents in Yulla's Realm."

He pressed his lips tightly together before storming out of her room. Mirra placed her head in her hands and weighed the prince's survival against her own sanity.

WITH A SWING OF HIS SWORD, GAITLAN CUT THE DUMMY

nearly in half.

Idiot. Fool. Hot-headed imbecilic prince!

Why couldn't he keep a rein on his emotions? He was lucky Mirra had stayed with him as long as she had. If the roles were reversed, he'd have abandoned her ages ago.

Gaitlan yelled in frustration, slicing the head off a dummy.

"Anger will not serve you in battle."

High Priestess Usoa stood behind him, her face tight. She regarded him with contempt before extending her hand. A golden pendant swinging from her fingers.

"This will help mask your appearance until you reach the Abbot. As long as you reach him within seven days."

Gaitlan eyed the pendant with suspicion.

"Mirra is tied to you, for better or worse. I will not do anything that could cause her harm."

Gaitlan sheathed his sword. "I doubt that my death would make that great an impact on her life."

The corner of the high priestess's mouth tugged upwards. "Perhaps, but the world would suffer. As of right now, you are the only thing standing between Lord Julian and his goals. He cannot move forward whilst you roam free. If anything else, your continued freedom protects the rest of us from utter annihilation."

Gaitlan let out a bitter laugh. "If you truly think that, then you're a fool."

High Priestess Usoa chuckled. "Perhaps." She extended the pendant again. Gaitlan crossed the distance between them to take it from her. The pendant felt warmer than it should have, nearly scorching to the touch.

"Don't put it on until you leave our woods," Usoa instructed. "I already explained things to Mirra. She'll be able to fill you in. Once she's calmed down."

Shame-filled Gaitlan. The High Priestess gave him one last pointed look before leaving him alone in the training yard.

THE TOWER LOOMED HIGH OVER MIRRA'S HEAD, AS unwelcoming as ever. She placed her hand against the door, opening herself to it. Like before, she fell through the door, only this time, when she opened her eyes, she was greeted by the sight of hundreds of bookcases filled with books.

Several Ilmarrions already pursued amongst the shelving, their arms ladened with books. A burly man dressed in a simple homespun tunic greeted her.

"Welcome, young one," he boomed. "I haven't seen one of your kind, but I doubt you're much different from the others."

"The others?"

The man nodded. "The Düa, Su'la, and Haror. They spend too much time thinking above the earth, but without us, the Fasht, they would lose themselves to their gifts."

The man shook his head at the vacant expression on Mirra's face.

"Grounding, my young Nexian. That is what you need to learn first. You must find your way to keep yourself tethered to this world while you wield your gifts."

"And how do I do that?"

The man's grin carried a feral edge. The man led Mirra to a pot of dirt half her height and handed her a seed.

"Make it grow."

He left Mirra without offering further instruction, leaving her to stare at the seed in her palm. Regular seeds could be planted and watered until they sprouted without any magical aid. But something told her that this particular seed wouldn't follow natural law.

Either way, she buried it in the soil and poured water over it from a nearby pitcher. She thought about the door and attempted to apply the same ideal. Closing her eyes, she opened her consciousness, drowning out all other sounds and sensations until there was nothing left but the wet earth and sleeping seed.

At first, Mirra felt nothing except for her own energies flowing throughout her body.

Go deeper.

Pressing her lips tightly together, Mirra went deeper into her own consciousness until she stood outside the pool of swirling night that was her power. This was the first time she'd ever seen the power that resided inside her like this. Until now, she only felt it, pulling it up before casting it out into the world. Seeing it in its natural state inside the center of her being filled her with a small sense of pride.

She reached out, trailing her fingers through the swirling darkness, smiling at the stars scattered in the ripples.

The dark pool reached out for Mirra, just as happy to finally meet her as she was. It coiled around her like a cat, warm and inviting. After a time, it settled back down, waiting for her command.

Make it grow.

Mirra reached out again, calling forth a tiny portion of her power, no larger than seed. Clasping it closely to her chest, she turned to face the great nothingness that existed beyond her senses. She walked up to the edge and peered out into the vast void. Some part of her kept her from crossing over the threshold of her consciousness. It warned her that if she left the safety of herself without a path, she'd be forever swallowed by the void.

"Show me the seed," she pleaded. "Show me the seed. Let me help it grow."

An eternity passed. Or perhaps it had only been the span of a single heartbeat. Whatever it was, Mirra lost her grip on her power and was thrown back into her physical body, covered in sweat, gasping for breath.

The burly man was still there, his massive arms crossed over his barrel chest. "Not bad, little one. Not bad at all. There's something to be said about growing up on the outside, learning to trust your inner voice."

"What do you mean?" Mirra used a nearby table to get to her feet. Her legs wobbling like a newborn foal's.

"You were born outside the clans, yes? That means that you never learned any of the bad habits that tend to inhibit the true understanding."

"True understanding?"

The burly man turned away, not answering her question, disappearing down the bookcases. Mirra remained where she stood, partly because she wasn't sure if she could leave, and partially because her legs were still shaking under her.

The man returned, thrusting a small bound book at her.

"Read this," he ordered. "Should cover most of the basics."

He turned to leave, and this time, Mirra did call out after him. "What should I do now?"

"Read," he said like it was the most obvious answer. "Read and make that seed grow. Until you do both, you can't move on."

Mirra stared at the man's retreating back, questioning his credentials as a teacher. Then again, he never said he was a teacher. Shaking her head, Mirra pulled out a chair at the same table she was using to stand. With no other options, she opened the book and began to read.

OYA WAS WAITING FOR MIRRA OUTSIDE THE TOWER. SHE took one look at Mirra's haggard expression and laughed. "I see Thrane is as brutal as ever."

"Is that the name of that big guy?"

"Yes, he's what you would call a master. He's not known for his gentle nature. But he is the most talented Fasthin we have."

"Lucky me," Mirra groaned, running a hand through her hair.

They walked in silence for a while, tension building with each step.

"The high priestess wanted me to give you this." Oya handed Mirra a small wrapped object.

Mirra unwrapped it to reveal a pendant brimming with power. "Is this the pendant she told me about?"

Oya nodded, her bright mood wholly gone. "She also told me to tell you that everything is ready for you to leave in the morning."

Mirra stopped in her tracks. "So soon?"

"She said that time is of the essence. Where you're going, you'll have access to knowledge even we don't have."

Mirra heard the longing in Oya's voice, and she wasn't sure if it was because Oya wanted to go with her or wanted to get her hands on the ancient texts.

"I guess I should go talk to Gaitlan."

"If you must," Oya said tersely. She took a step back and bowed her head before walking away, her steps quick and sharp.

Mirra watched her go, confusion written all over her face. Rubbing her temple, Mirra pocketed the charm, her mind and her heart at odds with each other.

CHAPTER SIXTEEN

GAITLAN PASSED AROUND IN THE ANTECHAMBER, HIS MIND
A tumultuous sea. He needed to get away from Moakwyd, away
from these people that looked at him with contempt. He needed
to leave this crumbling city that filled him with guilt. Needed to
get away from a priestess with midnight skin and ice in her eyes.
He never thought he would miss being on the open road with
only Mirra at his side.

"There you are; I've been looking everywhere for you."

Gaitlan spun, his heart fluttering as Mirra walked up.
There was a thin layer of pain behind her smile. Perhaps she
didn't really want to go with him as Oya had said. Perhaps his
foolhardy and brash words had finally driven her away.

"So," she began. Gaitlan closed his eyes against the
coming rejection. "Apparently, the high priestess works fast; we're
leaving tomorrow."

Gaitlan's eyes shot open.

"I know, right," Mirra said, misreading his surprise. "I
was really looking forward to a few more days, but things can't be
helped. We've been here too long, anyway."

"Are you sure?" Gaitlan asked. "I mean, you don't have to come with me. You can stay here, learn, connect to your people, and then come help me reclaim my throne when you're ready."

He could see Mirra's mind working, weighing her options and possible outcomes of each path. "I've been with you this long, princeling. I might as well stay."

The following words he spoke were like dry sand poured down his throat. "If that's what you want. I won't stop you, no matter what you choose."

Mirra arched a brow, her eyes peering deeply into his. Gaitlan held his breath, waiting for her answer.

"Let's go get some food," Mirra said. "This might be the last decent meal we have for a while. I don't even want to imagine what those priests think a good meal is."

Gaitlan plastered a cocky grin on his face. "Whatever they have is probably better than what you ate as a child."

"Anything is better than what I ate as a kid. Don't even get me started on what they pass off as food in the orphanages. That's the first thing you should fix when you take the throne."

"There are a great many things I want to change," Gaitlan said.

They let the conversation die, falling into an easy silence. Though Mirra hadn't entirely swayed his concerns, he knew that she was going with him all the same. And that was a comfort of its own.

OYA WAS NOWHERE TO BE SEEN. MIRRA CHEWED HER thumb, torn between leaving it alone and going after her. The latter was an entirely new mode of thinking for her. Since breaking down at Em's, Mirra felt like a stranger in her own skin. Though she was still uneasy about opening up, she wasn't entirely averse to making connections as she had been in her youth. The cause for this change was still a mystery to her, but the one thing she was sure of was that being in a state of unknowing was not something she could easily tolerate.

Mirra filled her plate and sat near the fire, half paying attention to the people around her and half to where High Priestess Usoa sat.

The high priestess met Mirra's gaze and gave her a small shake. Oya was not coming tonight.

Disappointment bowed her shoulders, turning the food to ash in her mouth.

"What's wrong?" Gaitlan sat down next to Mirra.

"Nothing."

Gaitlan looked across the space to where the high priestess was. "Did you two have a lover's quarrel already?"

Mirra bristled at his tone. "It's none of your business, but we're not lovers."

Gaitlan held his hands up in placation. "You're right, but as your friend, don't leave on bad terms. You may not get the chance to repair it. Trust me."

The snide remark building in Mirra's mouth died, taking her rage with it. "Whatever," she grumbled into her food, shoveling it as fast as she could into her mouth.

After dinner, Mirra's body hummed with anxious energy, the same energy she got before a job when she was a thief or pretending to be someone else for Nora. Sleep would be hard-pressed to find her. So, instead, Mirra went for a walk, taking her time to visit all the places she'd come to know during her short stay.

Leaving would be bittersweet, but she needed to know. Needed to be completely sure that the power Lord Julian presented was nothing more than a fluke, some remnant Ilmarrion blood come to life. Only then would she be able to cut her ties to the prince. If Lord Julian was nothing more than a man, Gaitlan would be able to defeat him with little help from her. Her future could finally be her own. But if he wasn't ...

Mirra tensed, her ears straining. Somewhere ahead, she picked up the sound of footsteps. They were light, nearly undetectable, but she was born of shadows, and nothing could remain hidden from her. Curious as to who was ahead, Mirra blended into the darkness around her.

Every time she called on her magic, it came to her faster and faster. She hardly had to think about it anymore, like she did as a child. She smiled wickedly and crept forward, nothing more than a passing cloud in the night's sky.

She peered around a corner, spying a small courtyard she wasn't familiar with. In the middle of the courtyard, Oya stood, bathed in moonlight, before a small altar. Mirra couldn't see what was on the altar, but the air in the courtyard hummed with the same energies as the temples she visited with the princess.

Oya chanted softly, her eyes closed, raising her hands, the golden light of affinity pooled in her palms. When she finished the chant, Oya raised her glowing hand to the sky in offering. The light that shimmered in her palms spiraled upwards toward the sky like stars, fading away into the night.

The air in the courtyard relaxed as the power Oya

summoned drifted away. Oya remained at the altar, her eyes cast downward.

"I know you're there, Mirra."

"How?" Mirra asked, stepping out of the shadows.

Oya turned around, eyes wide. "I didn't, but I hoped."

Mirra laughed. "What was all that?"

Oya looked down at her feet, tucking a braid behind her ear. "Nothing important."

Bells chimed in the back of her mind, exposing the lie, but she chose to let it slide. "You left in a huff this afternoon, and I didn't see you at dinner."

"I had ... to work through some things, and I'm sorry for any distress I caused you."

Mirra waved her off. "No worries."

They fell into a heavy silence. Mirra fiddled with the bead in her hair. "Do you wanna go for a walk with me?"

She was rewarded by Oya's bright smile, and they walked arm in arm until the sky turned from blue-black to rosy pink.

THEIR WORLD WAS PAIN. THEIR WORLD BURNED. THEIR world froze. Their world was an insufferable pit of hel. They cursed the woman. The one with eyes that burned, eyes the color of the palest ice. Her kind shouldn't exist anymore. They should have died out centuries ago. The creatures used their collective hatred to keep themselves tethered to their stolen flesh as their wounds slowly healed. They were used to waiting. They had plenty of practice—centuries, in fact.

The woman and the prince wouldn't get far. The creatures had their scent seared into their memory. They could track them to the ends of the earth through all planes of existence. The largest of the mercenaries, the leader, smiled, cracking the bloodstains on his face.

It had been a good long while since they had a prey worthy of their skills. They would have fun playing with her before the end.

TWO FINE HORSES WAITED, ALREADY SADDLED AND packed, for Mirra and Gaitlan by the city gates. Mirra ran a hand down one of the mount's necks, more for her comfort than the beast's.

"Long night?"

Mirra opened her mouth to answer, but a giant yawn came out instead.

Gaitlan chuckled. "I'd probably stay up all night too if I was you."

High Priestess Usoa walked toward them, saving Mirra from explaining what she did that kept her up all night. More importantly, who. Oya told Mirra her whole life story in one evening. She told her about her village, her family, and the dangers she faced before coming to Moakwyd. She spoke at great length of her time as a slave in the floating city of K'ashi and her desperate escape for freedom.

Mirra replied in kind, sparing none of the gruesome details. All the time she'd been forced to kill for survival or because of an order. The people she stole from and the secrets she unearthed. If Oya wanted her, she'd have to accept all of Mirra, even the dark bits. That's what happened with Em, and she seemed happy.

"Mirra, your time with us has been too short. There is much that we weren't able to teach you. Please accept this to keep up with your studies until you can return to us once more."

"The Songs of Mist? I've already read this book. They had it in the palace."

High Priestess Usoa smiled and ran a finger over the pages. The words rippled and changed, forming new shapes and words until the pages were unrecognizable.

"There are few of these left in the world, but they are there. For those who do not connect to the Ileing, it is a simple story about brave knights and good Mystics. But for us, it is a small collection of the most basic spells and enchantments of our people."

Mirra stared up at the priestess. "Thank you."

High Priestess Usoa turned to Gaitlan. They studied each other, their mutual animosity rippling in the air between them.

"I can only hope that the time you've spent here has illustrated how your actions can have long-lasting effects. If you can regain your seat of power. Do not forget that it was built on the bones of people that are clinging on to existence."

A muscle in Gaitlan's jaw flexed. He surprised Mirra by bowing to the high priestess instead of retorting.

"I thank you for your hospitality and the hospitality of your people. I hope that in the future, we can find ways to mend the damages of the past while moving onto a brighter future."

The corner of the high priestess's mouth tugged upwards briefly before returning to her neutral expression. She gave Mirra one last nod of the head in farewell before returning to the heart of the city.

One by one, the other residents of Moakwyd returned to their daily tasks, offering words of encouragement to Mirra and silent promises of harm to Gaitlan, should anything happen to Mirra.

Mirra tried to keep the smirk off her face, especially when she saw how much those looks got under Gaitlan's skin.

Before too long, only Oya remained.

"Take this with you," she said, handing Gaitlan the sword he used during training. To Mirra, she passed a small recurve bow. "This will be easier to use on horseback and a bit less conspicuous than the glave."

Mirra chuckled and accepted the gift. "Thank you. I wish I had something to offer in return."

"Your return can be your gift."

Closing the space between them, Mirra cupped Oya's face, running her thumb across the curve of her cheek one last time. Oya closed her eyes, her hand going up to clasp Mirra's. They would have kissed, but both women were keenly aware of Gaitlan's unabashed staring. Instead, they pressed their foreheads together, mingling their breaths.

Oya was the first to pull away. She strode back to the temple without looking back. Mirra watched her go for a moment before swinging up into the saddle. "Shall we, princeling?"

"After you," Gaitlan said, following suit.

They reached the edge of the woods by midday. Mirra scouted ahead to ensure that there would be no witnesses to their emergence or to their transformation.

"All's clear," she called, stepping out into the road.

Gaitlan came through a moment later, leading both the horses. "So, how do these things work?"

"Usoa said they will change our appearance so we can travel without fear of being caught. Remember, once they go on, they can never come off until we reach the Holy Isle. Or until the magic wears off in about seven days."

Gaitlan held his pendant by its band, a dubious look to his face. "If you say so."

Mirra rolled her eyes and put on her pendant. The pendant's magic rippled over her like a warm bath. Gaitlan's utter shock was almost worth having to leave, almost.

"You look like a boy!"

"Well, put yours on, and let's see what you become."

Gaitlan pulled his pendant on and closed his eyes. He shuttered as the magic rippled over him. Mirra watched, fascinated as Gaitlan's image shifted and melded into the visage of an elderly man, still fit, with a full white beard and hair.

Gaitlan opened his eyes and peered down at himself, but like Mirra, he couldn't see the changes. "What do I look like?"

"You're a voluptuous woman with large breasts and full lips," Mirra said with a wicked smile.

Gaitlan blanched, his hand going to rip the pendant off, protection be damned. Mirra doubled over in laughter. "I'm sorry," she said, wiping her eyes. "I couldn't help myself."

Gaitlan turned away, his face flushed. He muttered under

his breath, silently cursing Mirra until he regained his composure. "So, how do I actually look?"

"Like a retired knight," Mirra said. "I think we're made to look like a family. The entire kingdom is looking for a man and woman. Not an old man and youth."

Mirra swung herself into the saddle. "Let's get going, grandpa. Remember, time is of the essence."

Their journey to Eastport only took a matter of days. They made an excellent time not having to hide their faces, avoiding large crowds. And the best part was that they got to sleep in soft beds at inns every night.

Like before, Gaitlan let Mirra lead, this being something she received training for. He could never in a thousand years come up with intricate backstories using real places and people from places he'd never seen. And yet, she wove stories like she'd been blessed by Lothin, the goddess of tales.

"We need to find the captain of the Fallen Star. He's the one who'll take us to the island."

"Does he know who we are?"

Mirra shook her head. "I don't think so, but that's not the bad news."

Gaitlan shot her a look.

"Our pendants only last seven days. This is the fifth, and we don't know when the Fallen Star is slated to set sail.

"Oh!" was all that Gaitlan managed to say.

Mirra urged her horse onward, heading toward the docks, hoping she'd be able to find their contact before he set sail.

Eastport was a large town, with all its wealth tied up in the ships that sailed in and out. But for all its wealth and dependence on merchant ships, it didn't cater to their needs. There were only a handful of taverns for the sea weary sailors to find their convalescents, which worked out in Mirra's favor. She found the captain of the Fallen Star in the first tavern they checked. It was the priciest and most prominent in the town.

"Aye. I'm the captain, and you are?"

"Grathem and Micha," Gaitlan said. "We booked passage with you to the Holy Isle."

The captain eyed Mirra and Gaitlan with unveiled suspicion. "And what business would two strapping fighters have with those soft-handed scholars?"

Gaitlan froze, but Mirra swooped in with a believable lie. "Turns out fighting's not my thing," she said with a shrug. "My da's real pissed about it, but gramps figured if I can't be a fighter, I might as well be a priest or something."

Mirra somehow made her disguise look soft and unthreatening. The captain eyed her up and down before he nodded. "Aye, 'tis better than being a lout, I suppose. Well, you've gotten here just in time. We're shoving off in de morning. Be at the docs no later than the first bell after sunrise."

"We need to sleep on the ship," Gaitlan interjected now that the conversation shifted back toward his practiced script.

The captain shook his head. "I ain't about to have two strangers on my ship unsupervised."

Gaitlan pulled a gold coin out, money made from the sale of their horses, placing it on the table between him and the captain. "I'm sure a captain such as yourself wouldn't leave his ship completely unguarded. There's no room in any of the inns in this town, and my old bones aren't up to roughing it like they used to be."

The captain eyed the gold coin pointedly. Gaitlan sighed, pulling out another. The captain beamed up at them, swinging his long legs to the floor. "Understandable, gentlemen, if you'll follow me."

Gaitlan cast a relieved look at Mirra, who maintained her previous composure. Cursing his carelessness, he re-schooled his expressions and followed the captain to the ship. They would stay in their cabin until they reached the isle. Completely cutting themselves off from the others. Some type of mild, noncontagious illness would keep even the nosiest sailor at bay.

Their cabin turned out to be a room no larger than a small closet. Two hammocks swayed from the rafters, with an empty fruit crate in the middle. It took every ounce of Gaitlan's royal upbringing to keep the look of horror from his face. There was no way in all the realms this room was worth the money they paid to book it and the two gold coins to get into it early.

Gaitlan started to turn to say those very thoughts to the captain when Mirra firmly but inconspicuously grabbed onto his arm. "Thank you, captain," she said. "Gramps and I really appreciate it. These last few days on the road have been real hard on 'im."

"Not at all," the captain said with mock humility. "One less thing I gotta worry about tomorrow. And since ya here, no passengers are allowed on the deck during send-off. You only get in the way."

"Noted."

Gaitlan waited until he couldn't hear the captain's footsteps to approach Mirra. "Do you think we should take them off?" he whispered.

Mirra let out a massive yawn, shaking her head. "Best turn in, gramps. We got a long way ahead still."

She stowed her belongings under a hammock before swinging herself in it, falling asleep as soon as she closed her eyes.

It took Gaitlan longer than he'd like to admit to figure out how to get into the hammock without rolling all the way over. In the end, he managed it, cautiously adjusting until he found a comfortable position, his last thoughts filled with his sister and her wellbeing.

The pendant's magic gave out well after the Fallen Star had set sail. Mirra and Gaitlan were able to hold up in their room without too much fuss from the crew. With nothing else to do, Mirra occupied her time, studying from The Songs of Mist.

There didn't appear to be any semblance of order with the contents. Most of the information inside was more on the practical side, with spells for protection, healing, concealment, and a few combat-related ones. Mirra surmised it was just enough information to keep an Ilmarrion alive on the broader world, and nothing more. She spent some time tracing her finger over the pages, using her magic to make the words shift and change between the human myths and Ilmarrion magic. She shook her head at the wonder of it all.

"Is it that good of a read?" Gaitlan, unfortunately, had nothing to entertain his thoughts but Mirra. He'd already spent hours studying the emotions flitting over her face. He'd witnessed many different facets of her personality by this point. In court, she was sharp and reserved, always watching. As a fighter, she was graceful and vicious. She bullied and pulled him from the dark recesses of his mind until he could stand on his own. She was hot-tempered, private, and fiercely loyal. Gaitlan picked at the frayed cordage of the hammock, wondering for how much longer she'd feel the need to stay with him.

"In a way," Mirra said with a shrug. She tucked the book beside her before crossing her arms under her head. "I think it was made during the Purge or some time shortly afterward. It's nothing more than a few basic spells and enchantments meant to keep you alive and hidden."

"Are you going to practice casting these new spells?"

Mirra snorted. "Gods no. Use that learned brain of yours, princeling."

Gaitlan's face flushed, and he turned his back toward Mirra. He pretended not to hear her light laughter nor the way it made his heart soar.

The voyage lasted four days in total. Fortune smiled on Mirra and Gaitlan because their arrival was met by a small storm. Not enough to prevent their departure from the ship, but enough that the hooded cloaks they wore to mask their true identities went unnoticed.

A small gathering of robed people stood at the end of the docs. Most wore simple gray robes, but Mirra spied a few with colored bands sewed along the hems.

Usoa's instructions ended at their arrival to the island. Her last directive urged them to find the Abbot and explain their situation. The current Abbot was an ally, according to the high priestess.

A woman in a robe trimmed in red walked up to Mirra and Gaitlan. Her gaze rolled over both their faces, lingering a bit longer on Mirra, her eyes in particular. "The Abbot received word of your arrival. Please follow me." Her accent was melodic, sitting heavily in the back of her mouth. Though she couldn't have been much older than Gaitan, there was a hardness around her eyes that made her appear older. Or the hardness came from the geometric tattoos that dotted her forehead and cheeks.

"Where are you from?" Mirra asked. The memory of another woman with a tattooed face flashed across her mind's eye.

"Bardon," the woman replied without turning around. "Now, if you please?"

The woman led them up a winding, rocky path, passing fields of crops, goat pastures, a small orchard, and dozens, if not hundreds, of small huts.

"We strive to be self-sufficient here," the woman said. "When not receiving instruction, supplicants tend to the needs of the island."

"Impressive," Mirra said when the pause became too awkward.

The woman made a noncommittal noise in the back of her throat, and they walked on in complete silence.

The road led to a large stone building, strikingly identical to the citadel in Moakwyd. The woman continued up the steps. Those dressed in plain gray robes moved out of the woman's way, lowering their gaze as they passed. A few made reverent gestures, and one man even went to the knee, not rising until the woman had gone some distance ahead.

Gaitlan sent Mirra a questioning glance. A slight shrug of the shoulders was her reply. For now, the silence was best.

Inside the structure, several braziers burned to keep away

the chill. Most of the open space was filled with long wooden tables. Perhaps half a dozen people sat at the tables, some eating, while others were surrounded by books, jars, or bits of metal.

The woman led them further inside, turning down a series of corridors until they reached a singular door near an open courtyard. She knocked thrice before leaving Mirra and Gaitlan bewildered before the door.

"Enter."

Mirra and Gaitlan exchanged glances, locked in a silent conversation as to who should go first. In the end, Mirra shoved Gaitlan toward the door.

"Princes first."

"Some deadly assassin, you are," he snipped back.

"I'm not the one on the run from the crown," she said with a smirk.

The room they entered could only be described as semi-controlled chaos. Side tables and chairs were covered top to bottom with letters, scrolls, books, stone tablets, and other curious items. At a small desk sat an elderly man dressed in a scarlet robe. His eyes were as warm as coffee, framed by deep lines of laughter. On his head, he wore a small knit cap that stopped before his graying temples. The rest of his face was hidden by a thick black beard threaded with white.

"You must be the ones that Usoa wrote to me about." He rose to take their hands in time. "Prince Gaitlan. While I am happy to learn that you weren't responsible for your parents' deaths, I offer my condolences for their loss. May Yawah lead their souls to his kingdom."

"And you must be Mirra." She liked the way he rolled

over the Rs in her name. "The first child of the void in a thousand years."

Mirra wanted to smile, but the way he spoke of her lineage sent a chill down her spine.

"I am Abbot Josef. I offer you the food of my hearth and the safety of my home."

Gaitlan bowed deeply. "Thank you for your kindness."

Abbot Josef's chuckle rumbled through his chest. "Don't thank me yet, young prince. You cannot walk as freely as you did amongst the Ilmarrions." His face turned serious. "I cannot attest to the loyalty of all on the island. Your viper may have made a nest here as he did in court."

"What must we do?"

"Keep your identities hidden. I think this should be easy for you, dark one."

Mirra shifted under the Abbot's intense gaze. "I might have done that a time or two."

Brief lines of laughter crinkled around the Abbot's eyes. "You will live in the supplicant's loggings, share in their lessons and chores. That is until we can discern a way for you to communicate with your allies, should you have any."

Gaitlan paled and swallowed. "And if I don't?"

Abbot Josef clasped Gaitlan by the shoulder. "Then you may stay here for as long as you need to. But remember, we will not fight for you. Here, we work to strengthen our minds, not our might. Though many of the supplicants have some background in the fighting arts. The cost of fighting other people's war has become too great a burden for them to bear."

Gaitlan lowered his head. "I would never ask anyone to

go against their nature. But trouble may come to your door all the same."

"That may be, and we do have some defenses. But enough of that; you've had a long journey, and I have work to do." Abbot Josef clapped his hands, and a young boy in a plain gray robe entered the room. The boy's hair caught the light from the lanterns, reflecting their color back. When he stood, he eyed Mirra and Gaitlan with unabashed suspicion in his storm-cloud eyes.

"Kov, this is Lan and Mir. Take them to the House of the Unbanded. They will meet the masters in the morning."

Kov bowed deeply to the Abbot before motioning for Mirra and Gaitlan to follow.

"You'll stay in the House of the Unbanded until your course is decided."

"Yes, our course," Gaitlan said, his words coming out more like a question.

Kov stopped, his expression suspicious.

Mirra clapped her hands together. "I think I would like to be a Binder. I've always loved learning about histories and reading in general. What about you, Lan? Do you think you'd like the Alchemist, Smelter, or Binder like me?"

"Smelter," Gaitlan said, choosing the one that sounded the easiest. "What's your course?"

Kov turned his nose to the air. "I was born on this island. I will choose my band when I turn fifteen like the others."

"So, do you live in the House of the Unbanded too?"

Kov shook his head. "I live with the rest of the children in the Houses of Dawn." He chuckled at the confusion growing on Gaitlan's face. "You'll see for yourself soon enough. Here you go."

He pointed up a small hill toward a long row house. "Ina will take care of you."

Kov trotted back down the road toward waving over his shoulder. "See ya around."

Gaitlan waved back. He turned to ask Mirra about the courses, but she had already reached the door and talked to a small dark-haired woman. He scrambled up after her, slipping in the mud and gravel.

"Just let us know what we can do to help, Ina," Mirra said to the dark-haired woman.

"Yes," Gaitlan gasped, not entirely sure what he agreed to.

Ina's dark eyes glittered with disapproval. Gaitlan's gaze was drawn to the three-dotted lines that ran from her bottom lip to chin and the sharp V on her forehead.

"Marks of womanhood," Mirra whispered. "Cemont."

Gaitlan's eyes widened with understanding. "Forgive me, I didn't mean to stare."

"Come inside," Ina said.

The House of the Unbanded was nothing more than a long, singular room. One massive, open-aired hearth sat in the middle of the space, billowing smoke into the rafters. No one bothered to look up from their tasks when Mirra and Gaitlan entered. Several supplicants sat around the hearth, enjoying a hot meal from the cauldron bubbling over the fire. They laughed easily amongst themselves with the familiarity of long friendships.

Toward the eastern end of the building, three long tables sat up against the walls. There even more gray-robed supplicants poured over scrolls and models. One supplicant cried out in frustration when he calculated the incorrect angle for the third time.

"We complete the work from the masters there," Ina said, indicating the tables. "And sleep over there." She gestured to the western end. A series of cubbies were built along the wall, each holding a bedroll and a few other belongings.

"Find one without a name, then find two robes from the chests." Ina eyed Mirra's bow and Gaitlan's sword. "They stay here. You may practice in your free time, but other than that, you are not permitted to carry them."

"Why?" Gaitlan asked, his hand going to the hilt.

The room around them fell silent. The eyes of the supplicants focused on Mirra and Gaitlan.

Mirra coughed pointedly. Gaitlan released the hilt of his sword, his hand shifting to unbuckle it from his belt. "Forgive me; we haven't had the easiest time getting here. I'm still a bit on edge."

He held out his sword to Ina. She looked from it to Gaitlan for several tense moments, her face completely unreadable. At long last, she took his sword and Mirra's bow, stowing them with a small cache of weaponry.

Ina left Gaitlan and Mirra to their own devices. Mirra chose the first cubby without a name, stowing the little possession she had inside. "That was quick thinking, your highness."

Sparks of joy spread from his fingertips to his toes. "I

told her the truth."

"Yes, and that's your first lesson, knowing when and how much of the truth to tell." Mirra dug around in the chest labeled 'woman' and pulled out one well-worn gray robe. She held it up, contemplating whether it would fit her or not. She laid it on top of the chest and started to remove her rain-soaked clothing.

Gaitlan started, his face as hot as a furnace. Taken back by Mirra's nonchalant manner that he didn't think to turn around until he saw the pale plains of her back and breast band.

"Second lesson," Mirra went on, unaware of Gaitlan's shock. "Only change what needs to be changed; limit the lies. There's no way we can pretend to be anything else but wealthy merchant kids. You might not be able to pull that off. Let go of some of your formality, the stiff way you carry yourself. Here, you are nobody. So, act like a nobody."

Mirra selected a second robe, storing it with the rest of her belongings. "I don't know about you, but I plan to plant myself by the fire and not move until bedtime."

Gaitlan watched Mirra flounce toward the fire, settling amongst their fellow unbanded. She smiled and laughed with them, quickly solidifying her part in the group. Gaitlan ripped off his clothing, snatching the first two robes from the men's chest. Luckily, the first one fit him without too much fuss, but the second would be several inches too short. But Gaitlan was blind to all that. The only thing that consumed his thoughts was Mirra's carefree smile and laughter she bestowed on complete strangers. She only looked at him with pity or outright contempt. Their relationship improved slightly during their sojourn in Moakwyd, though a new wall was now thrown between them. However, this new wall wasn't as foreboding as the previous one.

Gaitlan got the impression that Mirra was only trying to keep clear lines between them.

Feeling the weight of the past week, Gaitlan grabbed his bedroll, keeping his back to the rest of the room.

Mirra peered over her shoulder at Gaitlan's prone form, already missing the calm and quiet of the woods and the scent of magnolia oil mixed with herbs.

Gaitlan pretended not to hear the laughter behind his back. He pulled the covers of his bedroll tighter around his face to hide the steady flow of tears that fell from his eyes. The void in the center of his heart latched onto the flow of emotions, clawing its way to the surface. Images flashed across his mind, terrible visions of blood, smoke, and suffering.

Over and over, he watched his parents die. Their blood leaking out between their blackened fingers, with tears brimming in their wide eyes. Those dreams were bad enough, but the ones where Julian and his men encircled Braelyn and the torture they put her through wretched him from his sleep time and time again.

CHAPTER SEVENTEEN

DAWN BROKE COLD AND DREARY. THE STORM CLOUDS from the day before lingered over the Holy Isle, making everything look gray and dingy. There was nothing more Gaitlan wanted than to be inside where it was undoubtedly warm, even if it was only marginally warmer than the outside. He woke bleary-eyed and stiff from the night before. Many of the people in the House of the Unbanded huddled together like dogs to keep away the chill. He couldn't bring himself to ask to join. Not even Mirra, who unshockingly seemed to have no problem curling up to strangers.

She grew up an orphan on the streets, you prat! a small part of him chided. She'd probably done worse than curling up to new acquaintances to survive as long as she had before Lord Julian sunk his fangs into her.

"Oi, new boy, get your head out of the clouds!"

Gaitlan nearly dropped his shepherd's crook. The trio of youths he'd been assigned to laughed unabashedly.

The youths were a trio of brothers, all tall and gangly,

with masses of unruly curly hair on top of their heads. Though they could speak in the common tongue, they could converse in their native language, leaving Gaitlan feeling even more like an outsider than he already did.

He scowled at the youths, whose names he hadn't bothered to learn, and trudged up the hill after them. Goats and sheep grazed freely around the surrounding hills, the bells tied around their necks jingling with every move.

For the most part, the herd looked after itself. There were no predators on the island, but many of the cliffs were weak, prone to crumbling without any provocation. Gaitlan's and the youth's task was to keep the herd away from the cliff sides during the day and bring them in at night. It was boring, tedious work, one that was well beneath a prince's station, even if he was in exile and hiding.

The wind picked up, carrying spray from the sea with it, adding further wetness to his already damp robe. Gaitlan tapped a wayward Kidd with the crook of his staff, sending it back to the herd. He peered into the distance, his mind returning to the horrors that had stolen his sleep. The visions were worse in the daylight somehow. The cold air around him seeped into the nightmares, bringing a sense of realism with it. The cries of the goats became his mother's and sister's voices, equally begging for help and spitting blame. Stones scattered by careless footing transformed into the crumbling walls of his home.

Gaitlan's grip on his staff turned white as his breath came out in short, rapid spurts.

"Oi, Lan!"

Spinning around, Gaitlan's shepherd's crook struck one of the brothers across the face. His whole body turned, limbs going limp. His brothers shouted, rushing to their brother's aid. They cursed Gaitlan in their foreign tongue as they checked for life in their fallen sibling.

Gaitlan stepped back in horror, dropping his blood-splattered crook as he ran.

A SUPPLICANT WITH BROWN BANDS SEWN ONTO HIS ROBE came for Gaitlan during his midday meal. "Come with me to the Citadel. The masters are waiting for you."

Gaitlan blanched, his hands roving over his robe as if it was stained by the young herder's blood. "Should I change first?"

"The masters don't care what you look like. It's your mind they will judge."

Tugging on his robes one last time, Gaitlan followed the supplicant. He wondered what tests or challenges the masters would present to him. He hadn't trained to be a priest or scholar. And he had been summoned to the fields before he and Mirra had a chance to work out their plans.

You're going to muck this up! a small part of him screamed. You've messed up everything else in your life, so why would this time be any different? Your friends, your parents, your sister, and even Mirra. All you've ever been to them is a burden, a source of shame. Everything is your fault. Your fault. Your fault ...

"They're waiting for you inside," the supplicant said.

Gaitlan blinked, coming back to reality. He stood before a set of oaken doors without any memory of how he got there. The words from the pit in his soul echoed in his ears, churning his stomach.

The supplicant rolled his eyes and knocked on the door before leaving a stunned Gaitlan scrambling to collect his thoughts.

"Enter, please," called a cheerful voice.

The voice was feminine, confusing Gaitlan.

Two of the masters were male, and the third was a tiny woman who beamed brightly at Gaitlan, seemingly unaware of the soot streak across her face. She'd cut the sleeves of her solid black robe off, displaying muscular arms crisscrossed with scars and burn marks. The bottom of her hair brushed her chin, and it looked like she'd run her fingers through it a moment before.

"I am Madadh, head of the Smelters. These are my counterparts: Ujurak for the Alchemists, and Nen for the Binders."

Ujurak was a stoic man whose features were similar to Ina's. Like her, he, too, bore tattoos along his face, though his markings were sharper than Ina's. The tanned pallor of his skin stood out against the vibrant green-gold of his robes.

Gaitlan inclined his head in reverence. Ujurak made no move to indicate whether he accepted Gaitlan's deterrence or not.

On the other hand, Nen offered Gaitlan a small smile before rolling back the sleeves of his blue and brown robe that set off the richness of his skin. Various gold bangles clanked against each other as he freed his hands from his robe. "Thank you for coming today, Lan, is it?"

"Yes."

"Be at peace, young man. Ujurak may look terrifying, but he's quite friendly once you get to know him."

Ujurak rolled his eyes, a ghost of a smile on his lips.

"From Abbot Josef, you've indicated that you are not a part of nor have any desire to join the priesthood."

"Or priestess-hood."

Nen closed his eyes and shook his head. "But you have had some schooling in your upbringing."

Mirra's words echoed through Gaitlan's mind, and he haltingly spun a modified version of his life.

"My father held a minor position in the Undrosean court. He spent a great deal of money on my education, claiming it would help prepare me for my future."

"And what future would that be," Nen asked, leaning forward to rest his chin on his folded hands.

"He wanted me to take over the family tradition when he died."

Ujurak's voice was lighter than Gaitlan expected, causing him to jump when he spoke. "Where is he now?"

Gaitlan clasped his hands in front of him and mumbled out, "He's gone."

The panel of masters fell silent, exchanging looks amongst each other. "What do you want to do now, Lan?" It was Madadh who spoke, her lively face turning serious.

Gaitlan froze, his mind going blank. The words that came out of his mouth next were the words he'd struggled for so long to keep in. The answer to the question he'd been asking himself since Mirra pulled him, along tied to his horse.

"I don't know."

GAITLAN'S HEAD POUNDED AS HE TRUDGED DOWN THE citadel steps an eternity later. Gaitlan scoffed. His tutors in the palace hadn't ridden him as hard as the three masters did. Numbers, herbs, battle tactics, languages, and histories danced in a jumbled mess inside his head. All he wanted was a warm meal and to crawl into his bedroom and sleep until the sun came up again.

Mirra wasn't in the House of the Unbanded when he returned. But there were only a few others besides him. Perhaps the rest would return after their daily chores.

Gaitlan ladled a steaming portion of stew into a clay bowl, taking a seat at the end of the nearest table.

"You were examined today?"

Gaitlan looked up from his bowl. A young man, close to his age, sat across from him. His black-brown hair dripped into his hazel eyes. His expression was bright and open as he waited for Gaitlan's reply.

"Is it that obvious?"

The young man laughed. "Don't worry; we all look like that afterward. I'm Daimon, by the way."

"Lan."

Daimon's palm was rough from years of hard work. Though Gaitlan couldn't tell if it was from the sword or field.

"Have you been examined?"

Daimon shook his head. "Not yet. I grew up on a small farm near the mountains. I never learned how to read, write, or anything. Gotta pass that first before choosing a course."

"If you didn't go to school, then why'd you come here?"

Daimon leaned back in his seat. "I realized I couldn't

force myself to fit into what my folks wanted me to be. Ya know?"

Gaitlan blinked. Not be what his parents wanted? That had never been an option for him. The whole reason for his existence was to be one thing—king, to spend his life in service to others under the guise of rulership. The ability to choose your own path, your own destiny, was something someone like him could never have. That's what separated him from his friends amongst the noble families, Mirra, and even his sister at times. He'd been born with the weight of the crown already around his neck.

"You all right, Lan?"

"Yeah," Gaitlan said slowly. "I thought that if things hadn't changed so drastically, I'd still be on the path my parents laid down for me. I wasn't unhappy, but I don't think I could say I was happy either. I just went along with it, not questioning if it was actually what I wanted."

"That's not a bad way to live," Daimon said quickly. "People can lead full lives, no matter how they choose to live. I just knew I couldn't stay there."

Daimon stood quickly. "Hey, man, I didn't mean to drop a serious question on ya right after the masters put you through the wringer. Enjoy your meal; get some rest." Daimon winked at Gaitlan, leaving him with more questions than answers.

After cleaning his bowl and changing out of his damp robe, Gaitlan crashed on top of his bedroll. There he stayed until Mirra shook him away several hours later.

"Lan, it's time to eat."

"Already did," he mumbled, rubbing the sleep from his

eyes. The scent of freshly baked bread wafted from her clothes and hair, making his stomach growl. Heat burned at the base of his neck, but Mirra didn't seem to notice.

"You look like death."

"Thanks a lot," he grumbled, getting to his feet. "I'm sure anyone would if they'd been up before dawn and questioned within an inch of their life."

Mirra's brows furrowed. Her grip on his arm was tight. "Questioned?"

Gaitlan placed his hand on top of hers. "The masters 'examined' me today. Were you?"

Mirra shook her head. "I'm going tomorrow."

"Good luck."

Mirra snorted and headed toward the hearth to receive her portion of dinner. Having already eaten, Gaitlan bypassed the line, picking two still-warm rolls and a tankard of cool water before looking for a seat. He spied Daimon sitting near the same spot from before, enthralled in a conversation with another young man. Daimon reached up, brushing a stray lock from the young man's face before leaning in for a kiss.

Realization erupted. Daimon's eyes locked on Gaitlan as he deepened his kiss. Gaitlan blushed, turning away. He chose a seat where his back faced Daimon and ate in terse silence.

THERE WAS NO SIGN THAT A BATTLE TOOK PLACE IN THE road, yet they were confident that this was the place where they lost a comrade. Each creature felt the loss akin to a missing limb; gone, yet somehow still hurting.

The leader got down from his horse, gathering a bit of dirt in his hand. Holding it up to his nose, he inhaled, separating each scent that lingered in the space between the grains of sand until he zeroed in on the one scent he needed. The bitch that killed his brother. The prince's smell was there, but it was of little importance to him. He'd get revenge on that bitch once and for all.

The trail led into the woods. Standing on the edge, the creatures picked up another scent that hung overall beneath the shadows of the trees.

Identical ruthless grins spread across the four mercenaries' faces. The Ilmarrion bastard had taken one of their own. It was only fair that they paid her back in kind.

THE MONOTONY OF THE NEXT FIVE DAYS BEGAN TO WEAR on Gaitlan. It didn't help that he only got a few hours of sleep between his nightmares. Every day, he woke up before the sun even started to rise over the horizon, to spend all day in the elements, keeping stupid beasts from walking headfirst into their demise. Then bone-weary and aching, he trudged back to the house, shoveling food he barely tasted into his mouth before collapsing beneath the threadbare sheets of his bedroll before the sun disappeared below the horizon again.

He saw so little of Mirra that he feared that she'd abandoned him on the island to live out the remainder of his days as a nameless face amongst the rest.

The masters had yet to call him back to discuss their decision, which added to his frustration.

"Oi, Lan! You hungry!"

Daimon waved at Gaitlan from atop a small boulder. "I managed to sneak something extra tasty from the kitchens today." Daimon removed a small bundle from inside his sleeve. "That friend of yours knows some delicious recipes."

Daimon unwrapped the bundle, revealing several sweet cakes so fresh steam still rolled off them in the chilly air.

Gaitlan picked up a cinnamon swirl roll covered in thin icing. He held it up to his face and breathed in the spicy aroma. It smelled of home. Tears welled in the corners of Gaitlan's eyes. He hastily wiped them away with the edge of his robe before Daimon noticed.

"She picks things up wherever she goes," he said, taking a bite. Gaitlan's eyes rolled back into his head. How many years had it been since he tasted something so delicious, heartwarming, so comforting? The fact that Mirra was the one who made it held no bearing on its flavor. Daimon could have told him that the sweet rolls had come straight from Verance that morning, and he wouldn't have questioned it.

"I can imagine. I heard the masters were impressed during her examination. They offered her a seat in any of their courses right then and there."

The sweet roll turned to cement. Gaitlan forced it down with half the water remaining in his skin. "She's already banded?"

"Not yet. There's gonna be a big celebration in a couple of weeks. They like to move large groups to 'encourage bonding' as if we need any excuse to bond, eh, Lan?"

Daimon's suggestive smirk fell when he took note of Gaitlan's face.

"What's wrong."

Gaitlan blinked a few times before answering. "Nothing. I just got something stuck in my throat. Thanks for the snack. See you later."

He rose and walked away without leaving Daimon any chance to respond.

She's leaving me behind after she promised to stay with me.

They had come to the island to figure out their next steps together as a pair, as partners, and now, once again, Mirra was leaving him behind for a world he couldn't be part of. Clearly, the masters thought him unsuitable for any field of study. Otherwise, they would have already summoned him. Gaitlan collapsed to the ground, heedless of the small stones that dug into his knees. Several of the goats and sheep crept closer, drawn in by the sweet aroma of the bun that still lingered on his skin.

Throwing his head back, Gaitlan screamed, with no one to hear him but the sea and the cruel gods that delighted in reminding him just how useless he was.

THANK YOU AGAIN," MIRRA SAID, BOWING DEEPLY TO THE three masters.

"Don't mention it," Medadh said with a wave of her hand. "You know where to find me if you should change your mind."

"As with me," Ujurak said.

"She's made her decision," Nen joked, throwing his arm around Mirra's shoulder. "You can't steal her away now."

Ujurak shook his head while Medadh made a crude gesture over her shoulder as they left.

"In a few weeks, there will be a ceremony for all those who are to be banded. You'll get a new robe and move the houses set aside for your group."

"Group? Not class?"

Nen shook his head. "We don't want to instill division amongst the different orders. We all work together to achieve similar goals. So those who are to join the ranks will live together. This helps to foster unity as well as the free exchange of ideas."

"Makes sense. What about Lan, the guy I came with? Did he do well during his examination?"

Nen frowned slightly. "He is a difficult person to place. He has a good foundation of knowledge. He's particularly skilled in diplomacy and strategic warfare, but to make those strengths translate into something purposeful here?" Nen waved his hands in front of him.

Mirra chewed the corner of the thumb. "Lan is a good fighter, but he's also been through a lot since the death of his parents."

Nen nodded. "Actually, I wondered if you could provide any additional input that might help us place him?"

"I think it might be better to put him in a place where he isn't comfortable. The Smelters deal with repairing and building as much as they do defense, but those are his strong suits."

"Do you think he'd fare well with the Binders?"

Mirra snorted, her hand slapping across her mouth. "God's no. I think he'd run a blade through his heart out of boredom. He cares more about forging history than preserving it."

"So that leaves the Alchemists."

"I guess so," Mirra said. "It might shock him, but it could help to break him free from whatever is holding him back."

"And what about what's holding you back, Ilmarrion?"

Mirra stopped dead in her tracks, magic bubbling behind her eyes.

"Peace, I mean no harm. Do you think the Abbot is the only one who knows your and the prince's identities?"

"I'd hoped so."

Nen chuckled, clasping his fingers under his chin. "Oh, my young one, you still have so much more to learn."

Daimon snagged Mirra's arm the moment she entered the House of the Unbanded.

"Hey, Mir; have you seen Lan?"

She shook her head. "Isn't he back already?"

Daimon released her arm to chew his nails. "I haven't seen him since I brought him the sweet rolls you made."

"Okay. Did something happen?"

Daimon ran a hand through his hair. "I told him you were already chosen by the masters. His face went scarily blank, and then he stormed off. The lads that are in charge of the herds haven't seen him since then either. You don't think he'd ..."

"No."

Mirra stormed into the house, snatching her bow and

quiver from the weapons cache. She barreled back out, heedless of the startled stares that followed.

He wouldn't. Gaitlan wouldn't be as stupid to take his own life over a silly test to get into an order that he didn't even want to be a part of, to begin with. But he'd been slipping since the death of his parents. His mind wasn't entirely in the right frame. Who knows what the breaking point of a person would be? Sometimes it could be something absolutely minuscule. Mirra ran faster, her legs and lungs burning. Not now, not after everything they've been through, everything they still needed to do.

She found him sitting on the edge of one of the many cliffs on the island, his feet swinging over the edge. His face was turned toward the same direction as Undros as if he could see his homeland if he looked hard enough.

"Gaitlan," Mirra gasped.

Gaitlan turned, his eyes nearly as void as the day she whisked him out of Verance.

"What are you doing?"

He pulled his feet back over the edge, slowly standing. "Thinking."

Mirra took a cautious step forward. "Thinking about what?"

Gaitlan turned and looked across the gray sea, defeat written on every inch of his body.

"What's the point? What am I even trying to do?"

Another step. "You're trying to take your kingdom back from the man who killed your parents and save your sister."

"What have I done to accomplish that? All I've managed

to do is hang onto your coattails. I've done nothing ... I am ... nothing."

The wind picked up, causing Gaitlan to teeter on the edge. Mirra dropped her bow, springing across the remaining distance to reach him. Digging her fingers into his arm, she wretched him away from the edge.

"You're a damned fool; that's what you are! What you need to do is get your head out of your ass and see that you've done the best, given the circumstances."

Gaitlan yanked his arms free. "What do you know! You try to leave me at every given chance. You're all that I have. The only one I can trust, can turn to. How can you leave me so easily?"

Mirra looked at him, confusion written all over her face. "Where am I supposed to be going?"

Gaitlan growled in frustration. "The masters have offered you a space. While I am left here to become the king of shepherds, ruler of goats and sheep!"

Mirra stepped forward slowly, her hand stretched out between them. "They've chosen you too, Gaitlan. You were just a little harder to place. We're staying together like I promised. I'm with you until the end."

Gaitlan looked at Mirra, his eyes wide. He reached out and clasped her forearm, pulling her in close. He wrapped his arms around her, burying his face into the crook of her neck. Mirra patted his back briefly before pulling back.

"Are you all right?" Her gaze bore into his, searching for any sign that he would harm himself if she let go.

Gaitlan reached his hand up to cup her cheek.

Mirra frowned slightly, attempting to pull out of his touch, but Gaitlan held her face with both his hands. Before Mirra could protest, Gaitlan brought his mouth crashing onto hers.

HER LIPS WERE AS SWEET AS SUMMER BERRIES. HE reached A hand back to cup the back of her head as he deepened the kiss. Her hands moved from his arms to his chest, resting over the frantic beating of his heart. The wind grew stronger, nearly pulling them apart, so he tightened his grip.

Soon the need for air grew too demanding to ignore. Gaitlan leaned back, smiling down at Mirra.

Stars erupted behind his eyes.

Stars and pain.

"What in the hel are you thinking! I was trying to stop you from throwing yourself off a cliff, not admitting any romantic feelings for you."

Gaitlan rubbed the place where Mirra struck him. Indignation molded with anger, turning into a spiteful poison that clouded his mind. "We're supposed to be together. You saved me, cared for me, and fought alongside me. Why should she get all your affection while I languish on the edges of your consciousness?"

Mirra stared open-mouthed. Gaitlan moved to embrace her again, but she stepped back, shaking her head. "Don't you touch me. What gives you the right to question my relationships, dictate who I should feel attraction to?"

"I met you first," Gaitlan said, continuing forward. "We

formed a connection. You can't deny that there's something between us."

Mirra continued to shake her head, pain splattered on her face. For every step she took backward, Gaitlan took two forwards until he could gently hold her arms.

"I know this is a confusing time, but why should we keep denying ourselves what we want?"

He leaned in for another kiss. White-hot rage coursed through Mirra. Curling her fist, she struck Gaitlan across the face and in the diaphragm in quick succession. Gaitlan fell to the ground, gasping, blood oozing from his lip.

"If I did what I wanted, I would have left you in Croglen and disappeared. I would have stayed in Moakwyd with my people. I would have never agreed to help Bossman Jax kill the High Priest of Yulla. I would have never signed my life away so I could live past twelve! My life has never been about what I wanted, and someone like you would never understand that!"

Mirra ran away, letting her feet carry her wherever they willed. It didn't matter where she ran to; she'd still have to return to Gaitlan ... eventually.

She ran until she breathed fire instead of air. Hands on her knees, she gulped for air. How could he? How dare he! Straightening, Mirra swept back the sweaty strands of hair plastered to her forehead. She started to pace, her hands on her waist, going round and round, cursing his very existence. This is why she kept people at arm's length. If she let people get too close, they start to get funny ideas that will undoubtedly destroy everything she'd worked so hard for.

Oya wasn't like that.

Mirra took a step and met only air. She whooped as the ground gave way beneath her feet, sending her plummeting into the unknown. She tried to catch a ledge, but there was nothing but open space around her. Somewhere in the darkness below, the bits of the cliffside that fell before her crashed against something hard.

As fast as she could, Mirra drew a rune for protection in the air in front of her. It shimmered white before spreading to form a sphere of light around her. With its light, Mirra could now see the instrument of her demise rapidly approaching. She sent a wave of her magic downward, hoping to either slow her descent or cushion her fall. The sphere of protection bounced against her wall of shadows and shattered. Mirra tumbled to the ground, scraping and bruising her body against the debris.

Coughing and sputtering, she pushed herself up, peering into the darkness around her. Bits of rock and sand still fell, forcing Mirra to linger against the wall. A faint light shone from the opening above, washing the open space in gray light. Once it appeared that no more rocks and debris were going to fall, Mirra stepped away from the wall, her hands raised slightly, magic waiting just in case.

After a few tense moments, she relaxed and slowly turned about to better grasp her situation. At first, she thought she'd fallen into a small cave of some sort. Still, the oddly uniform shape of some of the walls and the smoothness of the ground beneath her feet suggested otherwise.

Mirra pooled her magic in the palm of her hands until it turned into a small orb. Over the orb, she drew the rune for light. The black orb transformed into a small sun or star, casting enough light to fully illuminate the room around her. Mirra gently tossed the burning orb into the air where it remained, rising slowly until its light stretched to all corners of the space.

Standing in the middle of the room, Mirra spun around, looking for any signs of an exit. She couldn't see one from where she stood, but she did notice four alcoves carved into the wall. She walked over to one, the orb of light following overhead. Inside the alcove, there was a mosaic piece depicting a young man holding something in his hand. Mirra wiped away dust and grime to see the image better. It was a burning lamp, the color of blood. Around the youth, there appeared to be the bodies of the dying. The bodies at the youth's feet didn't make any sense to Mirra because their face wasn't twisted or hateful; it was kind and comforting.

Leaving the alcove, Mirra went to the next one to see if it, too, bore an odd mosaic image. The following image was of a young girl sitting on a stone, playing the flute. Her eyes were covered by a cloth band, and several roads spiraled out from beneath the rock from whence she sat.

"A flute and a bloody lamp …"

The sound of crumbling rocks drew Mirra's attention away from the alcoves and back to the open space of space.

"Gods above," Mirra whispered, her blood running cold. Beneath the heaps of earth and stone laid a mosaic floor ripped from her nightmares.

Mirra cleared away the debris and dirt with a wave of her hand, leaving the tiled floor pristine and illuminated. Like her nightmares, the images created told a story. This time, she was determined to pay attention to it.

She walked around the images twice to discern the beginning of the story, and when she did, what unfolded turned her stone to lead.

The land was once green and good. Humans and Ilmarrions lived in peace. The humans had fled their lands, carrying a tale about a demon that ate all life; it didn't matter, people, plants, animals. The Ilmarrion elders heard their warning and began developing relics in preparation for the demon's arrival. They made five relics; four to weaken, one to imprison. One day, the land began to turn, crops withered, streams dried up, friends turned on one another; the demon had arrived. The Ilmarrions tried to use the relics to defeat the monster, but it didn't work.

The queen of the humans suggested using her people to wield the relics since humans have no power to interfere with the relics' purpose. Four humans were chosen, and this time, they were successful in imprisoning the demon. The world healed, returning to as it had been before, and a great time of peace followed.

"Until the humans turned on the Ilmarrions," Mirra said to no one.

Mirra glanced at the remaining two alcoves, suspecting they would depict two more items, relics, giving hints about the nature of their abilities. The one thing that was missing was the fifth relic, the prison for the demon.

There was an empty space in the center of the mosaic story just large enough for a pedestal to sit. She stood on the open space and saw that the alcoves crisscrossed on the point where she stood. Dread filled her stomach as the ancient tale written on the floor sounded nearly identical to the present day.

"Mirra, are you all right!"

Gaitlan peered over the edge of the cave-in, worry

etched over his face. "Are you hurt? Can you move?"

"I'm fine, uninjured. Go to the keep and summon the Abbot and the other masters. Tell them the Ilmarrion found something."

Gaitlan jerked back. "Are you sure?"

"Yes, now go!"

Gaitlan disappeared, leaving Mirra alone with the ghosts of the past.

Gaitlan ran as fast as his legs could carry him along the dirt path that led to The Keep. He ignored the stares as he barreled past supplicants at their posts. He ran up the steps of The Keep two or three at times, ramming himself into the door, leaving it wide in his wake.

"I need the Abbot or the masters," he gasped to the startled students inside. "Now," he bellowed when no one made a move.

"Now, what's all this?" Master Nen asked, walking up from behind. "Lan, my boy, what's the meaning of all this?"

Gaitlan turned to face the master, a moment of hesitation freezing the message Mirra tasked him to pass on. She trusted the masters, and the Abbot knew who they were. He closed his eyes and swallowed his fear. "The Ilmarrion has found something. I need the Abbot and the other masters."

Master Nen's face didn't change. "Where?"

"Near the southwestern ridge. There was a cave-in. Mirra fell and found something interesting."

Master Nen nodded and turned to the supplicants with black and green bands around their hems. "Go fetch your masters. Tell them the same message Lan told me. And let them know I am fetching the Abbot."

The supplicants bowed and then turned to carry out their directives.

"Oh, and tell Medadh that we'll need something to get in and out of the cave-in."

CHAPTER EIGHTEEN

LIFE IN MOAKWYD RETURNED TO NORMAL SHORTLY AFTER Mirra's and Gaitlan's departure. That is the nature of life, ever moving forward, with minor blips of excitement. Each day, the sun rose and set on the Ilamrrions clinging to the crumbling ways of their past; though for one, their heart now looked more outward than it had before.

Every morning, Oya returned to the small space she claimed as her own, performing the same ritual she did the day Mirra left. She prayed to the Ileing, to the All-Mother of her clan, and to her ancestors to watch over Mirra and begrudging the prince as well. To keep them from harm and to help them succeed so that Mirra could return to her.

It had never occurred to Oya to leave until much later, but neither had Mirra offered. Perhaps she, too, hadn't thought about it, or maybe she knew that Oya's place was still in Moakwyd.

Oya gathered the implements of her ritual with a heavy heart. Maybe she could go to the Holy Isle herself and join Mirra in her quest. Surely the high priestess wouldn't oppose her leaving. She could mask her eyes to conceal her identity.

A silent alarm jarred Oya's bones, forcing her to drop the items in her hands.

"To the citadel, everyone! Leave everything and come!"

Usoa's voice rang throughout the air, solid and clear. However, Oya detected a hint of apprehension in her tone.

Feet flying against the paved stone, Oya ran to the Citadel, urging everyone she saw to hurry toward the sanctuary of the temple. The compiled eyes wide with fear, children crying in their parents' arms. Oya spied Roux issuing commands to the scouts, armor strapped over her clothing.

Panic urged her feet faster, even though they were already burning. She skipped up the steps, offering a helping hand when one of the panicking masses stumbled on the crumbling steps.

"High Priestess," Oya shouted once she spied Usoa.

The high priestess stood atop the stairs, directing people and members of the order with equal precision.

"Gather all the healing elixirs on hand and start making more. We will need fresh water and bandages, just in case. Get the kitchens going and make the people something to eat. Something sweet too for the younglings. Anyone with combative and defensive abilities need to be called up. Hopefully, the barrier will last, but if it doesn't ..."

Her words fell off. She didn't need to explain what would happen if the barrier failed. It would mark the end of them all. The barrier had been erected in ancient times to ward against the most dangerous of foes. If it stirred again ...

Oya's thoughts turned to a small island nestled safely in

the sea, protected by the vast kingdoms of this world. For the first time, she was glad that Mirra had left. Her only regret, should things go sideways, was that she never got a chance to tell her how she felt.

Oya shed her priestess robe for fighting gear, grabbing a staff gifted to her by her father on the day of her first moonblood. The power stored within the staff hummed under her touch. This was her home, and she would defend it, and there was someone she wanted to see again.

THE LONGER MIRRA STARED AT THE MOSAIC FLOOR, THE greater the hollow feeling in her stomach grew. She paced around the outer edge of the pictures, her eyes scanning for any detail, no matter how small. Perhaps she was completely mistaken, and the dreadful thought that was solidifying was completely wrong.

A shower of dirt and small pebbles showed down on her head, heralding the arrival of someone.

"Are you well, young Mirra?"

Mirra breathed a sigh of relief at the sound of Abbot Josef's voice.

"For the moment."

"Heads up," Medadh shouted before a heavy rope came cascading down. Wooden pegs were woven in along the length of the rope, making it a precarious ladder. "We're coming to you."

Mirra held on to the rope's end to offer some stability as Abbot Josef, the four masters, and Gaitlan climbed down to her.

"By the gods," Ujurak said, his voice soft. "I thought this was destroyed centuries ago."

Abbot Josef's face was pained as he looked about the space. "It was never lost, only hidden."

"You knew it was here," Mirra accused.

"Only that it existed, not its location." He paused, staring at the blank pace in the center of the room. "This is not the place for such a story. Medadh, see what can be done to secure the opening. I don't want anyone else to fall in. Nen, I need you to find the Book of Five and bring it to my study. Ujurak, tend to the injuries Lady Mirra sustained during her decent."

"I used magic to brace my fall; I'm fine."

Abbot Josef placed his large, warm hand on Mirra's shoulder. His eyes were filled with a warmth Mirra was unfamiliar with. "Indulge an old man, will you, my dear? I need time to collect my thoughts. There is a story to tell, and it's not pleasant."

Abbot Josef's study was as chaotic as the day she first stepped in it, though the Abbot had cleared off a few of the buried chairs.

She let Ujurak administer medicine to her minor injuries, if only to appease the Abbot and hear his tale. Gaitlan remained standing, leaning against the wall furthest away from Mirra. She guessed he was still a little sore over her rejection, but at least he was willing to set that aside for the greater good.

Medadh and Nen entered the study simultaneously, the latter carrying a large, ancient-looking, leather-bound book.

"I secured a bit of netting over the opening. It should keep away even the most curious of our people, but they will need answers soon."

Abbot Josef nodded, accepting the tome from Nen. "And

they will have it." He ran his long brown fingers over the cover of the book, a variety of emotions flashing across his face, guilt being the more prominent.

"I never took much stock in the financial legends of heroes, magic wielders, or the gods. I am a practical man by nature. If I can see it and touch it, it's real. But even I understood that buried beneath all the fanatical parts were bits of hidden truths lost to time. There have been many scholars who spend their lives, digging for the truths beneath the myths. Two such men arrived on the Ilse, not long after I assumed the mantle of Abbot. I believe you both know one of them intimately."

"Lord Julian," Gaitlan said, his voice dripping with venom.

Abbot Josef nodded. "At first, he was like so many others who come to this island for the library within The Keep. However, Julian was more interested in figuring out if the Ilmarrions had ever existed. He believed they were a real race of people predated humans and that most of our civilization was built off their ruins."

Mirra scoffed. "Well, he wasn't wrong about that."

"Along the way, he and his friend became obsessed with a particular story, the one written here in this book. If I had only stopped them."

"You couldn't have known what would happen, Abbot."

"No, but there are some things that should be left alone, and this was one of them because what they discovered was much worse."

CURSE THOSE LIGHT AFFLICTED SORCERERS AND THEIR POISONOUS charms. The attack on Moakwyd hadn't entirely gone as the mercenaries had hoped. The barrier around the Ilmarrion city was too strong, their defenses too ready for the four of them. In the end, they'd only been able to injure a few before they were forced to flee.

They'd shown their hand too early, let their vengeance blind them to their need of secrecy. They'd hoped their master would never hear of their failed attempt at revenge, and possibly tipping off the one race of people who actually knew how to defeat him.

Perhaps if they were able to capture the Ilmarrion woman and prince, he'd …

He'd what? roared a voice inside their head. Look over the fact that you blithering imbeciles thought you could make a decision that I wouldn't know about!

The mercenaries screamed in pain as their muscles ceased, causing them all to fall from their horses, convulsing on the forest floor.

Remember, there is nothing that I don't see, nothing that I don't know. You come from me. Every part of you owes its continued existence to me.

The pain subsided, allowing the mercenaries to breathe freely.

I don't care if you all die in the process; get me that woman!

The presence of their master faded away, leaving them hollow and beaten. They pushed themselves to their feet, remounted their beasts, and followed their prey's scent trail out of the woods. They would find their master's prize, but they would have a bit of fun with her to pay back for all the suffering they had to go through because she foolishly thought she'd escape him. No one ever escapes.

THEY FOUND THE RELICS, DIDN'T THEY?"

"Yes. At first, I was as fascinated by the relics as they were. I couldn't tap into the power trapped within, but I could feel it brimming just beneath the surface. Magic, real magic, had once existed in the world. We thought it could exist again."

"All things have a time on this earth," Ujurak said. "You should have left it alone."

"We all would have done the same thing, Ujurak," Medadh countered. "None of us here are actually priests. We're all practical people. How many times have you been swept up in the discovery of some new concoction?"

Ujurak narrowed his eyes but held his tongue.

"But we should always know when to stop," Nen said softly.

"And Julian did not," Abbot Josef said. "One day, there was a great rumbling on the island, followed by one of the worst storms to date. I never saw Julian again after that, but his friend ... his friend arrived a few days later, covered in blood, with a look on his face that I still see in my dreams."

"I'm sorry, he told me, clutching the relics and broken prison in his arms. I didn't know ... my friend ... I'm sorry."

A heavy silence fell over the room after Abbot Josef finished his story. The masters' faces were stoic and unreadable, their minds already whirling with possible solutions to the problem, of ways they could help.

"So you're saying that Lord Julian is possessed by some ancient evil force?" Gaitlan chuckled hysterically. "So I should run a blade through my heart before he devours me too?"

"No," Abbot Josef said. "We do what our ancestors did. What this book tells us to do."

He opened the book, its spine cracking from disuse. "You and Mirra must find the relics and reseal the evil that lives inside Lord Julian."

"Reseal in what," Mirra asked. "The jail was broken."

Abbot Josef shook his head and stood, reaching for a box that sat on the shelf behind him. "It was only cracked, and that crack was enough to release the great evil into the world."

From the box, he revealed a cracked crystal orb, no larger than a sweet melon. A long crack nearly cleaved the sphere in two, but otherwise, it was whole. Even in its fractured form, Mirra felt the layers of magic rippling off it. She reached out her hands to take it from Abbot Josef.

He tipped the orb into her hands, and just like when she touched the face of God so many years ago in the Temple of Yulla, the power of the orb burned along her body. She hissed but kept her hold onto the orb.

A bit of The Eater's essence still lingered within the confines of the orb. It battered against the broken prison, looking for any way to escape. Something about the hungry darkness called to the darkness that dwelled inside her, beckoning to become one.

"Mirra, Mirra, Mirra!"

Someone called her name over and over again. The darkness that lingered inside the orb was nearly at her fingertips. The connection was severed sharply, sending Mirra stumbling back into something warm and sturdy.

Gaitlan wrapped an arm protectively around her middle, his hand going to cup her ice-cold face. "Mirra, speak to me! What happened?"

"What is your affinity?" Abbot Josef asked, holding the orb once more. "Are you of the Nexi, the Shadow Walkers?"

Mirra could only nod her head, her strength utterly spent.

"What does that have to do with anything?" Gaitlan spat.

"Like calls to like," Nen said. "From my understanding, those who are claimed by the Nexi have abilities akin to The Eater. It wants to destroy all life. They draw their power from the absence of life. A small difference with tremendously different approaches." Nen rubbed his chin. "It could mean that you are more susceptible to this demon's power. You could be the key to his ultimate success."

"What about Julian?" Mirra asked. "He has Ilmarrion blood in him, as evident by his eyes. That was enough for The Eater to manipulate. Your blood, however, is more powerful."

Mirra's legs gave out beneath her. She should have died. Should have let herself meet the gallows that day in the dungeon. She should have died a hundred times in the streets of the Merchant District. She should have died in that cesspool of an orphanage her parents left her in. She should have never been born.

Never been born? Never know Bao, Em, Kril, Tull, and Sorro? Never experience the gentle care of Brian? Learn to read with Nora? Befriend Braelyn? Meeting High Priestess Usoa? Oya ... It didn't matter what evil force wanted to use her, there were too many good things in her life; things she hadn't always appreciated, that she was glad to have. There were still things she wanted to do, places to explore, facets of herself to discover.

Using Gaitlan as a crutch, Mirra pulled herself up. "Send the orb to High Priestess Usoa. Ask her to fix it. It doesn't matter what we do if we don't have a place to put it." She eyed the book on the table. "Could you send the book as well?"

"Of course," Nen said, stepping forward. "It is their history, after all. Perhaps, in the future, we could help your people reconnect with your past."

"After The Eater was freed, I received a surprise visit from your high priestess. I still don't know how she managed to appear in my dreams, but she berated me for not heeding the warnings written in her people's stolen history. I tried to defend my ignorance, but she can be quite forceful when provoked. The next time we spoke was when she reached out, seeking sanctuary for the two of you. It is past time I extended the same branch of communication. What you ask shall be done."

"Thank you," Mirra said. She then turned to Master Nen. "I guess we should get started. I need to have as much information as possible before we leave."

"Come with me, prince," Ujurak beckoned. "You have a fine mastery of the sword. It is time you learn something new. I warn you now; I am not an easy teacher."

"Come find me if you need to work out your anger," Medadh called out. "It was through unity we first defeated that bastard, and with unity, we will defeat him again."

Hope blossomed in the dark pit of Gaitlan's heart. Yes, they were up against a force with unimaginable strength and abilities, but they faced it together. He was no longer alone.

THE URGE TO RAZE EASTPORT TO THE GROUND SET THEIR teeth on edge. That and the strength of the scent that led them there. Their prey was only a few days ahead of them. Soon enough, they would slate their hunger for blood. The mercenaries split up following a split in the trail. One trail led the leader of the mercenaries to a well-to-do tavern, reeking with the stench of humans. If not for his driving anger, the leader was almost certain he'd have lost her scent amongst the unwashed masses.

He followed the girl's scent to a table where an over-flounced man sat, with his feet crossed on the table. The man eyed the mercenaries with suspicion, his hand sliding to the blade at his side.

"What can I do for you, gentlemen?"

"Have you seen a young woman with unnatural blue eyes traveling with a man?"

"Can't say that I have, sorry."

The leader of the mercenaries growled. "You're lying. I smell her on you."

"Look here, friend," the man said, swinging his feet to the floor. "I haven't seen any girl like that here or anywhere. I've only just gotten back to port."

The mercenary lashed out, grabbing the man by the throat. The man struggled in vain to free himself, his skin becoming red and blotchy. "The name of your ship."

"The Fallen Star."

A fine red mist splattered the mercenary's face, and the man went limp in his grip. "Thank you."

The mercenary dropped the man like a sack of potatoes, turning his attention to the patrons of the inn who had gathered at his back, blades drawn.

Twin feral smiles, too large to fit on their mortal bodies, stretched across the mercenaries' faces. They threw themselves into the fray, swinging, stabbing, and slashing with wanton delight as the screams of the dying filled the air. The other two mercenaries soon joined in, drawn to the inn by the scent of blood and death. They'd slaughter everyone in the inn and anyone who dared to oppose them on the way to the Fallen Star. From there, they find where the little bitch had run off to.

OTHER THAN THE ORB, THERE ARE FOUR RELICS IN ALL. The Seed of Life, The Song of Heaven, The Blood Lamp, and The Phoenix's Wing. Each one possesses a unique ability tied to one of the four pillars of Ilmarrion magic. The Seed with Fasht. Song with Su'la. The Blood Lamp with Düa, and The Wing with Harar."

Mirra flipped through The Book of Five while Master Nen gave her the crash course of its contents. "I guess that means the orb is tied to the Nexi?"

"Perhaps," Master Nen admitted. "Although I don't think any of your kind were around at the time of creation."

Mirra made a noncommittal noise, turning another page.

In The Book of Five, there were detailed descriptions of what a wielder could do with a relic and the cost of using them. The relics weren't a free pass to unlimited power. They were unique in the way that they were, more of a focus for power. The power still had to come from somewhere.

"How are we to find the wielders?" Gaitlan asked. A large red mark spread across one of his cheeks as a result of the long hours spent leaning on his palm while he agonized through the book Master Ujurak gave him to memorize.

"That, I don't know," Master Nen said, rubbing his chin. "Only Abbot Josef knows the name of the man that fled with the relics. But in the subsequent years, he has yet to relocate him."

Mirra turned another page in the book, and her heart leaped into her throat. She pulled the book close to her face, her eyes boring holes into the illuminated drawing on the page.

Mirra threw her head back and cackled. "That sneaky woman."

Both Master Nen and Gaitlan stared at her in alarm. Mirra thrust the book under Gaitlan's nose.

"Do you recognize anything about this picture? And I mean anything."

Gaitlan took the book and glanced down at the page Mirra indicated. It wasn't any overtly special. Just one of a dozen depictions of a relic and its wielder. This one was of The Seed of Life. A young woman wreathed in an amber light while crops grew from the ground.

"I don't know. Do you recognize the tree line or mountains in the background?"

Mirra rolled her eyes and tapped the necklace the

woman wore around her neck. The necklace was nothing more than a brown streak against the white of the woman's dress, but the pendant stood out like a drop of blood. Much like the …

"The high priestess!"

Mirra nodded, nearly bouncing in her seat. "She has The Seed."

"That makes no sense," Master Nen said. "Ilmarrions couldn't use the relics, for whatever reason. What use would she have of it?"

"Nothing," Mirra said, "but that's not the point. Where did she get it?"

Understanding shone through Master Nen's eyes, his mouth forming a small o. "The man."

"He must have stumbled onto Moakwyd or gone looking for it," Gaitlan said. "He must have been looking for places to hide the relics to keep them out of its hands."

All the joy of discovery deflated out of Mirra with a straightforward question. "Why didn't she tell me?"

Gaitlan slumped in his chair, brought down by the question as well. Not telling him wasn't a big deal. He was an outsider and heir to the crown that drove her people to near extinction, but Mirra. Mirra was one of their own. They celebrated her discovery, welcomed her with open arms. Why hadn't the high priestess told Mirra that The Eater had been released and that she possessed one of the relics that could shackle him?

Master Nen reached out, gently touching Mirra on the arm. "Only she could tell you why. Perhaps she hoped that nothing would come of that demon regaining its freedom. It was jailed for centuries beyond count. She could have been waiting for the right time to tell you. A nasty habit of us, teachers. We want you to come to your own conclusions and decisions about things. This means that we often withhold vital information until you've done the work to receive it with the 'right frame of mind.'"

"That's a load of bullshit," Mirra said, crossing her arms.

Master Nen shrugged his shoulders. "That, it may be, but please withhold judgment until you find out for yourself."

"Now you know where to start," Abbot Josef said, walking into the library. "What we have is yours until you can leave."

"What do you mean?"

"We have no ships here, none that can cross large open waters. You must wait for a larger ship to arrive."

"And just how long might that be?" Gaitlan asked.

"No more than a week," Master Nen replied. "We get regular shipments in and off the island."

Mirra did a few calculations in her head. "So, any day now?"

Both Abbot Josef and Master Nen shrugged their shoulders.

Gaitlan ran his hands through his hair. "Great. Well, since we don't know when we're sailing off, do you think I could write a few letters. I have some friends in the other kingdoms. They might not have bought Julian's lies. We might need their armies in the end."

"That's actually a good idea," Mirra said.

Gaitlan tried to not look offended. "I've been known to have them."

Mirra made a face with a teasing smirk. "If you say so, princeling." She stood, gathering The Book of Five and other historical text into her arms. "Well, we have a lot to do in a discriminate amount of time; best get to it, then."

THE GULLS SQUAWKED AND FOUGHT WITH ONE ANOTHER over the tenderest portions of the rotting corpses that littered the deck of the Fallen Star. Some of the ships had been laid to ruin, shattered, and scorched, yet enough remained for her to limp along the waves toward a small island in the middle of the sea.

If what the sailors confessed before meeting their paltry gods was true, the mercenaries knew they would have to tread carefully and quickly.

At the helm, the leader of the mercenaries kept the ship at the proper heading. The wind in his face distorted his target's scent. Still, on it, he detected something old, something familiar, something that could mean the end of his master's plan, should it ever make it off the island.

He and his men would ensure that it ceased to exist. Then nothing would stand in their way.

What a fine day for hunting it was turning out to be.

CHAPTER NINETEEN

THANK YOU FOR HANDLING THIS FOR ME," MIRRA SAID, handing over a sealed letter.

"Not at all," Abbot Josef replied. "I'm only glad I was able to help, in any capacity."

A series of sharp raps at the door drew their attention. The woman who greeted them at the docks pushed the door open. Her face was just as serious as the day they met. Yet, Abbot Josef picked up on something just under the surface.

"What is it, Largath?"

"Dark tidings." She held a tiny bit of parchment between her fingers. "I have a friend in Eastport who raises messenger birds. I've been working with them to improve our communication with the outside world."

Abbot Josef nodded.

Largath continued. "She's written that an inn in Eastport was burned to the ground, and a ship stolen."

The bottom of Mirra's stomach twisted into knots. "What ship?" she asked, half fearing the answer she knew was coming.

"The Fallen Star."

Things moved quickly after that. Those with no combat training broth before coming to the isle and since were conscripted into service. Master Medadh assessed each combatant, assigning them to strategic points on the island.

Meanwhile, all the noncombatants were ushered into the catacombs below The Keep. The same catacombs the former residence, the Ilmarrions, used to escape the marauders that took the island for their own.

"Do we know who's on the ship?" Master Madadh asked the day Largath brought the news.

Gaitlan shook his head, but Mirra remained silent, chewing on the end of her thumb.

"Mirra?"

"During our initial escape, Gaitlan and I ran into a group of mercenaries ... mercenaries with black eyes." The room fell silent. "I was only able to kill it by mixing my magic with my blade."

"Could you do something like that now?"

Mirra shook her head. "I did it during the fight. I wasn't thinking; just acting on instinct. If I have to think about it, I can't do it, if you get my drift. I was supposed to learn more about Ilmarrion magic, but we had to leave because ... well, you know."

Master Medadh pinked the brow of her nose. "Not exactly what I'd hoped to hear, but I guess I understand. You and the prince stay together and run if things take a turn. I don't care," she said, holding up her hand to stop Gaitlan's protest. "Your survival is paramount. We will make do, fleeing to the fishing boats if we must. But you two—if you're caught or killed, if that orb gets destroyed, then all hope is lost."

"Sometimes, to win the war, you have to lose the battle," Gaitlan muttered, looking down at his feet. "That's what my father used to say every time he beat me in chess. He would make small sacrifices to keep me too focused on what was happening and not what was about to happen."

Master Madadh nodded grimly. "Your father was a wise man. You should heed his lessons."

Gaitlan fell silent, his eyes looking far into the distance.

After two tense days and nights, the Fallen Star sailed out of the mist like a harbinger of death. It sailed straight into the docks, shattering them until it ran aground on the rocky shore. Master Medadh and Largath shared a look, communicating the way only fighters can.

Largath crept toward the ship with a small squad of fighters armed with bows, staffs, and swords. Largath led the way, peering over the top of a round, battered shield and a nimble battle ax swinging loosely in her hand. Behind her, someone gagged as the overpowering smell of offal and decay wafted from the deck above.

This is too quiet, Largath thought, tightening her grip on her ax. I think we should …

Largath would never get a chance to finish her thought. An arrow through her eye silenced her forever. More arrows rained down on the small band of fighters. Not a single one would ever make the long trek back to the citadel.

Master Madadh watched higher up the road in horror, unable to run to Largath's aid because the arrows hadn't come from the ships. They'd come from the cliffs above, where billowing black smoke had already reached the gray sky.

The creatures watched with wicked glee as the small band of fighters crept down to the abandoned ship, a perfect resting place for their arrows. They rushed toward the most prominent structure on the island, setting fires as they went. If the humans thought that stone walls would protect them, they were in for a nasty surprise.

As the creatures converged on the citadel, Gaitlan watched from a vantage point on the parapets. Mirra crouched next to him, darkness shimmering over her body like a fine mist. She still claimed to be insufficient with magic, but she wielded her strange abilities with grace and accuracy to him.

"Those bastards arrived in the night." Mirra ground her teeth as she watched another building going up in flames. "It wouldn't take much for me to go down there and …"

"No," Gaitlan ordered. "This isn't some back alley fight in the Merchant District or wherever it is you learned to fight. These things won't go down easily, remember."

"But I know more now."

"And they know we know. I highly doubt they'll just let you kill them."

Two large explosions sent burning debris into the air, forcing Gaitlan and Mirra to take cover. Twin towers of black billowing smoke rose into the air, spreading in the air, completely cutting off their line of sight. Below, the sounds of curses and short orders echoed against the stone.

Mirra slumped, the glittering night around her seeping back beneath her skin. "Let's go down; there's nothing more we can do up here."

Below in the citadel, the remaining citizens of the island huddled together. The explosions rumbled deep below, sending small showers of sand and silt showering down on those below. Children cried, clutching to the adults or their parents with all the strength in their tiny bodies. Many of those clustered stared off into the distance, their eyes glazed over with old horrors.

Ina held Kov tightly to her body, speaking soothing words to him in her native language. Kov couldn't understand the meaning of her words, but sometimes messages from the heart come through, no matter the barriers.

PREPARE THE LONGFIRE," MASTER UJURAK SHOUTED.

Down the lines, his command rippled, sending members of his order scurrying to move the small clay pots into place. They moved as fast as they dared, for if a pot broke prematurely, it would mean death for all those around.

Once the all-clear had been given, Master Ujurak gave the second command. "Archers, make ready."

Dozens of bows creaked, waiting for the signal to let loose. Their arrows would shatter the pots, exposing the oil inside the air needed to make ignition. The flames would burn, no matter the wind, rain, or lack of fuel, until the fire consumed every last bit of itself.

A dark mass grew in the rolling smoke that blocked their view. "Contact front!"

Every archer swiveled their bows to point at the encroaching mass.

Mater Ujurak's eyes widened as he recognized the person approaching. "Hold your fire!" He vaulted over the hastily erected barriers just in time to catch a badly beaten and bloody Madadh.

"What happened to you?"

"They took us by surprise. Ambushed us as we tried to get back. I'm the only one ..."

Master Ujurak shushed her, brushing a strand of bloody hair aside. "They've set off smoke bombs, but we haven't seen them yet. We were about to set off the Longfire."

Master Ujurak carried Madadh behind the barricades, setting her down gently before standing to issue the command for the archers. The sooner they light the Longfire, the better chance they'd have.

A flash of silver streaked across his vision before pulling away, stained with red. Hot liquid poured from his throat, stealing his words. He raised a hand to his bleeding throat, turning around, confusion painted across his face.

Madadh stood with a bloody dagger in her hand, her mouth stretched into a too-wide smile. Master Ujurak fell to his knees, staring up at his long-time friend, wondering what would cause such a sudden betrayal.

Madadh opened her other fist, three pitch-black forms flowing from her fingers to the ground before slithering off to find their next host. The dark of Madadh's eyes grew until they were completely covered. The perfect mirror for the horror forever etched on Ujurak's face.

SCREAMS ECHOED UP THE CORRIDORS, HASTENING MIRRA'S and Gaitlan's descent. Something had changed, something dire. They just reached the main floor, set up to heal the injured, when the great doors burst open, supplicants falling like wheat before the scythe across the threshold.

At first, Mirra couldn't comprehend what her eyes were telling her. Why were the supplicants killing each other? One would strike someone down, look down at their blood-soaked hands in terror before being hit down themselves by another. And so the pattern continued until Mirra was forced to defend herself against a supplicant she'd joked with over dinner not three days before.

"Their eyes," she whispered in shock.

The supplicant she struck down winked one of his pitch-black eyes before falling into a crumpled heap on the floor. A long black serpent slithered away from underneath the body, circling up another unsuspecting victim's leg.

The creatures leaped from person to person. Sometimes, they took the shape of black serpents, and other times, they were nothing more than a fine mist, contaminating several people at once. Soon, it didn't matter if the person's eyes were black or not. A single person might have been able to maintain control over their panic, but a mob—a mob was dangerous, easily consumed by panic, and driven by the most primal portions of the human psyche.

"Gods above," Gaitlan uttered beside her. He took one look at the chaos below, grabbed Mirra's arm, and pulled her toward the nearest corridor.

"What are you doing?" Mirra shouted, pulling against Gaitlan's iron grip.

"What we promised them we would do."

"We can't just leave them!"

Gaitlan stopped whipping Mirra around to face him, his hands going to cup her face. "How is this any different from the attack on the palace? You knew then that there was no hope in victory and fled. This is the same."

The fire in Mirra's eyes faded. "I know," Mirra said, bowing her head. "But these people ... those things will ..."

"I know," Gaitlan said, his voice dripping with pain. "Lose the battle to win the war."

Mirra pushed down the ache in her heart, stepping out of Gaitlan's hold. He was right. They needed to run. They already had their packs on their back, the orb safely stowed inside, along with the letters to those they hoped would answer their pleas for help.

Together, they turned to sprint down to the catacombs, the signal for the others to flee as well when a familiar voice carried over the din.

"Peace, brothers and sisters! Peace. Lay down your arms!"

One of the fighters stilled, turning toward the source of the shouting.

Abbot Josef slowly descended the staircase, his hands stretched wide to show he carried no weapons. Mirra and Gaitlan peered at the floor above, breathing a small sigh of relief when they saw his eye's regular warm brown coloring instead of inky black.

All but four of the combatants dropped their weapons, stepping away from the slaughter committed by their hands.

The thing that possessed Madadh smirked, blood

splattered across its stolen body.

"Hand them over, holy man," the thing said, speaking through Madadh.

Abbot Josef shook his head. "I cannot. The only thing that allows evil to prevail is for good to do nothing."

The thing threw its head back and laughed. "We are not evil. We are as much a part of the natural order of the world as you are. What is life without death and suffering? Isn't that right, little Shadow Walker?"

Four heads swiveled upwards, their black gazes focused entirely on Mirra. She took a half step back, halting when their cruel laughter reached her.

Squaring her shoulders, Mirra turned to face her pursuers. "I am nothing like you. I don't spread death in my wake or take pleasure in the pain of others. Your darkness is an unnatural one brought into this world by some means of betrayal or trickery."

One of the creatures laughed. "You'd like to think that, wouldn't you? But since your education is lacking, you should really thank your people for our arrival. We haven't tasted anything as sweet as your world."

Madadh spun, slashing the speaker's neck. Black blood poured from the victim's neck until it ran red, their body falling to the floor.

The black blood flowed into a serpent, coiling around into a tight mass to protect itself.

Mirra peered down at Madadh, hoping to see her normal eyes. The black still remained. The leader silenced its subordinate before it spilled any more things that should remain secret.

"Don't go slithering off for a new host just yet," the leader ordered. "We mustn't say things that ought to remain forgotten. You know that they say 'ignorance is bliss.'"

"Don't twist words to suit your own ends," Abbot Josef said. "We will not hand Mirra or Gaitlan over to you. You must leave this place and tell your master that the world turns its eye on him. I hope he's ready for it."

Madadh chuckled. "Oh, he's ready, holy man. He's had centuries to learn from his mistakes."

Moving faster than the eye could see, Madadh surged forward, her blade sinking up to its hilt inside Abbot Josef's stomach. She pulled it free with a sickening squelch that no one left alive would ever forget.

Abbot Josef fell to his knees, his hands going to his abdomen. His life's blood poured freely over his already paling fingers, his red robe turning black.

The creatures laughed, turning their attention to the weaponless supplicants around them. Screams and the sickening scent of blood filled the once peaceful halls of the citadel. Once more, its ancient stones would drink the blood of the people who called it home.

Gaitlan tugged at Mirra, yelling words she was beyond hearing. He tried to pull her down the corridor that would take them below, but she wrenched her arm free. He attempted to grab her again, fully prepared to throw her over his shoulder, but she sent him flying with a wave of power.

Power rippled Mirra in angry waves, sending many below to the floor. The entity inside Madadh looked up at Mirra, challenging with the point of her sword.

Mirra drew her daggers, darkness pouring over them like oil. Gaitlan lunged for Mirra and missed by a hair's width. Mirra vaulted over the edge of the landing to the floor below, going into a roll the moment her feet touched the floor, springing to her feet and meeting the edge of Madadh's sword.

"Impressive."

"Go to hell!"

"No, thanks."

The other three creatures abandoned their unfettered destruction, forming a loose triangle around Mirra and their leader.

Gaitlan swore, turning to rush down to her aid and tripping over her pack. He hadn't seen her drop it before leaping to her death. He picked up and stared down at the woman, deflecting blow after blow from a creature not of this world.

She wanted him to run because she could not. When she let people behind her walls, there was nothing she wouldn't do for them. That was the same emotion that led her to risk death for Em when she was just a child. That same force allowed her to break free from Julian's control to save himself and his sister. If he didn't run, she'd never forgive him. But if he'd let her die today …

Gaitlan dropped his pack next to hers, following her footsteps, landing on top of the creatures waiting below.

A startled scream behind her caused her focus to waver for a fraction of a second, allowing the parasitic bastard inside Madadh to land a deep blow along her arm. Cursing, she spun away, spying Gaitlan locked in battle with the remaining creatures.

"Self-important bastard! I told you to run!"

"Actually, you didn't," Gaitlan shot back, slicing the creature across the chest. The host went down for a moment before standing, heedless of the blood soaking its front.

"I thought I couldn't trust you to read between the lines!"

"Reading was never my strong suit!"

"If you children would pay attention to the matter at hand," the creature snarled, lunging for Mirra with a renewed sense of ferocity.

"Here!" Mirra shouted, tossing one of her magic-soaked daggers at Gaitlan.

He caught it and landed a killing blow to his opponent.

Like before, the creatures let out a blood-curdling scream at the death of one of their own. Mirra's ears bled, but she kept fighting.

Madadh roared, tossing a dagger at Mirra.

Mirra ducked under the dagger, quickly coming back into a guard position. The triumphant look on the creature's stolen face sent a sickening wave throughout her body.

"No, no, no," she cried as Gaitlan slumped to the ground, the dagger's hilt sticking out from his heart.

Rage and regret tore through her, ripping away the last chains that held her power in check.

Mirra let go of her mortal bindings, transforming into a being of never-ending darkness and death. The world of the living shone with the blinding ferocity of a thousand suns, but not a single ray was able to penetrate her all-consuming darkness. Time ceased to have meaning as the world of light slowed to a near stop. Mirra turned to the creatures and nearly dropped her last dagger as she spied their true form.

Hundreds of hungry mouths took up nearly all of the creatures' blood-red skin, gnashing their rotting teeth. Black, oily tongues slithered out, tasting the air like lizards. They had no eyes, only the gaping mouths pulling toward the prone, bleeding bodies around them, causing the creatures to sway on heavily clawed feet.

"You see us now, Mashta," the leader of the creatures crooned, extending its spindly fingers out.

Mirra shifted into a fighting stance, her last blade angled against her forearm. "Call me that again, and I'll cut your tongue out."

The creatures laughed, every mouth on their bodies pulled back into feral grins. "That little claw won't last you forever."

"I don't have to last forever. I just have to last longer than you."

The creatures' laugh sent shivers down Mirra's spine. "Let's put that to the test, then."

They converged on Mirra as one, their midnight claws hungry for her flesh, but they only met smoke. Roaring in anger, they lunged after Mirra repeatedly, with every swipe passing through her like smoke.

Mirra's strikes, however, found their mark, splattering droplets of black ichor all over the floor of the citadel. But the creatures did not stop their onslaught until one of their strikes drew twin lines of scarlet down Mirra's arm.

She bit back her scream, maneuvering out of the

creatures' reach, gasping for air. The power that coursed through her body was retreating.

Sensing the shift in power, the creatures grinned, a cold, dark light emanating from their bodies.

"I told you your little claw wouldn't be enough to defeat us. The weapons your people crafted to kill us turned to dust centuries ago."

An image flashed from the recesses of Mirra's memory, and a desperate plan formed in her mind. She turned her attention to her only weapon, diving into the deepest part of her power. Once again, she stood on the threshold of her consciousness with the endless void on the other side. Mirra extended her dagger across the border.

Power rammed into her through the dagger, driving her to her knees. She kept her focus on the tip of her dagger until it turned the same shade of nothingness as the void in front of her, just like the knife in her dreams of the burning city.

"No!" screamed a voice from the void.

Dozens of faces emerged from nothing, each one paler than death, with dark brows over white eyes. Some of the faces were terribly young, and others were old. She even spied a few with intricate tattoos across their face like the woman from her dreams. The pair closest to her was a man and woman not much older than she was. Though much of their features were still shrouded by the void, familiarity nagged at the back of Mirra's mind.

"Do not do this thing," the faces demanded as one. "Do not give them what they want, not again."

"What should I do?"

The woman's mouth pulled back into a smile. "Trust."

The faces retreated into the void, leaving Mirra alone with her partially blackened dagger.

Mirra closed her eyes, loosening her hold, allowing the Nexi to flow back from whence it came until the only thing her dagger was imbued with was her own power. Mirra was slammed back into her physical body when the last drop fell away from the dagger's tip. Bleeding and gasping, she fell to her knees, weakly bringing up her dagger, still thinly imbued with her power. The lead creature swatted it out of her hand as if it were nothing, kicking Mirra to the floor at the same time.

"Pathetic," the creature spat. "But you won't die here today with your little friends, although you might wish you did in the end. Our master has charged us to bring you back alive. Just you. No one else."

Mirra watched, unable to move, unable to call up any more dregs of magic, as The Eater's bloodhound stalked toward her.

"I shall enjoy playing with you until I deliver you to my master. I wonder just how close to the brink I can push your body until it gives out."

"Long before yours."

Using Mirra's discarded dagger, Abbot Josef freed his long-time friend from the grasp of an ancient evil.

The creature screamed in pain, its cry shattering what remained of the glass, clawing at the dagger, buried in its right eye. Black blood oozed out of the wound, flailing around on the floor like a fish before disappearing into nothingness.

Abbot Josef caught Madadh's falling body, a ghost of a

smile on her face. "Go in peace, my friend. May your spirit find its way to the home of your gods and people. Your fight is over."

Mirra rolled over onto her stomach and pulled herself inch by inch over to where Gaitlan's body lay. Pulling up onto his chest, she buried her face and cried.

She'd failed.

Failed Braelyn.

Failed Gaitlan.

She'd promised that she'd help him reclaim his throne, free their people. Now that promise tasted like ash in her mouth.

"Mirra," Abbot Josef called, too weak to go to her. "It is all right."

"All right? All right! Gaitlan's dead! I can't save Braelyn and find the relics at the same time ... alone ... I need ..."

A large hand slid over Mirra's, drawing a gasp from her lips. "I didn't know you cared," Gaitlan said. He tried to laugh, but it quickly turned into a cough.

"What ... how?"

"I guess I was a fraction faster than it was. Remind me to thank Oya when we return to Moakwyd, all right?"

Mirra ripped open his tunic, and indeed, the dagger had plunged two inches above his heart. He still had a sword in his chest that could kill him if not removed safely, but he was alive.

Mirra sat back on her heels, buried her face in her hands, and sobbed. "I do care, you idiot. You're my friend."

Gaitlan let out a weak chuckle before lowering his head to the ground. "Well, now that's settled, can you be a lamb and fetch me a healer?"

"As you wish, princeling."

CHAPTER TWENTY

SHIPS OF ALL VARIETIES SURROUNDED THE HOLY ISLE.
Soldiers, dignitaries, and healers from four nations swarmed over
the island, putting up healing tents and questioning the island's
citizens. But no matter how many people the officials asked, the
story remained the same.

An unidentifiable band of mercenaries came to the
island, looking for their mark. They didn't believe the Abbot or
the Masters when they denied the existence of said mark, and the
rest didn't require any explanation.

Mirra and Gaitlan recovered from their injuries in the
empty rooms of the fallen masters. Whatever Gaitlan felt about
sleeping in a dead man's bed, he kept it to himself, or perhaps he
was simply too tired to care. Mirra tried to ignore the ghost of
Madadh that seemed to still cling to her possessions.

"I promise I won't let your death be in vain."

"Do not make promises to the dead. They just might
hold you to it."

"Master Nen," Mirra cried.

He held out his hand to stop her from getting out of

bed. "You've depleted your strength, both magical and physical. It will take time for you to recover both. And you must do so quickly."

"Why?"

"The ships will leave once things have settled down. It will be your one and only chance to disappear without a trace." Master Nen's brows creased. "Many of our people no longer feel safe here. There will be dozens flocking to the ships, sailing to dozens of ports. It will take him time to find you again. I doubt he'll send others like them after you a second time."

"I don't want to leave that to chance. Gaitlan and I will have to find some way to hide our scent, essence, power, whatever it was they used to track us before. I won't lead them to the relics or their wielders if I can avoid it."

"As wise as ever." Abbot Josef leaned heavily on a roughly hewn cane. "But still with much to learn." Abbot Josef gestured behind him.

"Glad to see you didn't die," Kov said, his voice revealing how near to tears he was.

"Me too," Mirra said.

Abbot Josef put a paternal hand on Kov's tiny shoulder. "Kov will be one of the ones leaving our island."

Kov's eyes fell to his feet, and everyone pretended to not notice the droplets of water that fell from his eyes. "Ina's coming with me. She says I'm too young to be with an adult."

"She's right, you know?" Mirra said. Kov's tear-streaked face shot up, and pert replay already shaping his mouth. "I've been alone in the world since I was younger than you. I've had to fight every day of my life for what I need to survive."

"Imma fighter."

"I'm sure you are, but there will always be people who are stronger than you." She pulled back her sleeve, exposing the serpent coiled around her wrist. "This mark was put there by a man who was stronger than me. He used me for bad things, just like the man who used me before. I don't want you to go through what I did. Be glad you have Ina, and make sure she's taken care of too."

"I will," Kov promised with all the surety a nine-year-old could muster.

Abbot Josef smiled over the exchange. "We should let Lady Mirra get her rest. She has a boat to catch soon too."

Kov blushed, sliding a large sack Mirra hadn't noticed from his shoulder. "For your trip," he said, laying the heavy bag at her feet, fleeing the room before he lost all control.

Mirra shot Abbot Josef a questioning look. "Books on the magics of your people. Please pass them onto your high priestess with the promise of full access to any Ilmarrion who wants to learn more. We've forgotten the past, and now it has come back to haunt us."

"It's time for her medicine," said someone from behind Abbot Josef.

He accepted the cup of medicine, making a face as a pungent odor filled the small room. "I would say that it tastes better than it smells, but that would be a lie."

True to his word, the herbal concoction caused Mirra's stomach to heave and roll, but somehow, she'd managed to keep it down. Exhaustion pulled at her eyelids until she succumbed to a deep, dreamless sleep.

Abbot Josef returned to his study and took a seat at his desk with a long sigh. It was in times like this that he truly hated the responsibilities of his position. He pulled out a large stack of paper, followed by a healthy stick of sealing wax, ink, and plenty of quills. It was going to be a long night, and he had many, many, many letters to write.

CHAPTER TWENTY-ONE

THE SERVANTS WHISPERING JUST OUTSIDE HIS DOOR would soon find themselves facing the gallows if they didn't move their useless meat sack somewhere else. He'd rise or yell, but he'd been confined to his bed for three days, wracked with a fever and weak limbs.

The foolish healers thought he'd come down with some kind of stress illness, but he only knew the truth. His minions, few of the many that dwelled within, had been erased from this world. He wouldn't place so much of his power into his agents going forward if their demise nearly took him along with them.

Perhaps that was why Braelyn remained free from his control. The power vacuum created by the fool's death must have destroyed the tether he placed in her, and he simply couldn't discern its loss from the others.

Julian sighed, turning his face to the window. Something was stirring. He could feel it in his bones. If only he could pull himself out of this god-forsaken bed, he'd be able to figure it out.

"What?" he growled in response to the knock at his door.

A quivering footman timidly slid into Julian's bed

chambers, his face as white a sheet. "Forgive the intrusion, my lord."

"Yes, what is it?" Julian snapped. "Just give me whatever you have in your greasy little mitts and leave me in peace."

The footman yelled and shuffled to the bed, his gaze locked on the ground in front of him. He presented Julian with a thick letter both bound with twine and sealed in a way. Julian waved the footman away, turning the letter over in his hand.

Had his strength not been wholly taxed, Julian would have destroyed the room with the symbol engraved in the wax, a temple on a wave, the seal of Holy Isle. Julian tore the letter apart, not caring about the damage he inflicted.

The white-hot heat of his seething rage only grew the more he read the report detailed within. It appeared his foolish henchmen had chased Mirra to the one place they shouldn't have. Not only was the island under the protection of multiple kingdoms, but there were also secrets long buried on that island that should never be recovered. And when he thought about how close that conniving brat of a princess came to rejoining with her brother …

The letter crumbled to ash in his grasp, staining the blankets of his bed. All, save for a tiny slip of paper entirely immune to his power.

The shadows of the past can be illuminated by the light of the present. Nothing hidden can stay so forever, and nothing in the light can stay.

Lord Julian's roar spread through the castle, startling many of the servants working its halls.

Princess Braelyn looked over her shoulder at the sound, a

smirk on her face. Mirra and her brother had dealt a mighty blow against the monster who would be king. They hadn't let the wounds inflicted by that monster keep them from doing what was right, and neither would she, even if she had to do it alone.

ABOUT THE AUTHOR

One part geek, one part crazy, K. N. Timofeev has been telling stories for most her life but left them as ideas swinging in her head. And she would have been content with that until the day her husband got her something that inspired a story that burned so brightly that she had to put it to paper. Now eight years later, she continues to give the people who live in her head permanent homes built of ink and paper bound up with a pretty cover. When not creating worlds and people out of thin air, she enjoys snuggling up on the couch with her hubby and two pugs watching comic book movies, science fiction, or anything anime related.

You can follow her on Twitter and Instagram @kntimofeev and on TikTok @the_modge_podge_girl

Find more at
www.timofeevbooks.net